Art

THE METEORITE CHRONICLES: EARTHUNDER

May the Heavens
drop a meteorite
at your feet!

The Meteorite Chronicles

BOOK ONE

EarthUnder

EDWIN *E.T.* THOMPSON

INKWATER
PRESS

Portland • Oregon
INKWATERPRESS.COM

Scan QR code for more information on this book.

Cover and interior design by Masha Shubin
Title page art by Robyn Wax
Cover Images: Bigstockphoto.com. Desert dunes sand in milky way stars night sky photo mount © holbox; Close up photo of beautiful young womans face with big eyes and vacant eerie stare © BCFC; Planet Earth with appearing sunbeam light (Elements of this image are furnished by NASA) © Sergey Nivens; An image of a comet in the deep space © magann.

Library of Congress Control Number: 2014922440

Publisher: Inkwater Press | www.inkwaterpress.com

Paperback ISBN-13 978-1-62901-196-7 | ISBN-10 1-62901-196-7
Kindle ISBN-13 978-1-62901-197-4 | ISBN-10 1-62901-197-5
ePub ISBN-13 978-1-62901-198-1 | ISBN-10 1-62901-198-3

Printed in the U.S.A.

3 5 7 9 10 8 6 4 2

To Mom, she always encouraged me to learn. She recognized my wanderlust early on and encouraged me to travel the world at an early age.

To Dad, who totally approved when I told him I wanted to turn my space rock collecting hobby into a business.

To all of the wonderful people I have known and loved like family all over the world. You are my true family and you are all in my books.

Contents

Ch. 1: Holy Grail of the Great Sand Sea............................1

Ch. 2: Nemesis...21

Ch. 3: The Heart Stops...35

Ch. 4: The Boys 65

Ch. 5: Simon's Ride 89

Ch. 6: The Void...111

Ch. 7: The Tube 153

Ch. 8: Endeavor 167

Ch. 9: Capture 213

Ch. 10: Gary's Lab... 223

Ch. 11: Flade...241

Ch. 12: Teranor Captive...257

Ch. 13: Fierce Offensive 267

Ch. 14: Love Lost 279

About the Author.. 289

From the Author 291

Acknowledgments 293

SNEAK PEEK—Book II of The Meteorite
    Chronicles: Thundering Skies...................................295

CHAPTER ONE

Holy Grail of the Great Sand Sea

Alone, relentlessly, numbingly alone, with nothing to do and nowhere to go, I sat covered with heavy wool blankets that stank of dander, hiding on the flat, cold, tiled roof of this desert home. I was alive and yet life had screamed to a screeching halt as warm, oily slime soaked down my side, life's blood slowly pumping its way out of my body.

A short time earlier, I had felt something slice the edge of my neck followed by three punches to my left arm; one of those punches lifted the arm overhead. I heard the bangs echo through the open window of the third-floor room, shortly after the slugs had struck. Everything whirled about as I seemed to float to the floor in quarter speed. So this is how it felt to take shots from a gun. It wasn't at all what I had imagined. Feeling sick, dizzy, and confused as things came back into focus, I struggled to stand again as the shock tried to take over my conscious thought. It made no sense that I heard the shots after the bullets struck their mark. It was like watching brilliant bolts of lightning flash to the ground in silence before the booms of thunder filled the air with explosive sound. Had I turned for any reason in that instant, there would have been three ventilating holes through my heart and another through my neck instead of small slices through only skin. The one under the arm that made the limb jump was a doozy. That one was going to leave a mark.

As my mind began to clear, I realized that it was time to run. Someone had decided they wanted my money and obviously would do anything to get it. In the blowing desert night, one could see only dust and darkness. Everyone had scattered and no voices could be heard. This was a bad day, but a lucky day all the same. I grabbed a small daypack I knew had a few things in it that lay near the bed and climbed up, thinking that the rooftops might be the best place to start running. It was easy to assume that getting a few buildings away might help avoid further ambush. I had nothing of value on me, but the guys with the guns didn't know that. As far as they knew I was just another fool from outside their borders loaded with cash to buy rocks. I liked to think they were just trying to slow us down enough to take what we had. But that was a lot of shots landing in one small area near my ticker; this gave me a new-found level of concern and sense of self-preservation.

So for now the program was: keep moving and don't leave a blood trail. Where was Zen, and how would I ever find him or he find me? Shuffling from wall to wall and roof to roof, I could taste the salty pall of thirst. Blood was drying in my shirt. This was good; since I could not see in the dark I had to trust that for now nature would care for these wounds. The daypack had a couple of old favorite shirts in it so by morning I could change. I wouldn't want to walk the morning streets looking like a zombie—I raise enough suspicion just being myself. Turning to go to the next wall, I heard the plunk of a lone drop of water as it broke the surface tension in a wash basin. Slowing, I listened and crept towards the last sound of the drip. Then it plunked again just below me. Traditionally laundry is washed and hung to dry on these roofs, and this wash basin would be the perfect place to clean up and take a drink before moving on to safer ground.

This is a land where nearly any insect will take a bite of you, a land where everything hides from the sun. The searing sphere in the sky that gives life also takes it away. I had to adapt in one day to an environment that kills the natives, who have had a lifetime to prepare for survival. Nothing here lives far beyond the shadow of its own demise.

My mind spoke to me in two voices: one screamed at me to run; the other told me to stay put and rest. Bleeding and losing strength, I easily made the decision.

Just a few foggy days earlier, I was among humans who spoke my language and busily bustled about, managing their own affairs. I blended with my own kind in great comfort and with lavish ease. Now I appeared as a bright beacon in a dark world: light hair, skin, and eyes in a land of olive skin and black hair. I recalled someone once said how I seemed to feel comfortable in my own skin. Today I felt that this skin I was in was the enemy.

I knew where I was going and had a guide who was a fine friend and whom I trusted with my life. My guide

Zen knows all of the local dialects, and I can boast that I am well versed in two words: yes and no. One always knows that life's path may lead to a fork, a place of difficult choice. But this time the choice was suddenly so easy. The lure of mystery, adventure, and reward was so blinding that it seemed there was no option. Right now the option of having stayed at home sounded simply swell; actually it sounded really corking great. Suddenly I was alone in another world: no food, no water, no friend, no path, only flesh, bone, and brain, standing on the same planet but surrounded by thousands of miles of other world. My mind's eye visualized a shanghaied sailor waking on board a ship in the middle of an ocean. But this is the Great Sand Sea, just as hazardous and difficult to survive as drifting on the open ocean.

Zen was gone and I feared the worst for his fate. Zen is a dear and loyal friend who has always been there at my side on our journeys through his land. He is trustworthy and sincere. He has a keen sense of humor and he never runs short on energy. Zen is a kind spirit who loves family and friends. His approach to life and business is very philosophical, believing that all things happen for a reason and that we are guided by divine power. He is generous and unselfish, constantly giving his time and energy to others. Everywhere we travel together, small children gravitate to him like the Pied Piper. Having him with me on trips like this always encourages me to do more, to go that extra mile or ask the hard questions. I miss his bright, constant smile and his inquiring mind.

Right now I needed to find shelter for the night. The desert can cook you by day and freeze you by night. My biggest concern was to stay off the ground and away from all of those creatures that would end my journey in this first night. As excruciatingly tense as this predicament felt, I had to remember that these are the times that make good stories when I get back to my little corner of the universe. A part of me remained focused on the grail that got me to this crossroads.

Since childhood, my life's direction has been driven by a lust to recover rocks from space. In my years in this science, I have become convinced that the first evidence of life elsewhere in the cosmos will be carried to Earth in a meteorite. Only the rarest types of achondrites appear to have the potential of bringing this evidence to Earth. Modern-day physics dictates that the most likely chance of finding life elsewhere in our solar system would come from the planet Mars. From time to time fragments of planetary basalt fall to Earth from Mars and are recovered soon after the fall. Currently, research is limited to these rare meteorites and from data sent to Earth by a limited number of Mars rovers. I am here trying to recover a piece of this material. Like the Romans who came here centuries before in search of precious stones, gold and silver, and other natural resources, I am here to find a stone many times more valuable than gold or even platinum. This harsh land has a long history of invasion by marauding forces. Each empire, having out-grown its own natural resources, turned to invading its neighbors. North Africa was a ripe plum ready to pick, and yet all that remains of those invaders over the millennia are the stone structures they left behind. The land and the sand always come back to the nomads: navigators of the Great Sand Sea. Each generation of nomads laughs at those visitors like me who thought they wanted to be there. I have to laugh at myself, as I am just another foolish rock hound like the Romans before me, but I am inspired to find where this leads me.

We were traveling from village to village along the edge of the Sahara, communicating to the local desert dwellers that we had money to pay for rocks from the sky. We were walking the knife's edge. It's risky to spread word that you are carrying cash to buy rocks, so I always make sure there is a back door in case the bad guys show up wanting something for nothing. This was one of those times when the lure of free money was more than someone could resist. Zen always refers to this type of people as mafia. Well, tonight there was a visit from the mafia. In the middle of the hot, dry, dusty night, Zen and I were separated in a flurry of shouts, shots, and fleeting footsteps. Zen had in his vest all of the daily notes and the money—my money and passport. In this land beyond electricity and telephones, I stood at the edge of the Great Sand Sea, on my left a village of homes made of mud and straw and filled with dark staring eyes. On the right...sand.

As I crept along the walls of houses, the light from the stars was snuffed by the dust blowing in the air. I recalled that late in the day we had met with a young man, Zed, to look at stones he had brought from the desert. We had met with him a week earlier in another village. He had three small children. One little girl, three-year-old Fatima, had overcome her shyness to peek through the fabric hanging in the doorway to the room where we sat on the floor discussing his stones. Her grandfather was in the room watching as we talked. Fatima had run to him and curled up in his lap to watch as well. The grandfather was an elder, one of the "Blue People" from deep in the southwest desert. Through his sun-baked olive skin glimmered a tint of azure blue that also flashed in his eyes. You could see in his face the deep weathered lines of years in the desert and yet his eyes had a youthful glint. He seemed to take a liking to me as more than just a curiosity.

It occurred to me that I might find my way to this house and that I could climb the outside stone steps to the roof, where I might huddle up to survive the night. Typically, there is laundry on the roof and heavy blankets that I might use to keep warm. If I was discovered they might recognize me and give me shelter in spite of my trespass. I reached the house, and found that, fortunately, the burly blankets were predictably piled in a corner of this rooftop haven. As I curled up under the layers of wool, the adrenaline began to wear off and sleep took hold of the night. A blanket thrown over the wall, creating a makeshift lean-to, kept much of the blowing dust and sand from my lungs.

Dawn came in a blink. Covered in dust, my throat was parchment and my tongue was sandpaper. There was more stirring under the blankets than just me. As I stumbled to my feet, the night's collection of insects scrambled to find new cover. Several children watched me limp half-awake down the worn stone steps to street level. As I turned to move on, their ball rolled in my direction. I deftly dribbled it a bit and passed it their way. They laughed and pointed; I felt the tension fade and could hear the amusement in their laughing voices as I walked away. One of them called out an almost nondescript thank-you in desert dialect. I simply waved over my shoulder the international symbol for "yep, no problem."

As the day grew brighter and warmer, one could feel it, taste it, smell it, hear it, and in my case...fear it. My stomach was howling at me that its needs were most crucial, while my brain was trying to figure out where to go and how to get there. The thought occurred to me that it might be better to move by night and rest by day. It might even be easier to forage for food and water in darkness. The idea was to continue on the quest for the stone that brought me here. Although it seemed to be an insurmountable challenge, this might make a really great story someday.

Walking alongside an ancient, massive stone wall, I came to a small cross-street where a group of boys noticed my profile. They descended on me as moths to a flame. A tourist in these parts was a rare novelty, and their shouts drew more attention until I was surrounded four deep in mischief and mayhem. Out from the shadows came the swift movement of a lone elderly man with a gurgling, gruff voice and loud shouts, arms flailing and cape flying as he slapped ears with the flat of his hands and gestured with swings of his arm for the boys to flee. As suddenly as he appeared, he was gone again through an archway in the wall. I stood for a moment as stunned as if I too had been boxed on the ear. Just then the old man reappeared from the opening, and as I looked up from my silent glare, I realized this was Fatima's grandfather. As he drew closer he smiled as an old friend would and blessed me with his greeting. He fired several brief questions at me, but I could only make meaningless gestures and failed attempts to communicate. He grabbed my arm, his walking stick in the other, and led me to a nearby café (two tables and a few chairs out-side a doorway). Some words were exchanged and hot tea was brought to our table, followed by pocket bread filled with sardines and hard-boiled egg. He saw in my eyes how much this meant to me and he gestured that I proceed to eat. A boy walked past and stared at us sitting there. My host shouted a few commanding words at him, and he ran off. We sat in painful silence, enjoying the meal. As people meandered by, I watched them watch me. Soon the young man that was abruptly sent away returned with one of the grandchildren, Fatima's older brother, in tow. This was the boy I had passed the ball to earlier today.

"Good morning, sir," he said as he came near. The elder slipped a coin to the errand boy and off he ran, shouting the same "thank you" I had heard from the soccer player this morning. The boy introduced himself as Khal. He explained that his father taught him what he had learned from others. Suddenly life felt filled with comfort and ease. Simply being able to speak and have my words understood was this day's greatest luxury.

"Wow, you speak English," was my astonished reply. Khal waited wide-eyed for my next words. I asked him to introduce me to his grandfather. His reaction was a look of confusion with suspicion. My guess is that he couldn't understand my request for an introduction given that he saw us there, sitting together, eating, and having met the day before. I looked at Khal, then his grandfather, and put my hand on my chest to say, "My name is Bryce Monroe Sterling." The elder understood better than Khal, and he laughed softly, looked to the boy, and spoke. Khal's eyes stayed with his grandfather, whom Khal introduced, saying, "His name is Sharif." We all smiled and laughed a bit.

Tension faded into a past memory. Fear and doubt drifted off. This was a great start. The question of why I was there, alone, was in all our minds. With gestures and drawings, I explained to them what had transpired the night before. As soon as I used the word "mafia," they both sat back, mouths open wide, and gasped "ah." This was enough explanation. To convey everything was a laborious effort of words, gestures, and expressions. Time between words often dragged like crawling in mud. Strange how much harder it felt to remain silent with someone to whom you can't speak, as if the silence was wasted space. This was how I had gotten started ten years earlier as an eighteen-year-old searching for treasured rocks in other countries. In almost every case there was an elder with the wisdom and knowledge and a younger scout, willing to learn, able to help, and a lot of time was spent hacking out ways to communicate the mission. No matter how rough, it always seemed to fall together, creating bonds of friendship for life.

Once he understood the need to find Zen, Sharif slowly rose to his leathery, sandaled feet, his desert robe hanging to his ankles. He told Khal I would be safe in his home. Khal looked at me with release in his eyes and said, "Ok, see you." I pointed to my watch and he answered by making a leap-frog gesture on his outstretched arm, replying "tomorrow."

Uneasy and reserved, I replied with "Ok, see you," and as he walked away with deliberate direction, he waved over his shoulder as if to mimic my gesture from this morning. The tide of fear and insecurity rushed in again as I watched my voice, Khal, turn and walk away.

My Berber host and newfound friend was speaking with two soldiers with machine guns. He pointed at me in their conversation and they all laughed; then the two sauntered off talking and chuckling to each other as they glanced in my direction. I had a good feeling about things, but would have given anything to know what was said.

I speak Arabic, but Berber is like a language from another planet. Here on the edge of the sand, most speak Berber and those who speak Arabic cannot understand Berber. Berber people, their language, and customs, all seem to come from another time and place. Tough, resourceful, tenacious survivalists, they are perfectly suited for life in the harsh, relentless, unforgiving desert. I can understand a simple life living close to the earth and living happily with so little, but watching them come out of the desert, seeming to appear from nowhere, bringing rocks from the center of the continent and beyond, I can't help wondering why anyone chooses to live in such a harsh environment. It is said they have just walked across the continent. How long did this journey take? Why would they do it? What were the dangers and the risks? How many countries did they cross? The heat of the day, the cold at night, the bare rock, sand, mountains, wind, the creepy critters—things that go bite in the night. How do these people set out for months of trekking in a pair of sandals? What is out there to draw them? Berbers rarely remain in villages for long before they set out again across the globe. It's as if villages along the edge of the desert are there to supply the nomads. And if the nomads didn't exist, the villages would not be there.

Somewhere out there within walking distance for these people is the "Cradle of Life," the place it is said that humans first came from. And somewhere out there on the surface of this endless ocean of sand and rock is a fallen stone from the sky, which holds within its matrix the evidence of life elsewhere in the cosmos, or better yet, evidence of where life here on Earth came from. The quest is to get that rock into the hands of science. Looking out over thousands of miles of desert horizon, I feel drawn to its legendary magic. There are feelings of wondrous memories and the spirits of millennia of generations of people who lived their lives in the Sahara. One can feel the magical energy from those millions of ancient lives. It's a feeling of worlds long since gone that are still there in spirit.

Sharif was a serious, steady, taciturn man who said more with a look than most can say with hundreds of words. As we walked together my mind wandered. I felt this simple man was far more worldly than he let on. More than knowing how much trouble I was in, he seemed to know just how much I needed his help. I didn't ask for his help; he simply took the job as if he had waited for my arrival. Also, he knew Zen very well and this made him my best chance of reconnecting with my guide and good friend.

When we approached Sharif's house, I snapped out of my wandering trance and nothing looked familiar. Once we stepped inside, it was like coming home, and there was little Fatima smiling and waving hello. She seemed more at ease with my appearance this time, but still she stood half hidden behind the edge of a door frame. Standing in the entrance to the house, Sharif called to Maryam to come help with my wounds. We sat in the kitchen while she bandaged the three slices and one hole in my arm. Burning stiffness was setting in, and the warm compression of the bandages felt good on the stinging cuts. The hit that lifted the arm had left a sizeable hole that continued to drain blood, heartbeat pounding under the gauze over each wound. Maryam had laid some kind of seaweed ointment on top of each opening to help prevent infection and kill the pain.

There was an invitation to sit on the floor in the main room, and instantly hot tea and food were brought to the table in the center of the room. It seemed that those in the house knew a guest was coming. Sharif's son Zed entered the room to greet us and spoke in his limited English. I hardly knew these wonderful people, yet they felt like family. Lunch was a king's feast. Sharif sent one of the younger boys off on an errand with a handful of food. Soon he returned and I could see behind him in the shadows of the entryway the outline of my dear friend and guide Zen. His ear-to-ear smile illuminated the room, his eyes glistening with emotional relief and reserved delight.

Zen is young, tough, and tenacious, his thoughts and actions based in pure emotion. Pride and loyalty mean everything to him. His greatest ambition is to be completely trusted by those closest to him.

There were hugs and pats on the back, laughter, and great smiles. After the meal Zen was pulled into a lengthy conversation with Zed and Sharif. I sat watching; it was easy to see that they were discussing a subject that would soon be presented to me, but Zen's English is "small," as he puts it, and this would be a lot to condense into "small" words. Just then they all turned to face me. Zen asked me to wait for the words. He said, "The words he does not know. But Sharif has an old picture, he must find it."

So after two to three hours of broken sentences in three

or four languages, gestures, and sketches, the picture was presented. It was so worn and tattered that I could hardly make out what was in the photograph. One could see from the outline that it was a stone resting on a small table. Zen pointed to the stone, looked at me, and said, "This is your Mars rock! This stone they see fall and they find. Is not this why you are here?"

There it was, the Holy Grail of meteorites. I had heard of this legendary stone years earlier. The shape and size had been described in detail. A small fragment had been chipped from the mass when it fell, revealing the interior matrix. The green and black crosshatch pattern and color was always a telltale indicator that the finders had another piece of planetary basalt and most likely a Shergottite. Shergottites are a group of meteorites named after the original fall of this type of material named Shergotty, which fell on August 25th, 1865, in Gaya, Bihar, India. After putting several landers on planet Mars, scientists have confirmed that these and a rare few other groups of meteorites originated on the Red Planet. This origin makes these stones priceless research material.

Since early childhood, my fascination with rocks from space was unquenchable. I have read countless papers and attended every lecture on the subject at local universities about this mythical stone. It is said to have fallen into the Cradle of Life in what is known as the heart of the Sahara. How can I be holding a picture of what appears to me to be the Holy Grail of all meteorites? This stone, it is said, was seen to fall to Earth many thousands of years ago. Legend has it that after the stone was recovered and preserved, this part of the world changed from lush life-filled forests and waterfowl-inhabited inland seas to the desert we know today. Sandstone cliffs covered with carvings of jungle wildlife as well as artifacts made by the hands of men testify to this dramatic change. My interest is not in the legends of this stone's terrestrial history, but rather in its extraterrestrial history. If this meteorite truly is a Shergottite, then locked inside its unweathered matrix there might be clues to the beginnings of life itself. But how does Sharif have this picture? It's as if he knew I was coming. This stone has become a religious icon to the desert people. No one of the so-called modern world has ever laid eyes on the legendary specimen.

Life loses all other meaning as I am consumed by the interest in this stone. This was my Rosetta stone. It might very well have been that this was in fact the Holy Grail that the Knights Templar had quested after for lifetimes. Descriptions of all other possible artifacts that might have been the grail were obscure at best, the most convincing being a chalice. But I had a description of a shape and size and color and origin, and this photograph matches all of those details. What is the Grail; was it the bringer of life somehow or maybe life change on a global scale? It also makes sense that the stone was revered and protected for so long. It had its own legend, but only limited detail had leaked out of its existence. After all the stories and rumors, it seems that for the first time I am getting close. Everything feels different this time. This feels close to the truth. There is a brief passing of time between the search for a stone and that instant when it is laid out before you when you know it is really going to happen. This never takes long enough to think about what comes next. If that event has happened often enough, then one can feel the truth coming. It's the feeling of opening a long-buried treasure chest, and the bounty within illuminates the faces around it. You know it's there before the lid is opened, but the years of searching create a doubt that only the final moment can erase. The feeling is palpable; the truth is being able to reach out and touch your goal.

Ten years earlier, at the age of eighteen, I made my first journey here to try to recover a rare stony-iron meteorite that had fallen in this area. Stories had made it through the scientific community that someone had recovered a piece from a recent witnessed fall and that it was possibly a mesosiderite, a fairly valuable type of stony-iron. I had seen this as an opportunity to acquire some valuable trade material while providing research material out of the field, fresh from space. After I spent weeks networking, a young man presented me with the first specimen: a gorgeous fusion-crusted fresh-fallen stone. There was no mistaking that this was a piece of that recent fall event. That young lad was Zen, ten years of age at the time, and beaming with pride to show his recovery to someone who had traveled halfway round the planet to offer him money for it. Zen is like a younger brother to me now. We have grown up together. We were both just kids on an adventure together then and now. I had no business instincts, just a passion for collecting space rocks and a love for adventure.

I saved every penny earned doing paper routes, caddying the local golf course, stacking firewood for a local boat builder, and painting houses during the summers. The goal was to buy a car at age sixteen and pay for college early. But a broken leg right out of high school set me behind my peers, and lying around reading books filled my head with wanderlust. This rock fell about the time my leg was healed, and I saw the chance for travel and possible profit. Weeks later in an unfamiliar land, I was holding in my hands a melted black rock that just a few weeks earlier had drifted aimlessly through the vacuum of outer space.

This encounter with Zen would be the beginning of a long and thrilling relationship. Now, here we were once again working together to recover all or part of a treasure fallen from the sky. I learned early on to always make the effort to be extra generous. To always take care of those who take care of you means you will always have help when you need it. When we left Sharif's home yesterday, I quietly handed his son Zed a gift of dollars for his children. I gestured at the children while shaking his hand filled with the gift. One can only assume that Sharif had learned of my generosity with no expectation of a return, and that the gesture had won his admiration. This fine man was relaying information about a stone that had been legend for millennia. How was I given to be this fortunate? This part of the world was invaded by countless empires through the ages. But why would invading hordes wish to conquer a land of rock and sand? Is it possible they had searched for the magic of this stone? If this meteorite was that important, then how could I ever get this close? In this part of the world there are stories of the limitless power of this stone—from healing children with polio to protecting the land and its people. Will I ever get closer than this, and is there a chance of ever obtaining even a small fragment for research?

One of countless legends had described that this stone was the entire contents of the Ark of the Covenant, and the powers of the Ark were imbued by the stone. All of this tied into so many stories from other legends. I stand stunned by the flow of thought and possibilities. Zen and Zed had come to share that Sharif held me in esteem as an expert on meteorites and that he felt that my efforts were purely noble to get a piece into the hands of researchers. That night after dinner we sat around a small fire and drank tea. It was story-telling time, and I shared with the mesmerized group that there is a new "space race." It is no longer about getting people onto other planets. The real space race is to be the first scientist or institution to find concrete evidence of life elsewhere in the universe. For now we don't have the technology to travel to other planets safely and quickly, but space rocks brimming with valuable information come to us. When a meteorite falls through the Earth's atmosphere, it melts in a fusion fireball caused by compressed atmospheric gases ignited by friction. This fireball forms a glassy crust on the meteorite, sealing valuable rare gases and volatile or soluble minerals within the matrix. There can also be bubbles sealed in impact glass in the matrix, glass created by the same event that ejected the chunk of rock from its parent planet. This glass can have that planet's atmosphere trapped within those bubbles. The night was filled with endless questions deftly testing the depth of my knowledge about meteorites.

The next day was one of rest. My day was filled with observations of a loving family happily going about their day. I was made to feel that this was my new family. The daylight soared by swiftly, and night fell on another summer-baked day. The children had come in to visit with us and to experience the curious light-colored visitor who was welcomed into their home with such ease. Zen also was invited to stay and accepted without hesitation as if there was no one waiting for him at his own home.

Zen's attention was drawn to the small children. He was asking them a multitude of short two- and three-word questions in rapid succession, and they smiled as they responded with similar curt answers. Affectionately their voices melted into a blend of warm laughter and elfin giggles, with youngsters sending occasional glances in my direction. I could tell there was only innocent curiosity and harmless humor in good spirit. The mother of the house, Zed's wife, Maryam, seemed painfully shy, yet I sensed that she ruled the roost. The young girls slowly shed their shyness and began to feel obviously at ease around me. But like everyone else under this roof, they all looked to Maryam for final approval. Dinner came and went, with a goat's milk yogurt drink that instantly became my most favorite thing in the world. Milkshakes had nothing on this drink. I could see myself back home with a double cheddar cheese burger, fries, and a vanilla/banana goat's milk yogurt smoothie. The evening and into the night was filled with questions and discussion of stones from the sky. Sharif revealed his insightful mind when his questions led to what I do with these stones, who I compete with, and how much corruption can be found in this business I call my passion. One could read concern from between the lines of his questions.

Soon it was time for sleep. This night was a world away from the prior night. This night had a cozy bed with linens, four walls, and a door. Knowledge seemed to be buying the time here. The questions tonight were seriously intense, but it was rewarding to have answers. I fell off to sleep with dreams inspired by our exchange of thoughts. As with every night for a decade, slumber brought the face of my first love, who comes to me in my dreams, her eyes so lovely they burn my heart.

Waking as the dawning sun just illuminates the edge of the world, I heard voices and mellifluous noises indicating I was not the first. Soon we all gathered for tea to begin the new day. Thoughts through the night inspired me to be more open with Sharif and Zed. Besides, it must be remembered that they can pump Zen with endless questions, which dictated that I must be totally honest and try not to hide anything. As we visited, I learned that Zen and Zed had stayed awake last night to activate their network in the village. Word here travels far and fast. Remembering our recent close call with the thieves, they were far more cautious with this effort. Apparently they were trying to find specific people with information.

CHAPTER TWO

Nemesis

We gathered again to continue last night's flurry of discussion. Having tuned in to Sharif's line of questions, I decided to trust him with solid detailed answers. When one is globe trekking this way, a turning point always presents itself when one must trust others implicitly to succeed. I began the day by sharing with Sharif and the others how over the years the monetary value of these stones has exploded, driven by the race to do research competing with a rabid collector market. In earlier days collectors were traditionally science-minded nerds who lusted after stones for their connection with space, at that time a place we humans could only dimly dream of going. As time marches forward, these cosmic treasures have drawn countless fortune seekers who have not a clue of the scientific value nor do they care. They only see a chance to make tremendous profit—dollars from a stone they can pick up off the ground and sell to an obsessed collector for more money than most people make in half a lifetime.

The lure of wealth brings every kind of greed and every manner of human with it. Moral values fade into obscurity when lust and greed rush to motivate. I explain to these men how I can only control my own actions, that there are others who race to compete with me. They will say anything and do anything to beat me to the finish. Over time these hunters have become far more clever, competitive, and corrupt. They have the backing of wealthy buyers waiting to be the first to own what falls next. This fuels an ugly side of what was once a very rewarding and innocent endeavor. These people have their own network of evil doers, ruthless pirates who sail the Great Sand Sea trying to control everything.

There is an endless flow of new fortune seekers now coming into this market looking to make their splash. For many it is all about the money; for others it is all about ego (I got it first); for others still it is all about the competition. Even worse are the uncommon few who are a conglomeration of all the bad elements. The very worst are the serpents that culminate all things bad and coat it with a sugar-sweet shell. They're like a pill that kills, coated with a smooth candy exterior to help it go down. My nemesis is just that bad pill. He is fast, relentless, ruthless, deadly, greedy, and obscured by a smooth tongue and a devious, deceptive smile. Just as the reef fishes must coexist with the shark and the land creatures must live with the serpent, we must live with this scourge of a human known as Claus Laurent and all the masses of his followers, allies, and clones.

Sharif listened nodding and looking deep into my eyes, reading my earnestness as Zen translated my words but preserved the message as perfectly as semantics allowed. There was a time when there was no race to the finish. There was no need for the sense of urgency or fear of competition. These rocks could be left lying endlessly, and tenacity was a useless trait. Now there is a rush of fortune seekers diligently scrambling to be the first to acquire something new, something to turn into cash. And that is changing as well. For the last decade the scramble was directed at finding wildly new and unusual types of meteorites in classifications never before analyzed. There is a far more competitive clamber to be the first to offer pieces of the most recent fall event. So when something truly unusual is found or falls fresh from the sky, the sharks can smell the blood in the water and first gets the most.

When I originally got into this, I was filled with passion. It was fun-filled excitement, challenge, and travel to strange new places, so much fun it felt like a sin. No part of this was work; it was all a thrilling roller coaster ride. It was all about the quest, and after completion, it was on to the next adventure. Now many parts of the endeavor feel freakishly stressful. So often now I use virtually every resource and strain all of my assets, only to find that Laurent or one of his wannabe clones has just left with the stone. Or worse yet, I acquire pieces and upon returning home or arriving at a research facility, I learn that I am too late. So often now I hear the words, "Yes, your specimens are very nice, but we already have all we can use."

I needed to be clear with Sharif and Zed that I was not there to take this treasured stone away, but that the effort was to obtain a small piece for research. They understood that I had known of its legend through the ages. But did they sense my reservation about its actual existence? This relic photograph might have been a picture of anything, but it did appear to be meteoritic. As always, the only way to confirm its authenticity was to treat everything and everyone as if it was the real deal. What struck me is how Sharif was already so concretely certain. Between his conviction and the ludicrous language barrier, I would never convince him otherwise. But that was ok; a true believer can be a priceless ally. What was going to take time was educating him about the dark side of my work.

We began spelling out this portrayal slowly, carefully, and with diligent eye contact. The eyes are the window to the soul, and shifty eyes sever the bonds of trust. A limited few words into our dissertation on our concerns for the safety of the stone, I mentioned the name of my nemesis. Zen was abruptly interrupted mid-sentence by Sharif as he pointed and shook his fingers, repeating, "Aurent, Aurent!"

Heart leaped to throat as I whispered, "He's already been here." Zen frantically bid for clarification. The Elder began speaking swiftly in soft, deliberate tones. I watched his gestures as Zen listened intently. One could feel the importance of Sharif's words. I struggled to choke back concern. It was nearly impossible to sit quietly while potential scenarios raced through the mind. Although not soon enough to squelch my angst, after a time Sharif's words ceased as he glanced into my eyes. His expression was unreadable, and I got nothing from his guttural, vociferous dialect and flailing gestures. But we all knew who he was talking about, and he had a great deal to express, which was a rare occasion.

Zenny, as I sometimes affectionately called him, took a deep breath and turned to me. "Ok, man," he said, "there is a lot to tell you. First, Sharif knows of this snake you call Laurent; everyone here knows stories of him. He is a bad man and he runs with a pack of bad men. Here many call him the devil. So it is good that you are a serious man (in this land serious means trustworthy) and the people know this. Sharif knows this, he trusts you, and he likes how you are. You have made a good friend here, man."

Sharif watched my face as Zen spoke. Zen went on saying how Sharif had known about our pending conflict the other night, but he did not know me and had decided to stay out of it for his family's safety. He realized later that night that he should have done something to warn us off. What unfolded in his words was an explanation that "the snake" was here and searching for the sacred stone. What Sharif seemed to be wanting from our encounter was that I might help stop anyone's advance toward finding the stone meteorite. As Zen continued, I thought to myself, *What can I do to help?* Just then Zen's interpretation got garbled and strange. It sounded like Sharif was offering to get me a piece of the stone. Zen had led our tentative robber-bandits three villages away to protect me. As in so many close calls before this, I knew I could trust this man with my life and with my confidence. At the very least I could trust every word of his version of Sharif's words. Zen's respect for Sharif was obvious in the words Zen used to interpret Sharif's message. But a piece of the stone; how was it possible that this was happening so quickly and easily, and was it the right meteorite? When Zen continued, he explained that Sharif knew all about me and the competition. His fear was that the stone could not be protected, and his hope was that getting a small piece into the hands of researchers might call off the dogs and slow the questing. They all looked at me as Zen asked, "Can you help them?"

"Of course I can help," shot out of my mouth without

an instant of hesitation. Sharif smiled as if he could understand every word. Zen repeated what I had replied, and
Sharif grinned in obvious relief.

Zen leaned in to whisper, "This is a great honor and a
huge responsibility. This elder man is known as one of the
protectors of the stone. It is said that he has lived lifetimes
to secure its secrets. He is a desert dweller and is only here
visiting for a small time. He must return to where he comes
from but he hopes to complete his mission and impart his
small treasure with you before he departs." Zen went on to
say that all of these words must remain sacrosanct and not
go beyond our ears. I was being drawn into a secret pact and
was being given the dire trust of a timeless sect of shamans
charged with every secret of this space gem. This was a win.
No matter my fate or future, I had won an impossible trust
beyond possession or value. The only way to live up to this
honor would be to fulfill the mission.

For now it would be nice to just lie around and mend
for a few days, but, as Zen reminded me, there were bandits
out there diligently trying to figure out where we had gone.
He had spread word villages away that we were there to buy
stones, and the hope was that this would lure the mafia in
the opposite direction. Zen, Zed, and I would push on fairly
under cover, in heavy camel hair robes, driving a tiny truck
filled with penned chickens and jugs of oil. Word had been
sent ahead to another dear friend, Ali, to wait for us at an
arranged meeting place. My biggest fear was that countless
corrupt people were allied with the mafia, so any stop along
the way of our journey could be risky.

Our vehicle heavy with goods, its tires nearly flat from
the weight, blended in nicely with smoke-belching trucks

and motorbikes along the dusty road. Our faces were covered with robes to filter the yellow dust blown by the wind and lifted again and again by each passing vehicle. I felt at home where we were, and it was hard to leave on this leg of our quest, but the plan felt perfect and it seemed to be working. I craved more talk of the Touchstone; my interest was piqued.

We would meet up with Sharif soon and I'd get to see what it was he had spoken of. Curiosity was welling up inside me. After years of stories I had dismissed it as myth, and now on a trip to find another fall, I was being guided to the Holy Grail. Part of me couldn't believe that this was really going to happen. Even if it was simply another fresh-fallen stone recovered by eyewitnesses of the fireball, this would be tremendous good fortune. And if it then turned out to be something wildly new to study, that would be way beyond the ordinary good fortune. But if it turned out that I was actually to be presented a small fragment of the mythical Touchstone, well this would be more frightening than any risk I had ever taken. Regardless of the risks, I would very much like to see this sacred stone.

As we traveled in the scorching heat, other vehicles trickled off until we were pretty much the only ones on the road. People sat in the shade of trees and buildings watching us drive by. Did they wonder if we were being brave or foolish? Zen knew that the Souk was this day in the next village, and so to waylay any suspicion he swung his arm low out the window, which was a signal to onlookers that we were in a rush. After this the people stopped the long looks in wonder. I guess the assumption was that we were late for something very important at the Souk.

The drive was a six-hour journey to the village. We are aiming for a magical place at the edge of the desert where the river Ziz flows out of the mountains. It fans out onto the desert floor and disappears into the sand, a river to nowhere. In this same region there are sacred fountains of salt water that blast up from the sand, gushing salt water onto the surface of the ground. These geysers have spewed salt water into the air since before recorded time. For years, it has struck me odd that fresh water goes in and salt water comes out. No person has ever been able to explain this anomaly reasonably well.

My guides simply shrug their shoulders and say, "It's sacred, God does it, it's a gift. Everybody needs salt in the desert." Much as a bee finds flowers for nectar, a desert dweller finds salt roiling up out of the ground. It is assumed to be that simple and natural. For me it is a never-ending puzzle.

Our day's journey would take us to the meeting place at an obelisk on the other side of the next village. There we planned to meet with Sharif and my oldest and dearest friend Ali. I enjoy calling him Ali Baba but over the years that had morphed into Ali Baby! Ali is more a brother than a friend, more a brother than my own birth brothers. We have been in a lot of trouble together, many tight jams and many more fun times. There is a trust between us beyond words. Ali was my first guide. Everything we did together for years was new to us both. We ventured onto the Twilight Zone together, equally naïve, countless times. Now we could reflect and laugh about our times together, but many of those adventures turned out to be far more serious and dangerous than we had considered going in. So here we were again preparing to join up for another endeavor.

Ali had saved me so many times that it was comforting to know he'd be near. A great talker and a good runner, he had limitless connections. Ali understood the importance of what we are doing, and he got it that we were relentlessly pursued by the bad guys.

We rumbled along the only road for a hundred miles, throwing up golden desert dust behind us until we came to the southwest end of the village. There stood Ali Baby, relief showing in his bright toothy grin. There were hugs, hand-shakes, pats on backs, pecks on cheeks, and great waves of laughter. Ali had a barrage of questions for us, but first praised Zen and Zed for all they had done already. Ali asked Zen to stay and visit for the night, which was swiftly accepted. I could tell that Zen was already planning to remain. Zed too would stay the night, but then move on to play out the ruse with our truck full of freight. I felt relief being reunited with Ali and was looking forward to open conversation and inter-pretation. We sat in the lobby of our hotel and talked over tea. First the two of them, Zen and Ali, compared notes on what had transpired. I could see a number of references to me or at least glances and nods in my direction.

The evening droned on and I listened. I was not really included in their conversation, but often in our travels together Ali Baby would leave me out for long periods of time before he would bring me up to speed with details. I learned years ago that he would tire easily of having to think in two languages and sometimes three or four. He always needed time to think before he would come to me for advice or decree. That night little was said to me, but Ali did make it known how pleased he was that we were rejoined. Next day the morning conversation turned to me and my purpose and intent. From what he was asking, I could tell they had been discussing the stone.

Ali turned to me and smiled, saying "Ah, so, you know of our legend?" I smiled and nodded as he looked at the others. "And what do you think of this thing?"

I began to answer when he interrupted with, "Do you believe in this thing?"

"Well, sure," I shrugged, displaying neither hesitation nor reserve, in reply.

"Good," said Ali with conviction and relief. "And do you believe this stone fell from the sky as a gift from God?"

It was easy to answer this quite convincingly because I was one of the few humans who actually tracked these things down. I didn't address the gift issue as I had learned years ago that it is important to let people believe whatever they needed to. In this case there was, in fact, a sacred touching stone that fell from the sky. I would do nothing that might lessen my chances of getting to see it or, even better, obtain a small piece of it. All I needed was a fragment no larger than a small finger for making a thin section and doing some probe work to figure out where this shooting star had come from. If it were wildly new material it might help add to the model of the formation of our solar system. But the real modern-day space race is about finding life. And if this stone is an SNC (Shergottite, Nakhlite, or Chassignite), then it may hold the key, a never before seen clue of where life came from in our solar system. The men had countless questions for me that eventually led to the stone's value.

I thought for a moment and said, "For me this treasure has no value, I simply wish to see it. If Sharif asks me to have a fragment analyzed, I will do as he asks. But for you this stone is priceless. If it holds the power that you tell me it has, then it is beyond insulting with a value." We all laughed a long, loud belly laugh. We continued to laugh as my two protectors joked about what the stone's power and blessing might do for me. They joked about how I needed lots of saving and how we all needed lots of help in walking the straight path. The laughter continued to grow louder as more humor fueled the group.

Later, following more laughter and conversation, hugs and handshakes, blessings and thanks, Zed left to return home. I insisted that he take money for driving us here. He refused my offer, saying, "It is a gift." It would be hard for this proud, poor gentleman of honor to refuse my offer. For him this was a lot of money.

As I've always said, "Any amount of money is a lot when you have none." Quickly I replied, "Ok, let me buy all of your chickens for one hundred dollars." He agreed and said that twenty of it would go to Fatima for caring for the family chickens. After we watched Zed drive his tiny truck off into the blowing dust and desert heat, we gave the chickens to the hotel kitchen. They were delighted and insisted that we stay for lunch. This was a chance for Ali Baby and me to catch up.

Ali queried wryly, "I hear that you gave $20 to the old man's granddaughter?" I nodded yes, knowing that Ali would scold me for giving too much as a gift. I know how much he does not want me to spoil his sources. Ali held up the flat of his hand as if to silence my defense. He continued, "That gift saved your life. This man would not have accepted money from you, but he could see that you intended it for the granddaughter. You sidestepped his pride and you touched his heart. You impressed him as another man of honor who understood life as it should be lived, and he had prayed to meet you again someday to repay your gesture. You two are now bonded for life by this memory of honor."

I was stunned by the magnitude of this life lesson learned from what I thought of as a small gesture of consideration. We both stood gazing at the sun-baked horizon as our friend disappeared into the skyline. Ali went on to say that he had never seen Sharif take a liking to any stranger as it seems he had with me. He added what an honor it was that this small gift of limitless value was coming our way. As we walked back into the hotel, I reflected on my own good fortune for having such fine friends in my life. So there we sat, three of us waiting for Sharif to join us. We all had the same "split and run" plan in our heads. We needed to discuss how to move on. Zen had ditched our car the night I was shot, and he called his loyal friend Samir to bring us another car to use.

And so we waited. The hotel lobby was soon filled with the aroma of roasting chicken wafting through the air. Since we had filled their pens with new stock, they were cooking all of the birds they had already prepared for that day. Ali leaned towards me at the table and said, "Listen, man, I want to share this with you in confidence." He spoke quietly while peering into my eyes with intense earnestness, "The sacred stone, it is a true story. A friend of mine, his grandfather touched the stone as a child. He said that the stone healed his illness."

Curiosity carving its way into my mind, I inquired, "What does this mean to me?"

Ali went on, "I had always planned to take you to see this man. When he was young, a secret sect had brought the stone to his village to help heal the sick. The stone was carried in a cask with holes for hands to reach through to touch the stone. When his turn came the boy reached inside the cask and touched the stone, and a small fragment fell into his hand as he withdrew it from the hole he had reached into. He was terrified and he knew that he might be punished for what he had done. As he withdrew his hand he held the fragment with his thumb and clenched his fist to his side. He walked home with the fist clenched, arm at his side, afraid to look at what he held." Ali told me that this young man was Sharif's grandfather. He looked deeply into my eyes and made an effort to gain my full attention. "No man knows how old Sharif is, but many have said that no man alive remembers him as a younger man. And there is no illness in his family." Ali leaned farther until we were whispering to each other. "How do you feel?" he inquired.

"Me?" I asked, looking puzzled by the suggestion of his inquiry., "What do you mean?"

Ali asked again, "How do you feel, are you tired? Do your wounds hurt? Could you drive for several more hours?"

I thought about this for a moment, my eyes trained off to the side, deep in thought, and then it struck me that my wounds did not hurt at all. The stiffness was gone along with the sting. I could raise the arm that was lifted by the hardest hit over my head and stretch it as if nothing had happened at all. "Huh, that's weird;" I added, "I couldn't lift my arm this morning to get into the truck."

"Exactly, man," said Ali, "it is magic. Well, plans have changed, and as soon as Samir arrives, we need to drive further into the desert to meet with Sharif. Word is that he too ran into bandits and he is giving us roads to drive to avoid being messed with."

CHAPTER THREE

The Heart Stops

Soon Samir did arrive and before long we were off again on another drive. Things are different with Samir; he is from the city, and we call him "the Prince." He likes to drive nice, fast cars and he listens to pop music while he drives.

So there we were, four guys driving down a dirt road in a car built for city driving. We were moving fast and leaving a wall of dust in our wake. The prince was singing to his music and tapping to the beat on his steering wheel. That afternoon we headed north to a road that would take us west and then south and deep into the Sahara to meet with Sharif. My mind never rested from analyzing detail. For me it was the smallest things that could add up to the biggest and best stories. I found in my travels that those little things made my days most interesting. A detail that caught my attention every time in this part of the world burned in my brain with tenacious fury. With all of the difficulties of transportation and communication across this harsh, undeveloped, ancient land, this question haunted my thought-filled mind. We could travel for days and when we got to where we were going, our host would be standing on the side of the road waiting and waving as if he knew we were moments away.

And here was another cluster of brain puzzlers that just ate my lunch. How is it that through thousands of years, countless armies had invaded over and over and all of them failed to conquer this land? Why did they try? Why had they always failed against a simple, unarmed people? Why did they want this land? And then, why was it that in the oldest populated area of the world, virtually nothing has changed? Things here in the desert were done as they were thousands of years ago. Maybe, I thought, they were living life as they were intended and that things here were already perfect. That would explain why people living on bare rock and sand could be so happy living such simple yet full lives.

I got to ride in the back; the boys were up front enjoying music, drumming it out on the dashboard. The car seemed to dance down the road to the beat of the music. Knowing Samir's lead foot, I thought the car would leave the surface at any moment and fly intermittently. Reflecting on Ali's question, I reached under my shirt to check on my new battle scars. Peeling back the bandage I was shocked—flabbergasted was a better descriptive term—the wounds were completely healed. No, this couldn't be. I was delirious from a day of motoring. Or maybe they cooked the chicken in hashish butter. But tonight I wanted to take a closer look with lights and a mirror if there were any.

We passed a tiny donkey burdened with two children and a three-foot-high stack of bundled grass. The small child on the back of the donkey rode facing behind and watched our approach. We must have appeared as an approaching sandstorm from our speed and the cloud of dust trailing just behind us. I wondered how many expletory curse words we will earn from this passing.

And so we rolled on speeding towards our destination. I found myself in envy of the happy, full lives my friends lived here. Every day was an adventure filled with life, love, and laughter. As we carved through the serene beauty of a mountain pass, winding our way along the massive canyon that once held in its breadth a raging torrent, we passed the ruins of magnificent hand-hewn stone bridges built by the Romans many lifetimes ago, ghostly architectural skeletons standing over ghost water. Scattered about the mountains were huge black tents shielding fragile lives much as these same tents had done thousands of years earlier when the failed bridges were built. We passed between mountains that pierced the blue blanket above, jagged gauntlets that have not hidden under snow in over a century.

I recalled walking through these mountains a while back teaching an ambitious group of Bedouins how to search for meteorites. Even this group in a remote mountain enclave related to me their version of the Touchstone legend. I remembered how it felt to walk with these sturdy men through the stone monoliths of these mountains. There were plants and bushes in the jagged crags but even the plants were foreboding, as every limb and blade was coated with armor and thorns. The only thing that could traverse this area was the wind.

Eventually our view changed from mountain boulders to luscious green oasis villages. Date palms and banana palms were everywhere. Here and there along the road was a wide swath of surface for vehicles pulling over between the roadway and the buildings and shaded structures. There were people walking, vehicles parked, and coming or going. The fronts of the shops and cafes were littered with tables and chairs, with both locals and travelers resting and watching the endless current of bodies and machines. The smell of diesel and gas blended in the air with the aroma of roasting chicken, lamb, beef, and black tobacco. Children pushed vending carts heaped with prickly cactus pears and watermelon. People sipped coffee, tea, or soda and stared blank faced at the blur of movement. Motor repair garages were hard to miss because of the black grease smeared onto the edges of the doorways.

We stopped for a few items and continued on our way south towards the sand once more. On a beach in Hawaii the sand is a white band of softness that draws you to the water's edge, a shifting pillow of cool crystals worn round by the sea. It holds a beachcomber's bounty and erases its impressions with each tide. The sand here is the foundation of existence that gives life and takes it away. The buildings are made from sand, mud, and straw, the epitome of environmentally sound recycling; the sand that is used to build is eventually taken back by the desert. Today's modern world is invading on multiple levels, but as in the years gone by, this invasion should fail.

Driving on, it appeared the slower cars were put on the road by some benevolent being to test the deft passing skills of our self-proclaimed, race car–driving chauffeur. In the driving game of chicken, our driver had nerves of titanium alloy. He was a silent, loveable guy who calmly smiles when cars pass far too close, horns blazing. He meant no harm or disdain—it's simply how he did what he did. Slow-moving vehicles simply represented obstacles to get around and go faster than.

Sitting in the rear and watching the outside world from behind Samir's calm, unmoving profile, we were like pawns in a video game. I could see an almost demonic smile in his eyes reflected in the rearview mirror. He delighted in threading the needle through the craziest traffic with the cool and calm of well-rehearsed choreography, and one hand lay relaxed in his lap as if to say, "This is only a fraction of what I can handle." But this was country touring and not city driving; he seemed bored without adding a dash of challenge as often as he could. And yet I had seen him stop a fleet of trailing drivers to allow a single stranger to cross the roadway in a land where pedestrians take lives into their own hands to risk crossing the highway. I thought back to childhood amusement rides and pondered how much would someone pay for a ride like this? The sun would be coming up soon; you could see a glint of yellow glow melding into the last of the night sky. Soon the scorching orb would rise above the edge of the dunes and consume the dark.

"Today," Zen said, "we will drive until the heat stops us." Zen announced that today we would visit his adopted aunt's home and rest through the heat of the day. The so-called aunt is Maryam's sister. Zen is so fond of her that he likes thinking of her as part of his family. This reminded me of my childhood, growing up with countless aunts and uncles and grandmas and grandpas. As I grew older I learned that they were just close family friends. I still have vivid memories of greeting Grandma Johns early every morning in her vegetable garden puttering with her plants as I walked through her yard on the way to school. I grew up believing that she was family.

We arrived at Zen's aunt's home just as the heat of the day began to force humans and animals alike to seek shade from the sun's searing rays. Turning down a narrow dirt lane, we soon pulled up to a cream-colored block building with olive trees planted around the house and rows of citrus trees behind the house watered from a tiny irrigation ditch flowing past the home.

As the car came to a halt, Zen cheered, "Ah there's Auntie!"

I was struck dumb by the stunning, simple beauty of this tall, green-eyed matriarch. I clumsily clambered out of the back of the car, legs stiff and half dead from our time driving.

Zen youthfully sprang towards his aunt, calling out her name, "Kadishya!"

I froze at the door of the car as my eyes winced from the light. That name grabbed at my heart like the clawed talons of a raptor in flight. I could feel my heart heave into my throat as I put the name with the exquisite face of my first love. How could this be? The young girl who had hosted me on my first stay in this land, a girl turned woman whom I had fallen intensely in love with when we were both still just kids, is standing here just a few paces from me. As much as I believed I would never see her again, I also knew she would always be with me in mind and heart. This pain in my heart was beyond description. The rest of me was simply numb. I couldn't talk or walk. I stood there in absolute question of everything. How could this happen? Where had she gone? Why was she part of this quest? She knew everything about me. I felt I knew nothing of her. She had disappeared mysteriously ten years earlier and left behind a broken young man filled with doubt and the pain of lost love. Each day since that day I had thought of how I might handle such an encounter. I was frozen, overwhelmed by the thousands of hours of thought, hurt, and reflection. I had been then just eighteen years of age; she was fifteen. She had taught me French and I had helped her with her English. We had been like brother and sister until the time together changed us both. The fun and laughter had turned, day by day, into love and adoration. But some intangible thing tore us apart in a day, and that day was followed by years of unrequited questions.

The guys had gone in. I stood there petrified with no clue of what to do next. The realization washed over me that all of my companions knew each other. There was some mysterious, underlying connection between all of us. There were relations here that I was not ever aware of. I was sensing some kind of grand deception. The more I learned; the more questions arose.

Kadishya knew I was coming. She too had no idea of what to do next. She took a deep breath, lifted her arm to offer her hand, and invited me into her home with words that came to my ears like a song. As I hesitated, she turned her head to peer out of the corner of her eyelids and asked the word I had heard her say so very many times in my dreams…"Compri?"

When we were just children, teaching each other our ways and customs and words, she would often look at my puzzled, struggling face and say that word. It was an up word, a single word that meant: do you get it? It was the thing I loved the most about her, she always took the time to make sure that I was with her on the same page. It made me feel safe and at the same time it was so intensely adorable.

The word always ended on a high note as if musical. Here we stood ten years later and it came out of her as if she had spoken it on the last day we had seen each other. A rush flooded over me. This was going to be a very difficult day. Kadishya stepped toward me, gently reaching for my hand to lead me into the house. She said nothing and looked to the ground as if deep in thought or searching her own mind for how to deal with our encounter. I could feel in the touch of her hand that this was real. I could feel her everything: her warmth, her compassion, her gentle nature, her strength and confidence.

Her voice was music as she asked in flawless English, "Are you good?"

I mumbled something with no idea what I said. She left me in a magnificent front room, tiled from floor to ceiling, and disappeared into the next room.

I stood on a thick hand-woven rug and stared at the vibrant colored tiles in the room. Soon my three travel companions came into the room. They all tried to speak, but I only wanted to pump Zen with questions about his aunt. I knew that Kadishya had an older sister. Kadishya had told me that she was her older sister's favorite. Her older sister, Maryam, was Zen's mother. Kadishya had a younger sister Jasmina, who had spent much of the time with us when we were together. Question turned to shock as I realized that many of my long-time friends were actually family. This realization simply raised more questions. It also raised doubts about my trusted friends. Why would this be kept from me? Who are these people, really? How many more are there? Can I still trust them? And where was Jasmina?

Jasmina had her sister's brilliant, piercing green eyes. She was always the imp. When she saw the friendship developing between her sister and me, she did not like it at all. Jasmina would constantly devise plots to trip us up. She was extremely clever and resourceful for an eight-year-old girl. She seemed to have the entire village wrapped around her finger. More than a few times through the years I had wondered if it had been Jasmina who made her sister disappear.

Kadishya walked into the room, her footsteps so soft and silent that she seemed to float. She brought towels, which she gave to Zen. She whispered a few words in her softest tone and turned again to breeze away. As she left the room, I could feel that I didn't want to let her leave my sight. Then it struck me that maybe our parting was her doing, and immediately my angst to learn what happened lost value. All of the reflections and emotions of the past decade were just snapped like an arrow from a bow, and all of those questions were rolling through my brain.

The bath did nothing for me. I felt I might lie awake for hours and listen to my inner voice scream. Eventually sleep came to us all. I dreamed the dreams that were burned into my night mind's eyes years before. When we wakened our clothes lay washed and folded near each bed. We walked together down the hall from our room to tiled stone steps leading down to the ground floor.

Waiting for us in the front room was Sharif. He had arrived early and was quietly anticipating our awakening. My head was clearer this morning and it began to occur to me that I was surrounded by many members of the same family, and the love of my life was here and part of this family. Had I been led here? Was this some kind of huge, elaborate scheme or was this a most ornate example of happenstance? How could I ever know? Could anyone possibly tell me what was happening? Was I simply following the trail of a mysterious new find or was all of this orchestrated by some divine guidance?

We sat circling a low table in the front room. Sharif had deliberate purpose as he lifted from his pocket a small linen-wrapped item. As he unfolded his linen, I caught a glimpse of what looked like just a piece of common concrete. As he uncovered the entire fragment, I could see the matrix and my eyes grew as my pulse raced. At first glance I was certain that he had just revealed a piece of Chassignite. This was the rarest of the rare: a Martian meteorite, but from an extremely rare group. It looked like no other meteorite except maybe an Angrite. It's a meteorite that looks more like concrete, and this piece had obvious fusion crust on it from falling to Earth. There was no speaking, no sound; we all just sat and stared at the specimen resting there on the table. Zen, Ali, and Samir could not bring themselves to even consider reaching out to touch the sacred fragment, and I would not for a host of reasons. And there was no need. I could see what it was. And yet the matrix made no sense to me. It was unlike any other meteorite I had ever seen. It was almost like someone had taken a piece of the Berlin Wall into space and dropped it just to see what it would do. I smiled as I visualized some Russian nerd, cosmonaut/pyro technician, trying to create the ultimate skyrocket from the ISS during his or her spacewalk by chucking a chunk of concrete at the Earth. That would make a dazzling fireball to witness from above. And who would ever know? The boys were puzzled by my silent smile.

"So, now for the serious discussion," I said. We had all

come a long way to get to this place. Something magical had brought us all together. Zen and Ali began to speak with Sharif when Kadishya came into the room. Behind her, children followed with trays of pastries and pots of tea, coffee, and juice, which they set on tables near the door. The children left the room and Kadishya sat next to Sharif. She began to ask him questions in desert tongue and soon she translated in perfect English with the loveliest and the slightest accent of both French and Arabic. The beauty of her eyes and face were only rivaled by the supple tone of her melodic voice. Her voice commanded the room.

We all fell silent as she spoke. Something in her tone made all stop and listen. It was such an overwhelming joy to see her again and to know that she was safe and thriving. But the questions running through my thoughts were a huge distraction to everything in the moment. I was able to suppress these thoughts long enough to listen to what Sharif was saying. He wanted us to get this fragment off the continent and into the hands of researchers with the wherewithal to rush the research and identify this stone. He said this was for everyone. He implied an intense sense of urgency. I could see in his eyes true concern and dire emotion. The message and the task were fairly simple on the surface. But the doing would be another matter. Zen, Ali, and Sharif all had reports of other teams that were trying to intercept what we were planning.

As I have said before, "the sharks can smell blood in the water." At this point I had no interest in even seeing the mass from which this piece had been taken. It would be of no use to me. But that might play out in our favor as we made a run for the borders. Those groups of thugs and bad shots with rifles would be lured towards the main mass and not towards us if they thought we didn't have it. Kadishya finished Sharif's message to me. He could see by my face and eyes that I took this in earnest, and I nodded my head yes and shook both of his hands, agreeing to do all I can. He seemed very pleased and relaxeed back against the wall behind him. Tea was brought to the table. I looked to Ali and acknowledged, "Ah, more tea."

He laughed in response, saying, "Soon you will be one of the green people, man."

We were in the land of the blue people. The people here use dye made from copper minerals to color the wool from their sheep. Over time this turns them blue: skin, eyes, finger and toe nails and hair, all a deep dark blue. One of the first reasons I came here as a younger man was to see the blue people.

Ali said, "Yeah, man, you drink so much green tea that we call you one of the green people." The room erupted in laughter as he repeated his words in Berber. Again Kadishya quietly left the room.

This was a happy home, I could hear children playing on the roof, happy voices speaking from room to room. Brooms brushed floors and kitchen utensils clanged while cars and scooters purred by on the road in front. Ali referred to me as a walking bag of green tea in laughter as we walked the halls and staircase winding through the labyrinth of this joyful home. I heard the calm commanding voice of Kadishya calling for one of her children to come help her, and in my mind's eye I could see her calling to me to come practice my French. "Vite, Vite," she would call to me and clap her hands. It was her voice, her expression, her energy and spirit. It hurt so bad to be so close after so long and feel so far away. She had children, which meant she had moved on and had married. Where then was her husband, and why was there no mention of him?

Through the day we had all scattered to rest. I walked down a hall listening to the sounds of the house and humming to music from one of the rooms. Growing closer to a doorway, I could tell whose voice was humming the tune, and as I passed, I caught just a flash of a glance from her eyes. I stopped just past the doorway to listen to her lovely voice reverberate with more volume. There was just a moment of silence, which reminded me of all the years I had missed her friendship and company. The emotion gushed from the eyes as I labored to calm my heart. I turned to move back to the opening and there she was: standing, eyes littered with tears and arms outstretched towards me. We collapsed together arm in arm, tear on tear. Both of us had held back our emotion for so many years, and it all came out right there in each other's arms. The encounter in front of the house the day before had been so hard for both of us. Neither one of us knew the right words to say. We were both in a daze, neither of us able to fully believe this was happening. The future and the past no longer mattered; only this moment right now mattered and we were both right there in that moment, tasting our tears and letting all of it go. It was as if we had both died and then both came back from that dark place and found each other. It was on this day that I learned that a part of you can die and still come back to life.

We sat crumpled in one mass, arm in arm, sobbing in disbelief and joy at having found each other. For me, no matter what came to pass in the future, my life was complete. The spectrum of my life had found its limits from the lowest low to the highest high. After a time we gained our composure and lifted ourselves up off the floor, fortunate that we had done this when we had so there was no need to explain our behavior. We talked a bit and agreed that over time we would be able to share the details of the missing years. Kadishya asked me if that would be all right in French, and followed the sentence with…"Compri?" I smiled and wiped another tear and she laughed a subtle chuckle; then we both went into daydreams from our past for a moment.

We had had six months together then and had filled them with two lifetimes of fun. When there was nothing going on, she would always have our days planned. She taught me how to haggle in the markets. She took me to the beach to swim, and we would lie on the sand and watch the dung beetles push their balls of dung backwards down the beach. It seemed like such a perfect design as if God had created the beetle to form balls of dung so that when the wind blew, it would blow the escaped balls of dung away from the beetles and roll them for miles until they came to rest at the base of a bush that needed the fertilizer. What a perfect circle: camel or goat eats bush, animal drops dung, beetle rolls dung into ball, wind blows ball under bush, dung feeds bush.

We found humor in everything. Sometimes we would belly laugh so hard we would both cry tears of laughter. She had invited me to her aunt's home for a formal dinner one night. This was a huge honor and my first lesson eating desert fashion with tagine and flat bread. For a teenage boy fresh out of Boy Scouts this was a dream come true. I got to eat with my hands. There was that feeling of my mind taking a photograph. Often in my dreams, in the years beyond, I would see that glance she shot at me out of the corner of her eye as I passed the doorway to the kitchen. This was the same look that I saw today. That was my picture of her. I had carried that mental picture in my mind and heart since then. And she was humming with the same dreamy, child-like voice she had been given by the angels as a small child.

For ten years I held the dear, sweet memories of Kadishya in my mind. Parts of my life I lived according to how I thought she would approve. Her moral conviction, her personal pride, and her belief in her own rights and free will had taught me to believe that she would someday inspire the world. In our humor, laughter, and friendship she shared with me how she thought what I did was "weird" but then she would bless what I did because it brought us together. To her this meant that what I did for a living was a good thing for the world. Then she would joke and say, "But only if it always brings you back to me," and she would rock back and forth. Her voice would go hoarse laughing her belly laugh as she slapped me on the shoulder in her favorite gesture of affection. She could play all roles. She would some days be my mother as she expounded her opinions and shook her finger at me. Some days she was like an older brother and knocked me around. Then there were the days when she would ask me on a date or she would critique my clothes or my hair like a sister. But mostly she was my best friend and I loved her for that. I loved her now as much or more than ever.

In a verbal ballet of catch-up questions, both of us starving for answers about what happened to the other, we filled in much of the gap. It was a surprise to learn that my little Kadishya had become a doctor. She laughed and said she considered studying geology in the hope it would bring me back into her life, but the need for medical personnel and her passion for helping others steered her towards her career.

Kadishya's eyes watered slightly as she admitted, "There was always hope that my road would lead me to yours. And," she laughed, "I prayed that it would not be in my emergency room." One could see she had hung onto her independent mind and her sense of humor. She had developed the calm reserve of a worldly professional. Just then she spoke in her childhood voice and reached over to pinch my side like she had done the last day I had seen her and so many times before that whenever she was about to tease me. As she pinched me, she said, "Still chasing the stars and your bigger than life dreams I see." One could see we were both happy with our choices, but we had always rather have shared them with one another. She added that now that she had her career, she could better understand the commitment I had to my own vocation. I told her that I have so much fun it feels like a sin. She rolled her eyes, laughed, and slapped my shoulder fondly. Just then Ali walked in and gave us a puzzled look. Ali was not part of the family and there was a chance he didn't know much of our past.

There were three tables of people at dinner that night. Kadishya and I were both straining not to burst with questions and stories. After dinner the children sprang into action, dutifully clearing the tables and bringing more tea. In time people began to slip out of the room. Eventually the conversation turned to exclusive question and answer between Kahdy and me. Ali sensed that we needed this time to visit, and he slipped away with the last of the children in tow. Kadishya and I covered everything: my life, her life, my work, hers also. It felt being apart all those years had brought us even closer together. It wasn't just seeing her there or hearing her voice or knowing that I could reach out and touch her; I could feel her presence fill the room.

I teased her by asking, "Where are your great girly glasses?"

She smiled, eyes closed, then cocked her head to the side, fired a look back, resisting a counter-tease, and said, "Contacts."

I teased again with, "I miss the glasses, they did so much for you."

Then, happy to reply to this one, she countered; "Then it's a very good thing that I kept them for you. I remember how much you liked them. I always planned that when you grew old, I would loan them to you."

We both laughed as we tried to get each other with some old tease target from our past. It was such fun to feel those feelings again. They were precious feelings and memories that had been locked away for so terribly long.

Kadishya had a more serious side that melded with her humor and it had always been there, but it had matured over these long years. Even though she was much younger than I, she had helped me grow up in those months we had together. She would always make me tow the line. She would mother me and berate me like her own child if I acted too foolishly or irresponsibly. She always had a keener eye, more like a sixth sense for risk or danger, and she could change her tone in an instant to warn me off or keep me in line. I liked that about her. Made me feel safe and secure, watched over.

"I see you're still chasing your stars and taunting fate

with near misses," Kadishya ribbed, gesturing for me to sit. She lowered her eyelids into a criticizing sneer and said, "You are a slow learner aren't you?"

Without agreeing I replied, "I like the term 'tenacious.'"

Then Kadishya opened her heart and admitted sincerely, "I never stopped thinking of you, not for one day. I have always wished you success and I have prayed for you. In these years I have kept a journal; in it are articles and notes, pictures and names of contacts. Everything recorded in this journal might help you find more of your treasures from space."

As she handed the scrapbook-like journal to me with photos and irregular papers and newspaper clippings hanging out of the edges, I could see she had spent an immeasurable amount of time building this colossal journal that lay heavy in my lap. As I flipped from page to page I could see the years of days of hours she had spent in hope that she might some day present this tremendous gift to me. These pages of hope that we would see each other again someday were pages of proof that she believed in my life's passion. She supported in me the same thing that she used to delight in teasing me about. They say that guilt is the enemy; well then, the enemy had me by the throat. This was such a monumental effort of support and caring, and I had nothing to show her that I had thought about her also and as much. Just then it occurred to me that I did have something to show her. In my wallet, which I had gotten back from Zen's vest, was a worn, tattered photograph of Kadishya and on the back it said, "My Kadishya, Compri?" When she held the picture in her hands, she gently ran her fingers over the ragged edges of her picture; the paper was tattered and curved from time, faded and stained from tears. She could see that I had spent countless hours staring into her eyes. The look in her face was as though the picture was speaking to her. Kadishya began to weep; we both leaned into each other and sobbed away some of the pain from having been apart for so long.

She disarmed the moment by cheerfully saying, "Now you must stay in my land and find all these specimens. I will find you a house so you can live nearby."

We had found each other in an insecure time of change, both our lives between childhood and adulthood. What we had left with each other was a trust that the spirit of that love and friendship would always be there in our lives. I still had many questions for Kadishya but they could wait indefinitely. I just wanted to be with her.

Kahdy pointed as she volunteered, "Here, this section is on your sacred stone. Ali says this is what brought you here to me."

I smiled as she said this, but replied, "I have never tried to find this stone. I have always felt that this stone has sacred significance and that it should not be pursued. It's more like this stone is trying to find me. In the quest for other meteorites, the stories and legends of this stone keep presenting themselves. For something so mysterious and secret, there certainly are a lot of clues and flags laid in my path."

She asked, "Do you want to find it?"

"I admit that I do have a serious curiosity, but only because I have heard about it for years and have never seen the mass."

She continued, "You must promise that you will be extremely careful in approaching this treasure. Anything of this much legend and intrigue will always draw a bad element. Even good energy draws bad energy in this world. You must make a solemn promise that you will always return to me. You have a family here and you are well known to my children. My husband, God rest him, considered you as family also and he had hoped of someday getting to know you better. He was a historian and an archaeologist. You would have liked him a great deal and he you. He had taken an interest in your efforts. He would have wanted to go with you on some of your journeys. It was he who found many of these papers on your sacred stone. Shortly before he passed, he had told me that he felt he had gotten close to its truth. At that point I asked him to let it go. A part of him was like you; he laughed at my request. I could see that he had your silly fever, that feeling that he was so close that stopping now was impossible to even consider. He used to tell me, 'Brightest star of my heart, does a fisherman work all day and then when his quarry finally shows interest in the bait, draw in his line and row for shore?'"

I nodded in agreement with his analogy. I liked this man that I would never meet. I felt that he would have been fun to work with; he was of a like mind.

"Ah, there is that look of yours," she pegged me. "I used to tell my father, Sharif, about your look and how you and he would get that same look when you would talk about this thing. Please tell me that you will be careful. I lost you once and cannot bear to lose you again."

I really wanted to ask her for her side of the story, but I knew that in time I would learn the details of our parting. So I simply said, "you will never lose me, you never have, nor I you. And now I can always find my way back to you. I will not let anything happen to me or to us. I promise to take care. I am not after this stone. I am only here on a general hunting and buying trip. I will get this piece of Sharif's into the hands of scientists who can tell him what he has. But beyond that, this is a routine buying and recovery trip." I said this as I impulsively reached over my chest and rubbed my arm. "Granted, there seem to be a few more glitches than usual, but I promise to be careful."

It occurred to me to show the wounds to Kahdy but then when I reflected on how rapidly they had healed, I thought she might find it strange and resisted raising any suspicion. "So tell me about yourself," I said. Do you still sing my favorite song of the Sahara? Do you still believe that there is magic in the sand? Do you still read late into the night? Do you still drink your tea in the morning brimming with cream and then eat your croissant with goat's milk yogurt?"

She laughed and gulped for air, leaning forward and throwing her long thick black hair back and flushing with a twinge of embarrassment. "Yes, yes, yes," she laughed. "And you?" She asked, "do you still snore like my grandfather? Do you still bite mint lifesavers at night and watch the sparks fly from your mouth? Do you still taste every rock you acquire? Do you carry more books in your pack than clothes?" We both laughed loudly and lifted our heads to breathe in from the laughter.

There were no barriers between us: none of culture or gender, none of age or emotion. There were no borders or beliefs that held us apart. We were as one. We protected what we had between us and would not allow any boundary or standard to interfere with our fun and friendship. I reminded her of the day she had taken me to a motorcycle race. We had collapsed to the ground, rolling in audible amusement when the first class of bikes came up the hill in front of us. The poor novices on their mopeds pedaling to reach the top were falling over as they lost momentum. It was a memory she had let go of and suddenly she realized what a treat she had shown me as I recalled every detail and we belly laughed all over again.

"And you, a doctor," I mused, continuing to tease her, "amazing, so can you save me if I break?"

She quipped, "Only if you are good to me and it will of course depend on how I feel about you on that day. I will always save you, but your behavior will determine how much it will hurt."

"Oh, I promise to be good." I pledged with fingers crossed, "In fact, I promise never to get injured again. If my arm falls off, I will just tape it back on."

"Oh," she said, "you never stop, do you?" Ten years had dragged by and it felt like we had no more than turned a corner and there we were. It felt so comfortable to be there with her. Kadishya released her serious side. I knew I was going to get an earful. "I am telling you, my dear Compri," she expounded, "I have deep concerns about this direction you are taking. I have often hoped that this thing would bring you back to me. But I have felt that this quest for the stone is somehow integrated into the lost life of my dead husband." I struggled with envy as I listened to her speak so highly of her lost spouse, Kamal. "He was a happy, healthy, loving, beautiful man. He was a fine, fair, loving father. There was no explainable cause for the stroke that took him. I have been forced to accept something that makes no sense. You will not want to hear this, but I believe that he was discovered in his research and was silenced. Since then part of me has not wanted you to get this close. I fear that now you will be even more intrigued to travel the same path."

Immediately I began to build my "it will never happen to me" rebuttal of invincibility when she hushed me. She knew where I would go with my defense and she knew my long-winded lecture about what I know of these things.

In her wisdom of my ways she simply said, "For me do this, be careful, be mindful of all those around you and honor your promise to always return to me." Her deep green eyes peered into my soul. I could feel the depth of her concern. I am not good at remembering that it is a responsibility to take care of oneself for the sake of others who care about your well-being. I felt cared for. I could feel how important it was to her that I keep this promise. I've never made promises easily because it meant to me a setup for failure. It was easy to make this promise but it would be much harder to keep it, based on the recent holes in my body and knowing that Laurent and many of his henchmen were on the same trail. In the back of my mind, I was thinking that I needed to leave with this sample.

Part of me felt a dire need to remain here long enough to see a piece of the new fall that had brought me back here in the first place. I spent time poring over this fragment with a hand lens and to my experienced eyes this piece looked like limestone or concrete with fusion crust. That was the clincher: this gorgeous crust that appeared as smoke-tinted glass with ripples and flow lines caused while falling to the ground. I have never seen a piece of meteorite this friable or fine grained. It was absent of any of the typical indicators found in most achondrites except for the lustrous glassy fusion crust.

My fear was that rather than being a new discovery of some unusual planetary material it would turn out to be just another amazing and yet anticlimactic ungrouped achondrite. This was the bane of all meteorite hunters. To find a new and uniquely thrilling type of meteorite only to learn that our researchers don't have a clue of its genesis was always anticlimactic. Then to have it get dumped into this nondescript, blandly disappointing group of lost toys was agonizing. The math was beginning to show that for every home run with a new chunk of Mars or the moon, there were roughly five new gems that got dumped into the pit of despair that is "Ungrouped Achondrites." Over the years, this anomaly has taken a great share of the excitement out of the searches. Even once a piece is in your hands, it is still hard to release your emotions and get excited about the possibilities. Pile on top of that the race to be the first to recover a piece. Once a specimen is obtained, then one's mind turns to all of the possibilities and scenarios whereby your competitor has beaten you to the finish line.

Kadishya had walked back into the other room and had gone back to her singing and humming. From the change in her tone I could tell she was deep in serious thought. I had made my promise to her and I had every intention of keeping it. I had found her and was never letting her go again if I could help that. I could see that there was a great deal she knew that she was withholding, but I felt it would all come out in time. She has such a strong character that I know she can carry a tremendous burden within. Now it was time to go. I walked out to the car, where the hood was up and Samir was checking the oil level with Ali looking over his shoulder. "Everything tip-top?" I asked, walking around to the front of the raised hood.

Head under the hood, Samir replied, "Oh yes, just always check the motor before and after long drives."

"Yes, professor," Ali reiterates, "every drive in the desert is long." He could see the question in my face and he answered it before I had the chance to form the words into a question. "And today we meet this Berber. Today we drive. We drive all day and we stop at the sacred springs to bathe and to drink for our health. Then we meet the nomad with the story and the curious stone. Say your goodbyes, my friend, but I have already told her that we will be coming back after several additional stops. We have a lot to see and many people to visit with."

Returning to the entry room of the house, I could no longer hear her singing flowing through the halls. Kadishya's voice called me to a room at the end of the hall lighted by a tall, slender window. She was seated at a massive hand-carved oak desk in the office. There were glorious antiques and ancient artifacts placed throughout the elegant room.

"This was Kamal's place of peace, solitude, and study," she said. "He is still here; I feel his spirit around me in this sanctuary." She gestured for me to sit toward what seemed to be a throne chair with griffins carved into arms, legs and back. It faced the desk as if its position was for interrogation. I could feel a dread that hung in the air as I sat. Kadishya appeared ominous and dark for a moment while we gazed through the dim light into each other's eyes. This did not feel like my bright little star of the Saharan sky. I felt a pained struggle with the anticipation of the coming words. I was seeing a side of Kahdy that I had never seen. She called for one of the children to close the door to the room.

There was a palpable tension in the air of things most needed to be discussed. I sat quietly as Kadishya placed her clasped hands on the desktop and drew a long, deep, slow breath filling her lungs to begin her words. She stared into a dark corner of the room as if looking into another time or place.

"My beloved Kamal took an interest in your sacred Touchstone. In his travels to ancient sites he began to feel that he was getting very close to its secrets. He wanted very much to meet you, to collaborate with you on this mysterious myth. It began to fill his days and nights with lust and energy beyond any of his prior passions. He was obsessed with its allure. I would challenge him to drop the quest. But no matter my approach he would often say, "My little honey girl, I simply wish to solve this puzzle and see the prize. I don't need to have it or even touch it."

"Then why, I would implore him, don't you please just let it go. Do this for me, I would plead. He would go on to explain the value if it were real and how much time he had invested in the quest. He said that since he felt so close that he had an obligation to finish his research and to document his findings. The more I pleaded with him to cease, the harder he would resist my influence. My husband was extremely determined in trying to solve mysteries of man's past. He was very much the same as you in this way. This stone, its fabled effects on the people, and the land of this part of the world was the pinnacle of his work. On his last return, he had shared with me that deep in the desert in ancient caverns they had found a place that once lay deep under the sea. He and his research crew had found what they believed was a shrine that might have housed the stone, based on carving they had interpreted. He talked about glyphs that recorded this stone having been carried throughout the land several times to help heal the people. It was from his next journey that he never returned. His men said that he died from an apparent stroke. They said it was caused by dehydration. But not seeing for myself makes me suspect foul play. Maybe he found something important or got too close and he was made to stop." She went on to say, "I have lost one of the men I love to this mystery and I will not lose another."

I assured Kadishya that I was only doing what I always do and that I was headed off to acquire some other specimens before heading overseas to meet with researchers. I told her that I was not doing anything beyond routine work in the field and that there was plenty of danger and adventure without looking for more and that I would strive to be extremely safe. This would be a short out and back so that I could spend more time with my dear friend Kahdy. "Besides," I quipped, "the boys and I could use a break in the action. Remember what I told you years ago, the only secrets these stones carry would be the stories they could tell of drifting through the cold of space for billions of years, if only they could talk." My eyes asked her not to worry; her eyes asked me not to give her cause to worry. We were held together and apart by the translucent, elastomeric tension in the room. I could feel it was the right time to leave. This was one of those transitional moments when true friends communicate without words.

As I moved to depart, I felt the slightest touch to my shirt sleeve. When I turned to acknowledge the touch, she lifted my arm and so gently placed a small token on a strand of chain in my outstretched hand with an almost ritualistic gesture. She said something softly, almost inaudible, as she ever so slowly released her grip; I heard the words in Berber something about peace, protect, and let it pass beyond me. She was glancing downward as she folded my fingers into a grip around the gift. She asked me to always wear this medallion around my neck and to bring it back to her. I smiled and bent to press my lips to her hand, then turned to step out of the room. As I walked the hall I could feel that her gesture of the gift held weight and importance to her beyond my understanding. I turned, and looking into her beautiful, soulful, intelligent eyes, I expressed a heart-felt thank-you for the gift.

As I stepped into the full daylight, my eyes winced from the sting of the sun's illumination. I relaxed the grip on the medallion in my palm and looked down at the golden disk. It was a coin, an extremely rare coin. I had only seen one of these coins at the Natural History Museum in London. It was a well-documented but rarely seen Greek coin showing the image of a meteorite on its face. Around 340 years B.C., Aristotle was said to have written the book *Meteorologica*. Although this book covered many terrestrial and atmospheric phenomena, it also held information on meteor events and meteorites and groups that held them in regard as gifts from the heavens. This coin was said to be used as a talisman by one of those groups. I held ancient history in my hand. Just as we climbed into the car I slipped the coin and chain over my neck. I looked out the back window and saw Kadishya standing in the doorway, Sharif standing by her side. He would remain behind while we made this stab into the desert. She raised a hand over her head to say a last farewell. It hurt so badly to leave her. It just didn't feel like the right thing to be doing. I felt so safe in her presence.

I could feel Kadishya's eyes on me as we drove away. I glanced one last time at her face. As we pulled away, I saw the exact same image of her that had been in all of my thoughts and dreams for so long. For years I had thought it was the image in the one picture I had of her with me. Now it felt like I had been looking at her through space and time. There is something mystical about time with her. She seemed so much in control of everything and everyone around her. The only thing that eased the pain of leaving Kadishya was feeling that I would see her again soon after this journey.

CHAPTER FOUR

The Boys

O ff down the dirt road we rolled, headed to our next encounter. None of us knew where this would ultimately take us, but Ali had a list of names and places in his head that we were planning to visit. Random stops along the way could produce any number of opportunities to view specimens found in the desert. You just never knew when asking a few questions would lead to a meeting with a new source. But those encounters could also get us into hot water again. So we were being much more careful about whom we talked to and where.

As we drove, discussion determined that we could swing into the next village to visit Rudy, a German mineral dealer who had moved here in order to get first pick and high-grade minerals for collectors in Europe. His home was a small empire of walled-in acres built on a hillside in his village. We drove up a small hill on the back side of this village to Rudy's palace.

Inside the twelve-foot stucco-covered stone walls was a paradise of fruit trees and livestock pens. Above an outbuilding was a well–laid-out lapidary shop with saws and polishing wheels, steel racks of cut stones, and wooden crates of rough rock to be worked on eventually. Rudy's live-in caretakers were hard at work on various projects around the orchard while the housekeeper was busy in the kitchen cooking lamb for our lunch. We were discussing our journey thus far with Rudy, a trusted confidant, when our story turned to the day of my shooting.

Rudy was very deliberate in his intrigue with our encounter. He was firing questions at us while we were distracted by all of the cool material to pore over. He seemed puzzled by the fact that all of the shots were obviously directed at me. Zen stopped him, wanting to know why he looked at it that way. Rudy, who had lived here for many years and had seen and heard of most encounters, turned suddenly and came at me with a strange piece of tech in his hand.

As he drew closer I could hear the obvious ticking of a Geiger counter. His usual application of this instrument was for buying radioactive minerals, but why was he coming at me with obvious intent? Rudy's face changed from an expression of studious observation to near horror, as he announced what he feared most, "You were shot with bullets of depleted uranium laced with strontium-90 and barium! I have heard this is being done here now. It is a shortcut so that Laurent can track the competition. He is following you and if you spend time in any location, then he will close in to see what you have acquired. But since you have not seen him recently I suspect that he is waiting for something important. If you are after a piece of this new fall that rumors say is Martian, then he is holding back to spring on you when he thinks you are there. That is the only thing keeping you or anyone else safe for now. We need to scrub you and remove any flesh that is heavily contaminated. This will take some time and it is best if we do this here behind high walls. I can bury the waste deep in the ground at the bottom of the property. I'll plant a tree over it and maybe grow some giant fruit."

Rudy smiled his wicked, crooked smile of self-gratification. He was very proud of his ability to make light of a dire situation. There was nobody better equipped to have found this problem and certainly nobody better equipped to help us. But we would owe him a lot of business in future years for his help. I was thinking to myself, *How could this have gotten any worse? This is just plain craziness!*

Our host went on to say, "Hazards are from shrapnel and alpha particles. Studies show no major risk to you, particularly if we remove all residual material. I can use a detector to find any pieces and we can scrub the particles." He looked over the rim of his reading glasses and paused as he stared at us. "This is what I used to do in my past life. I studied mineralogy and specialized in radioactive minerals. I worked for Mineral Resources in Germany. We replaced titanium with DU and then replaced Depleted Uranium with Tungsten Nickel Cobalt. I created the Q bullet and the kinetic energy penetrator, two very nasty, effective tank killers. Somewhere here I still have some surplus hazard kits. We'll get you scrubbed down a couple of times and then we'll check you for shrapnel. Well, at least you know now why they didn't kill you; they want you alive and kicking the can down the road. But you must all remember that you have shown your direction for days now. So once we eliminate the signal it will be just like stirring the hornet's nest with a stick, they will scramble to catch up with you again."

An uncanny happenstance was eating at me. When we pulled into the village, "the boys" laughed and told me that the interpretation of the name of this village meant "End of the Road." I was not feeling the humor right now. Rudy went on to explain that the biggest hazards would be caused by inhalation of dust, which he said was slight because I ran upstairs immediately, and from shrapnel, which had the highest degree of hazard and that within two weeks would do damage to the kidneys. So he rushed to give me some pills to swallow that he insisted would help protect me. As I removed my shirt he frowned with puzzlement as he looked at my wounds.

When I saw the look in his eyes I turned to say, "I know, right? Have you ever seen bullet wounds heal this quickly?"

Rudy's response was comical, "Must have been magical uranium."

We both let out a sullen chuckle of sarcasm. Rudy waved his detectors over my torso, looking puzzled as he set one on the workbench and returned with another.

"Hmmm," he frowned, "there is nothing here. I am not finding any contaminated dust particles in your lungs. I find no pieces of shrapnel, not one shred of material. It may be that since the bullets hit you before striking anything else they were smooth enough to simply slice right through undisturbed. Good for you, I should say; you seem to have a very influential guardian angel, eh."

Just then Rudy unwittingly swung his counter over my rucksack, still over one shoulder, and got a screaming signal on his machine. A bit of digging and we found a piece of bullet that lodged in the heavy fabric at the bottom of the bag. Rudy put the fragment of bullet under a microscope. Moments later, he excitedly proclaimed his new find as a "candy store" of radioactive isotopes. He described the projectile as having been layers of depleted uranium and lead contaminated with an assortment of nasty radioisotopes.

Rudy was obviously excited and intrigued by this new weapon. "Ok, so they are tracing the same signal that I am getting from the counter. This means that they are either close or they are using very expensive technology; either way it would be best if we build a decoy. This should be simple," he said as he walked off and down the steps to his house.

Rudy shouted back up the stairs to Ali in desert dialect. He would be sending a package back north on the back of a truck that would mirror my signal. We must prepare to depart at the same time his package takes flight. His suggested plan is that we should drive deep into the desert and circle far out towards the coast to return to the north and off the continent. Of course I needed to get a piece of the new fall, which might mean more excitement. Rudy's housekeeper fixed us a nice basket of lamb, flatbread, and fruit, a rare and welcome gift for the road.

Now we were heading into a part of the planet where I like to say that everything is angry. This is where the fun begins, where the sand can swallow a large truck whole, where large toothy vipers hide under the sand waiting to strike, where scorpions the size of saucers outnumber the roaches, and yet I have more fear of my fellow man. It seems odd to note that this was once the bottom of the Devonian sea and then a lush forested land with endless wetlands, and now a land of rock and sand. As we ventured further into the dry we were approaching some of the oldest tribes of humans. It has been shown that these tribesmen have a direct genetic link to the earliest beginnings of humans on Earth. They remain here as if waiting for life to return to what it once was. And with all of their struggle to survive in a place that threatens to take life from them each day, they remain here and they are happy to be here. Everything I see here raises the question: why?

At this juncture there was no longer a road beneath our tires. This was the beginning of the Great Sand Sea. We approached a tiny village far out in a great basin of bleached hardpan soil. As we rolled closer we could see a fellow waving and jumping for our attention. As we grew closer Ali said, "Ah, this is Liashi, our next contact." As we pulled up to him, he signaled us to keep rolling and he began to run alongside the car. Zen opened the door and helped pull the winded runner inside. Liashi was frantic as he announced that we are being followed, they are not far behind, and that they have beaten Rudy senseless in the pursuit to catch us. Fortunately, Rudy had a radio and his groundskeeper had called ahead.

Liashi pointed off to the right where a Quat Quat was dusting towards us. Quat Quat is a French abbreviation for Four By Four. Liashi went on to say that he was trading us his Range Rover for our Mercedes. Nothing more need be said. We all scrambled to make the swap to this luxury survival vehicle with the tank filled with fuel and a well-stocked desert kit in the rear. The rack atop this excursion rig was loaded with water and fuel cans, a tent, and blankets. This was a rolling fortress of solitude and it felt at this moment like the game had changed. I was learning just how

70

powerful networking can be. The boys were doing things right and I was just along for the ride.

Living here on the edge of the world, an explorer must be prepared to deal with every possible element. As I looked around our new home, I noticed the rear interior had steel plates bolted inside. This struck me odd since as we pulled the car switch, I had noticed that the outside was lined with beautiful polished sections of checker plate steel. I asked Ali if he knew what was up with the steel plates.

He smiled and called out, "Bullet proof, man; how we rock and roll here, man!" The boys all laughed as I grinned so hard it hurt. This journey had just gone from fear back to fun. For once it felt like we were on top of the situation. Liashi wanted to be dropped at the next village. He said he had some business to do there. Just then Liashi leaned over to dig into his pants pocket. Slowly he lifted out a piece of our next target. He looked over at me and the others and handed over this gorgeous, totally complete, jet-black, fresh-fallen, fusion-crusted individual of the new fall from just weeks ago. He was there; he watched it fall. He said he was there buying fossils when the fireball event occurred and he was one of the first to arrive at ground zero. He said there were stones like this hen's egg–sized specimen lying every fifty meters. This was the real thing! I could see melted into the fusion crust the angular basaltic, cross-hatch structure of the matrix and the rectangular clasts of breccia suspended within that matrix. It was lightweight for a meteorite, and the magnet I religiously carry in my pocket would not stick to it at all. All of these indicators showed a field identifier that this was an achondrite and from my experience this was an SNC.

I looked at Liashi and asked, "How many stones?"

He replied, "I got them all; it was 11 kilograms of stones, 31 stones just like this one."

My heart stopped. This was what our adversaries were after and they had no leads because the only man to have material was in the Quat Quat with us. Liashi was one of Ali's team and his loyalty to Ali was dauntless. This kind of loyalty was priceless and it was such an honor to be a part of this brotherhood. I feel compelled to take better care of the team members than even myself. My guys know this, which is the only reason that I get to witness this level of trust and loyalty. I put my hand on Ali's shoulder and said, "This is great!"

Ali smiled, shook his head back and forth, and waved his index finger in my face, preaching, "We're not letting the mafia get you, man." He repeated this to Zen, Samir, and Liashi; they laughed and loosened up a bit. They started talking amongst themselves. I wondered if Samir was trying to learn how he would get his car back.

For me, the journey was complete. I was sitting in silence, thinking that there was no need to continue on into the desert. We had been gifted a piece of the mysterious Touchstone that had been just a legend for thousands of years, and we had a fresh-fallen piece of the latest fall event. It was time to run for the barn. It was time to get these stones into the hands of science. I knew I'd need to address this with Ali and the boys, but first it was on to the next village to drop Liashi. The stop to drop Liashi was abrupt and swift. They had made this part of the plan and there was no time wasted on goodbyes. Liashi knew that Ali would take care of his concerns. He shook my hand and

blessed me with a hand on his chest, and off he ran. As we
continued, I ask what we would do next.

Ali could apparently read minds. He assured me, "Don't
worry, man, we are finished; other deals can wait. Now we
make a big loop into the Sand Sea to leave no trail and then
we go back by a different route. It will be long and hard to
go this way, but then we have a chance of getting your rocks
where they need to go." Then Ali went on to say, "You know,
man, this game is getting more dangerous and I now have
childrens."

It struck me funny that his English had gotten so good
and yet there were still these little slip-ups that were so like
him to use. It had become his unique way of speaking. Ali
had learned my language so much better than I had learned
his language, it was an embarrassment for me. He went on
to say that this danger was a big worry for him and his wife.
It was hard to hear what he was telling me, but I always
knew this would come. I also knew that I could never repeat
this relationship again. Things change and are never the
same again. He could see that I understood his message.
For now it was to complete this mission at hand and get his
friend home safely. First, we must make this loop through
the desert.

There was one final safe place we could head for. Kadishya's
little sister Jasmina lived here deep in the desert. Kadishya
had told me that her sister was out here and living well on
her own. She had married young but her husband also had
passed away. Jasmina had developed her instincts and skills
to manipulate people and had to live where she could take
charge of her world. She had become a shaman and she was
still using her rare gift to lead. I remember that Jasmina was

wickedly beautiful as a young girl, with Kadishya's eyes and her own youthful look, golden skin, perfect lean build, and just a few impish freckles cast across her nose. She knew how lovely she looked and she used it like a magic wand to help her get what she wanted. She had a devilish smile and she was destined to be a man killer. I felt apprehensive about seeing her. If she was still as gorgeous on top of these years to mature, I might feel uncomfortable spending time with her. We didn't have the same relationship I had with her sister. She was always against her sister's friendship with a guy from outside their culture, and I remembered seeing a burning look of envy in her eyes.

Often hatred comes first and is then followed by justifications that don't need to make sense. At the same time I was bursting with curiosity about what this lovely little sprite was doing, living out here in the sand and rock. She had the love of her family, but she had married a prince of the desert and apparently she was living his life, in charge of their tribe and ruling the roost as only she knew how to rule. It was interesting to me that the girl I knew at a young age was living exactly the life I had figured she was born to live. I knew I would find a young woman completely in command of the world around her, and hopefully a merciful leader of her people. She always had a sweet side, but I saw more of the devil in her and had assumed in my naïve youth just which direction she would follow. I did not know how long it would take to get to Jasmina.

The boys had an idea of where we were headed, but we were getting there much faster in this powerful all-terrain vehicle. There was no need for us to stop; we had food and water and pissed in water bottles. We all figured that a bit of discomfort was better than a bullet to the head. We had to assume that Ali's "mafia" figured we had reached our goal and were running heavy, meaning we had what we came for. This was our big chance to make the break-away and gain a big lead on our predators. And so we went; the plan was to trade off driving. It was laughable when my turn came up: I had a car full of side-seat drivers watching my every move, and nobody slept with me at the wheel.

Eventually the sun slipped below the edge of the Earth. The guy who said the Earth was flat must have been here once upon a time. We drove past a tiny oasis just at twilight. It was the first open standing water we had seen in three days of driving. This view inspired the thought that water in this desert must feel just like a desert island in an ocean. An oasis is a place of unparalleled beauty with date palm trees, olive trees, fruit, grass, and colors everywhere. The air is filled with the pungent, sweet scent of jasmine. The tiny white desert flower's delicious fragrance is everywhere in the air. Much like Jasmina living out here in the desert, jasmine—the delicate white flower she is named for—lives in a world of thorns and blistering heat.

Ali spoke, lifting me out of my waking dream. "Hey, man, the plan is to drive late into the night until we are all too tired to go and then we will pull well off the road and sleep for a time. If things go well, we see Jasmina in morning, ok?"

I answered with a simple, "Yep."

The night droned on. The headlights faded into oblivion out ahead and there was no opposing traffic, which helped keep things simple. We took our turns at the wheel and drove well into the late night and early morning. Ali took over as pilot after we passed a tall, natural stone formation that he uses as a landmark for where to leave the trail and how to return to the same exit point after daybreak. We ran off into the dark and continued far enough that if we slept after dawn, anyone passing would not see us out there. We all groaned as we climbed out to stretch before sleeping for the few remaining hours of dark. It was difficult to know where we were but Ali was confident he could follow Kadishya's directions to the home of Jasmina.

Morning arrived in a blink. We were all stiff, sore, and hard-pressed to wake, but motivated by concern that our stop might give the bad guys a chance to catch up. The last thing I wished was to draw any risk or hazard towards Jasmina. We climbed into the car after fueling up and turned back on our tracks. Soon we were back to the stone standing at the road and continuing on our way. Looking out my window, I noticed that automobiles were mostly gone, now replaced by donkey-drawn carts and people walking alongside their camel train. I thought about this image for a time and then asked Ali to explain why I never saw Berbers riding camels but often saw them walking alongside their beasts. He laughed at my inquiry.

He chuckled. "People riding camels?"

"Yes," I replied.

"Tourists," he continued. "Berbers walk, man. Berbers are tough, man; you have no idea how tough these people are. They love the Earth, they love to walk, and they walk all the way across, man."

One thing I have learned about having curiosity about other cultures: be ready to feel foolish and ignorant. But I don't know a better way to learn. Poor Ali and his mates rapidly tired of all of my questions. From time to time I had to remind myself to give the boys a break. I really didn't know what their motivation was for helping me other than the money, but the money wasn't enough for them to take risks like this. So I felt obliged to cut them as much slack as I could out of consideration for all they do for me. So I watched this strange world fly by and tried to remember my queries for a later opportunity to fire at Ali unfettered. He knew I would hit him with a barrage of inquiries during a quiet moment. Based on the subject matter, Ali would know exactly when I started saving up my curiosities to take advantage of his knowledge and familiarity with this amazing land and its people. Ali is proud of his land and I like to think that my questions remind him of just how fascinating his corner of this world really is. I hope that he gets that message from my constant picking at his brain.

The road diminished to nearly a set of tracks in the dust. Beyond here travel is guesswork for even veteran nomads. This is where the term "safety in numbers" originated. Most traverse these parts in caravans so there is plenty of help when some unlucky member gets stuck. And all carry tracks on or under each vehicle to set out and drive over on soft, fluffy sand. It can be exhausting, rigorous exercise running tracks, but we all prefer running tracks to digging people and rigs out of the sand. And it's not just the running and the carrying of the tracks. It's doing this over and over again in soft sand. Some teams will take turns driving. We enjoyed the gamble of drawing short straw. There is a sinfully sweet revenge in getting to drive the tracks on an uncommonly bad day of soft sand pits. Zen and Ali were very good at spotting the pits early and I was learning the indicators; Samir just wanted to go home to his fast-paced city life.

I paused for a moment to breathe and to look ahead. I heard my father, imparting one of his many pearls of wisdom, "elbow to the grindstone, shoulder to the wheel; don't look up at how far you still have to go, it will only slow you down"—he was the king of cliché.

I had looked up and my mind was instantly flooded with thoughts of how we could work so fast yet travel so slow. It was exasperating to work through this sand fluff. The driver got the glory of getting to sit on his ass, yelling and driving, but every time he hit another pit, he suffered a barrage of disdain as we cast dispersions on his inept abilities.

Soon we found ourselves back on top of what appeared to be a road surface. It was as if a section of road had been scoured off the surface of the Earth by the wind's corrosive determination and then this segue of bad fortune reversed itself. As fast as we had covered this track, the winds had removed our sign. For once the wind was our friend. After stacking the tracks temporarily on the rear bumper, Zen, who had drawn the short straw for the day, jumped back into the driver seat and the rest of us followed his lead and piled into the Quat Quat.

Off we went down this seemingly paved road. It was the short straw driver's responsibility to remember that as we flew down the road we had roughly two feet of grated steel track protruding from both sides of our vehicle. Popular opinion was that we didn't know how long this delightful road surface would last, and nobody wanted to lie down to formally store the tracks beneath the rig until we absolutely had to. It's a bit of a trade-off since driving this way was slow and noisy from the rush of air howling through our apparent metal sea anchors.

Ali had the two stones in his pockets. Zen again carried my wallet and passport in his vest. I felt safer knowing that I carried nothing. Then I remembered the chain around my neck and the gift that Kadishya had given to protect me, and my new mission to return it to her safely. Since the first sight I couldn't get thoughts of her out of my mind. Repeatedly her image appeared in so many of my favorite expressions.

Most compelling was how all of this was falling together and where this journey would lead next. I feared the tiny dynamo that is Jasmina. Her strength and direct demeanor have always set me aback. In our limited past, I felt mostly judgment and disapproval emanate from her direction. Any man will expound on her beauty and rave about her family eyes, those deep, piercing, green windows to the soul. But my Kadishya was always there to buffer encounters with Jasmina and now I was set to meet with her, one on one, for the first time. This simply didn't bode well for a joyful encounter. My gut told me it could be a disastrous prospect. I knew the boys would be smitten by their first impression, but they too would read between the lines very adeptly and would rapidly acknowledge her tough spirit and armor-plated shield. This way of hers had apparently kept most men out, though not all men, since she obviously had married before becoming a widow.

We traveled a while longer, Zen dodging the odd stone or high spot on the road that might catch hold of our air brakes. It was obvious that the surface continued, so he pulled the car off to the side, where we all piled out to heave-to reloading the tracks back under the car. As always my eyes wandered, hoping not to catch a glimpse of my least favorite critters:

scorpions, snakes, etc. I can't resist the look because it so often produces results. Ali loves to catch me looking around. He giggles the cutest high-pitched giggle whenever he sees me glancing about in fear. He knows now how good I am at spotting a pair of horned eyes peering out of the sand or the dark outline of a plate-sized scorpion strolling along in the dark with all of its assets poised at the ready.

I recalled where Ali and the boys first learned of my fear of things that bite and sting. Many years earlier before I was tuned into these annoying dangers, we were on a wonderful journey through mountains reasonably near this area when we stopped for a break and to visit with three small desert children who were standing on the side of the road at the summit of this range. They were very quiet, solemn, curious observers, there to watch cars and trucks go by as if they had never seen this amazing phenomenon in their short lives. I tried to give them candy or money in exchange for a few photographs, but Ali told me that they didn't know what these were or what to do with them and that they were not there to take anything, simply to watch. He said that on our way back we would bring paper and crayons and show them what to do with them, and that might win their approval. One could see these children were in utter wonder at the strangers that had stopped to visit. Ali said that they spoke an ancient dialect that he did not speak at all.

While Ali and Zen walked back down the highway to look at the view of the basin we had come through and the view down the range we had climbed for two hours, I went dancing from rock top to rock top so that I could get a couple of hundred feet away from our car to take a picture of the scene. It looked as if giants had been here eons before us and stacked these boulders side by side. As I turned to look back at the road and car, the kids, Ali, and Zen were back to the car with Samir and they were all vigorously waving and calling to me. I could see their sense of urgency and began hopping my way back in their direction. I stopped a couple of times to nose around in the rocks, but there was nothing to see. I had made it roughly halfway back when I stopped again and called out to ask what was the rush.

"Snakes, man!" I looked into Ali's face for a glint of a smile, but all I could see was the wrinkles of concern and a very serious posture.

Voice wavering, I called back, "Snakes?!"

He responded in direct reply, "Yeah, man, snakes!"

"What kind?" were my next, rushed, nervous, pointed words.

Ali clarified, "Cobra, man, lots of them!"

Earlier that day we had seen several snake charmers in the Souk we visited, with their cobras in baskets. I asked him about the snakes at the Souk while I danced on boulders from top to top. Ali called back in my direction while he gestured, waving his arms outstretched in all directions, "Yeah, man, where do you think they get their snakes?"

As we continued through the area, I reflected on that past journey through the very same mountain pass. Now the boys were laughing and speaking to each other in broken Berber so that I could not understand. I knew exactly what the joke was.

This encounter with my own ignorance opened my eyes for years to come. I will never again walk around aimlessly and will always keep an extra set of eyes on the ground.

Growing up in rattlesnake country with all of my childhood out adventuring, I had only seen one live rattler in the wild and that one was just a few years earlier on an island while fishing. But here, once I started tuning in to the possibility, I saw snakes daily: big ones, little ones, in the brush, in the sand, in the rocks, and often in the cities and villages. I think for me the concern with scorpions comes from that honking huge stinger sitting up there always poised for a strike. Snakes are a horse of a different color. My travel partners think it's hilarious that a great big human is intimidated by a little bitty insect. The snake episode simply reminds them of my pusillanimous fear of nasty bugs as well. This brands me a constant source of humorous entertainment.

Back in our rig and off we went now with Ali back at the wheel. Laughter erupted again and again as we rolled down the mountain road. The boys were having a great time at my expense, discussing my reactions to tiny critters, their voices elevating in tone and speed as they mulled over my behavior. Ali said we are close to the oasis where Jasmina should be waiting for our arrival. His voice cracked through the tears of laughter they are enjoying.

The hope was that Mina would have information on the path we have left behind and if our safety still remained at risk. Since she had been living here for some time, there was hope that she could give us best directions for getting back where we need to go. The plan in place at this time was for Ali and me to get these two samples to the London Natural History Museum. Once that part of our task is complete, then the risk of hazard would diminish for a time. Meanwhile, Ali had made arrangement for the 11 kilos of gorgeous meteorites to be taken out of the country to get them out of harm's way. The recent event of bullets through my arm and neck had given all of us a new sense of urgency. One of my biggest concerns and a constant underlying theme in my thoughts was that this work I had chosen was getting too dangerous and I might need to look for a new career. The concern was not for me, but for all the friends who come in contact with me. It was a growing burden of responsibility for me to worry that dear friends and family might be harmed because of my vocation. For now we had to complete the task at hand and get the heck outa Dodge.

The line of thought struck me in an odd way. It suddenly occurred to me that just maybe, our travel direction had been deciphered and our next step might turn out to be another trap. We had no wildly overwhelming need to meet with Jasmina. Here was my gut screaming at me again to listen. Maybe this is what others refer to as the inner voice. I had a gut feeling that there were more serious reasons why I feared meeting with the lovely Jasmina. It was almost as if someone had a way to communicate with these gut feelings and change my thoughts.

"Oh yeah, that's what this is," I sneered to myself with sarcastic rebuke. But that voice inside my head was undeniably clear and concise, telling me to ward off this pending evil doom and head for the deep Sand Sea. Putting my hands on Ali's shoulders, I told him to please turn right. He looked up into the rear mirror with puzzlement in his face.

"What are we doing, man?" Ali inquired, puzzled.

I retorted, "Please, my dear friend, I know this sounds crazy, but we need to move now; just turn and go; I have a gut feeling."

Ali knows all about my gut. He has seen it save us or

others so many times that it's as if there was another person with us who knows everything before it happens. Often I have felt that he trusts my gut more than I do. He always listens, and this time he smiled as he jerked the wheel with both hands and shouted, "Ok, baby, here we go!"

"Yes, Ali Baby, here we go again!" I yelled as the others simply whooped and cheered. Our mood had become sullen as we drew closer to seeing Jasmina and now that we had shaken things up and were flying blind, everyone was happy again and feeling on top of the world.

Ali shouted out, "Now we follow the gut!" Somehow such a random and illogical choice had changed the entire complexion of our journey. We all seemed happy about this change. It was as if we had all felt that our fate was sealed if we continued to that destination. Now we four were in total control of our destiny and that fate would work itself out just fine this way. We had just severed all connections with the world outside this car and that felt good.

"My friends, we need to make a new plan and it needs to be a plan that keeps us all safe," I directed. "I figure the best course is for us to split up in four directions; one remains near here for a while to observe activity. One we take out to the coast where he hops a boat and heads for the museum, one takes transport up the coast, and the last drives north for a while and then returns this vehicle to Liashi. Any of you have suggestions or better ideas?"

Silence filled the air for a time while our brains scrambled and sparked with possibilities. I went on to tell the boys that my wish was to get us all out of this danger unharmed. My thinking was that I would run decoy while Ali headed for London and the Natural History Museum. I wanted

Zen in place for me to reconnect with as soon as possible, and I just wished to get Samir back to his car and safely home to his fancy life. Beyond getting the fragments into a laboratory for classification, there was no need to take any risks. Also, not stopping to visit with Jasmina kept her safer than if we had gone there, or so I hoped. Everything up until now dictated that these bandits were hot on our trail. Right now, any of us could drive anywhere we wanted and we would be ok. But the sooner we changed our numbers, the better. Ali came up with a great suggestion: to stop in the next village and buy a scooter which he would then ride separate from the group. Eventually he could take another route to the coast.

Samir added his two cents, "I know, I know, I have a good plan, I will ride with Ali, I have a friend some kilometers from here where he can drop me. I can stay for a few days, visit and then he will drive me to my car. Then Zen can take this car north and Liashi will pick it up on his next trip to the city or he can ride with me to pick up the Quat Quat. He is due for a visit to the city to party with me!"

Plans fell together rapidly as we plowed through the dust and sand heading across country. Eventually we crossed another road and took it towards the west. We were making our huge loop after all, and it felt like we had made all the right choices. Just then our flying desert gauntlet zipped over a hump and flew out into the fluff of a sand trap. Before we ground to a halt we were thirty paces into the pit and axle deep in the soft shifting sand. Worse yet, the sand tracks were under the car. We were all so busy brainstorming our next moves that none of us were watching for the hazard. We had to dig out the tracks under the Quat

Quat before we could dig the car out. Everyone knew this process would take a full day. The trap was massive so it was easy to see that backing out would be the best effort. Surveying our surroundings, we could see the faint tracks of other vehicles that navigated around the edge of the pit. In this desert, slower is faster. This is where we would use most of our water. Bodies sweated like pots of boiling water. The heat of the sun began to radiate from the paint and metal of the half-buried car, the vehicle of glass, metal, and plastic becoming a Dutch oven buried in a fire pit.

We were working hard and fast, but soon the car was too hot to touch. The water and gas cans strapped to the top whistled from the pressure release vents as the liquids approached boiling temperatures. Soon we would have to wait until dark for the water to cool enough to drink. Quickly Zen removed a water can from the rack and wrapped it in wetted towels and clothing. The evaporating water would refrigerate the life-giving liquid in this can. We would have something cool to drink while we labored to dig our trapped ride from this pit of despair. As fast as we could drink water, it poured out of our skin as sweat. Legs and arms cramped from dehydration as we scrambled to dig the sand out from beneath the car to free the metal tracks we needed to place under the tires. As we dug away sand, more flowed in to replace what we took. Our only chance was to be able to get the tracks far enough under the rubber tires that they could grab hold of the perforated surface, then we could carefully climb our transport back out of this trap. Sweat and sand stuck to the skin. With each breath more water escaped our bodies as the sun slowly, silently made its daily attempt to take lives from the Earth. Ali had the greatest desert wisdom in our group and he wrapped himself in heavy clothing to insulate from the sun's rays as he shuttled sips of cool water to each of us manning the shovels.

Without words, we labored diligently: a well-rehearsed team all hoping for that moment when the engine would ignite and the tires creep their vulcanized way onto the tracks and atop the sand that holds us. Samir dug with surprising speed and relentless energy in his button-down shirt, creased slacks, and Italian leather loafers. For a city boy he handled the desert challenges seemingly better than any of us. Zen and I dug out the back while Samir managed the front and Ali scrambled about, serving water and coaching the group. In time we were backed out of the fluff and the Quat Quat was parked on firm ground. We loaded the tracks on the back in case they were needed again and began our journey once more, driving cautiously around the edge of the pit. As we followed the faint treads of predecessors, we could see the impressive size of this obstacle. These sand traps are a simple, natural phenomenon and yet the epitome of a passive-aggressive killer. In the deepest parts of the desert these traps are marked by rusted vehicles and weathered bones. Even when death is nigh from the heat of day, the eyes maintain their vigil for creepy crawlies and things that slither.

Later that day we reached a village where we negotiated cash for a scooter that Ali felt would make the distance to the coast. Zen and I gave Ali most of the cash so that he could make his way. We said our goodbyes and wished him to fare well. There was an indescribable difference between how danger felt in a tight group like ours and how it felt to send one of our own off alone into harm's way. I have never learned how to deal with that particular insecurity. How does one not worry for a friend in danger? It will change again once we have all gone our separate ways and each of us has to get along by our own wits. For now it felt unfair or out of balance. Just before Ali Baba departed, I took one last look at the stone and because there was enough for research I snapped a small end piece off of the Touchstone fragment.

Saying, "Just for luck," I looked at Ali and stuffed it into my shirt pocket. We wished each other the best of good fortune and safe return, then went our separate ways. Ali would go it alone and race for the coast on his scooter to catch a boat for London, England. Zen, Samir, and I head to get Samir to his friend's home; then we split again. Zen and I continued to a point where we too could split up to go our separate ways. Zen dropped me in front of a bus station after getting my ticket for me. He would be there to meet me at the destination and all I needed to do was sit quietly and keep to myself.

CHAPTER FIVE

Simon's Ride

Waiting at the station for my ride I took a seat; before long my eyes were giving up the battle as I started to fall off to sleep. It's all I could do to keep track of my departure. Suddenly, Jasmina was standing there in front of me. She reached out as she asked me to come with her. She was glowing with inexplicable beauty. She had matured into a figure of perfection that would stop the hearts of men. The symmetry of her face and the youthful glow of her flawless skin only served as the ideal frame for her hypnotic emerald eyes, eyes that burned into your soul. As a woman, she is her sister personified. In a whisper she beckoned me to come with her. She said that things had collapsed behind our plight and that our path had become one of destruction. She needed me to come to her home to help with problems that only I could resolve. And so as she stood there reaching out to me, I rose in response. People scurried by, horns honked, and dust filled my lungs as I awakened standing there in front of the station. I had fallen asleep and woke standing in place, looking into Jasmina's eyes as she faded into obscurity.

There went my gut again. Ticket in hand, I conclude that my direction can wait a few days while I figure out a way to get back over to Jasmina. Wandering away from the bus station was not in the plan, but then again, neither was reaching out to Mina in a waking vision. Something was all wrong, and my gut was telling me to follow her plea. This was simple really; all I needed to do was hitch a ride with someone back across a span of barren ground without roads or maps, in or on any vehicle with a driver who could understand my request. And having given Ali most of the cash, I was going to need to use my limited charm and inept ability to speak the desert dialect to get my weary body on board for another bumpy leg to this journey. The message from Jasmina was so irresistibly compelling that I chucked caution to the wind and tried pretty much every approach I had ever used to get attention that might result in a ride. In this part of the world, there are fuel stops along the roads and highways where people will stand or sit and wait for the offer to join a ride. Cars rarely travel with empty seats, and the riders help pay for the fuel. It seems an honorable way to economize and conserve fuel. Holding out a hand full of cash can get one a ride quickly, and often times a better or longer distance transport.

The first opportunity offered would have been fine, but it was so full already that when it stopped and nobody got out, I figured I would pass on the offer. Next was a large truck that had just dropped riders and since he was stopped, I ran over to see if he needed replacements to ride with him. When I used my lame dialect to inquire, he yelled back at me loudly, but in fairly decent, heavily accented English. I didn't quite catch what he said but I replied yes, regardless, and he waved me up to the seat next to him.

His truck had a lot of character. The interior of the cab looked like it was decorated for some type of holiday celebration, the kind of look that made you figure this truck must have a name. He talked to his truck more than he spoke to me. He was a colorful guy with a tremendous amount of energy. He drove his truck like a bicycle racer riding in a peloton. His hands and feet worked non-stop steering and shifting and never touching the brakes, but rather relying on the clutch and gears to slow down and speed up. His seat was only there for minor support and to hold him in place while he worked to keep us on the road. His face was pocked with deep sockets of missing subcutaneous flesh and his chin was littered with occasional heavy whiskers. Dark, black eyes peered out from beneath thick curly black brows.

The cab smelled of mint and the sun visors were lined with peppermint candy canes, one of them hanging from his mouth as if it were a toothpick. He asked me where I was going, but it was difficult for me to say since I had no name for Jasmina's village. The cane in his mouth waved up and down as he spoke, and the protrusion only made his words more difficult to discern. So I started to tell him about our journey and where we had been and who I was going to see.

When I mentioned her amazing green eyes, he interrupted me, "Ah, you wish to visit princess Jasmina!" He laughed as if I had just finished a world-class joke. "That is where we are going; we take this load of freight to her village. We take right to her door." When he said "we" it seemed that he was referring to himself and his truck. As I spent more time in his truck I began to think maybe "we" included the cane in his mouth. He would pull the sweet treat from his mouth and wave it around much like a professor, lecturing with a pointer in hand. He talked about everything he could think of while we rolled across the country. I liked this fellow more every minute we spent together. Something about his demeanor made me feel at home with a good old friend. He talked so much that I could just relax and listen. The rambling conversation and his proactive driving were a symphony of sound and movement. The surface of the road was only a random addition to the music and its rhythm. For the time I had no worries; I felt safe. It was simply a fun journey in the passenger seat much like sitting in a theater watching the scenes of a movie roll by.

Parched from a day in the dust and heat without a drink, when he offered me one of his precious mouthwatering suckers, I accepted without hesitation and took one from my visor. The flavor and scent brought back memories of wintertime fires in the fireplace at home and stockings hanging from the mantelpiece filled with nuts and fruits and one of these canes hooked over the edge of the knitted sock. I would never be able to decipher from our language barrier how he had discovered this favorite sweet of his but I would ponder this endlessly.

I smiled and chuckled to myself; how could anyone not find fun in this burly, serious guy who drove his truck around the country with a candy cane hanging out of his mouth? It's an odd anomaly traveling in another land where you only know a limited amount of the local language. Over time one can listen to the dialogue and pick up the general message, but you miss a great deal of the detail in what is being said. Still the general idea is enough to get by. And so as my new friend and tour guide chiseled our route from the desert floor, I picked up his introduction and that his name was Simon. Simon seemed to me to be the kind of guy that anyone would want for a friend. It was obvious that he loved his work and that his life was complete sitting behind the wheel of his truck seeing the world go by. He was happy and his life was simple. There were pictures of his wife and children jammed into the edge of the windshield, and when I pointed and made a short comment, he went off on a lengthy introduction of every member of his pride and joy family. His young wife was home caring for a large number of children: three boys and the rest girls. Simon's youngest girl was obviously his favorite; there were several pictures of her and I could see him glance at one of her photos often. He repeated her name, Meli, often and seemed to enjoy calling her "my Meli." There was a perceptively, powerful, tactile bond between the two as though she was there in the truck with us. One could almost assume that she was his guardian angel. I could see the love and the longing in his eyes to be there with her rather than here driving his beloved truck.

On we rolled as Simon happily shifted through the gears while navigating the nearly nondescript roadway. The only indicator of correct direction was the occasional human walking along our path. Simon seemed so confident in our direction that I would forget to care about that which I could not see. It reminded me of riding my old mare Chex on the trails near home. At the end of a long-distance ride I could drop the reins and she would take us directly back to the barn and she would always find the shortest set of trails to get us there. Simon and his truck were headed for the barn to take a load off and he knew the way better than a GPS.

So on we rolled while I learned to decode his accent and helped him with his English. As we drove closer to our destination I had more visions of Jasmina; she was speaking to me and waving me in her direction. I could feel her sense of urgency and I could hear her telling me that we were getting closer to where we would see her. Simon began to sing to the rhythm of the road; if he didn't talk he would sing. His singing voice was magical. These fluid, melodic, almost operatic tones came from the chest of this burly, bearded trucker of the sands as if in another life he had entertained millions with his voice. I was here alone gifted by his unbelievable talent. Time drifted by almost unnoticed as we logged the miles. I began to understand how Simon could love his work so much. His freight was the reason to be here, and his truck was his key to the doors of the outside world. He was a simple, happy man and he was living a full life doing what he could to care for his family.

While we rumbled along I thought about his family and what it would look like to see this great, happy man arrive home to his family with his booming voice and arms outstretched to catch the rush of children running and calling to greet their loving father. My impulse was to dig into my pocket to count how much money I had left that I could offer him for this ride. He glanced over to see me counting money and immediately he began to throw up a hand to block his view as he rattled off a blur of words all meaning that he would not take my money for this journey. I'll never understand why he wouldn't take payment for the fuel, but apparently he had made up his mind early on that this was how he would handle my effort to repay his kindness. I didn't have much, but I was prepared to give all of it to this new friend, and his refusal to accept it only endeared his jovial nature more to me. His demeanor reminded me of so many of my closest friends back home. I knew the day would come when I might be able to repay him in another way. For now all I could do was settle in for the remainder of our rocky ride and of course enjoy Simon's yammering and songs.

Clouds of red dust rose up from the horizon to our right, creating a wall of billowing flowerets of floating microscopic rocks that formed an impenetrable screen. In an hour we would be buried in this shroud of desert sand, but Simon seemed to have his own ideas of how this would all transpire. As if he had found another gear in the truck's transmission, we began to race along at greater and greater speed. I could hear in his voice the grin on his face as he sang a song much like a battle hymn. We were either headed for cover or we were so close to our destination that he knew we could make it. Racing to nowhere it was impossible to keep from looking at the pending doom moving to cut off our passage. There was nothing on the horizon but this descending dust storm and yet Simon plodded on into the nothing as though he knew some secret way to beat this storm.

Suddenly Simon turned his beloved beast of burden directly into the coming storm on a small dirt trail. Things were happening so quickly that there was no time to try to communicate my concern or ask any of the questions racing through my mind. I could only sit, hang on, and ride it out with my new guide and friend. Just then the road dropped into a narrow canyon carved out of solid stone and soon we were under the cover of a stone roof and driving through carved walls on a slick, clean, cobble floor. As I looked over at Simon in astonishment he looked at me and gleamed with a proud smile of someone who had just made the finish line ahead of the pack. We were in some kind of a warehouse below ground and were headed toward a loading dock. We wheeled around to back up to the dock, and as Simon happily shut her down and locked up the brakes, he leaned over toward me and smiled, saying, "Jasmina here!"

As I climbed out of the truck, my legs rebelled in a slow, painful reaction to the first movements. We had sat bouncing for so long that it seemed our legs had lost the strength to carry weight. While stretching and groaning, I looked around and overhead, recognizing that we had pulled into what must have been an old war bunker of some fashion. I couldn't imagine anyone going to this much trouble to build this man-made cavern just to load and unload freight. The design made perfect sense in this part of the world, and the opening was deep enough that the wind and dust seemed far off. One could see the rain of grains falling into the ramped opening, but nothing made it to the solitude at our end of this well-engineered hole in the ground.

Simon smiled and chuckled in obvious satisfaction as he sat against the front bumper of his truck and rolled a cane in his mouth, joining me to look back at where we had just come from. He made a gesture with cane in hand and commented, "Much dust."

We both grinned in knowing silence as we listened and watched. Then Simon pushed off from the bumper and fondly patted his truck on the fender as he walked to the back. He climbed up, pushed up the door on the back, and offered me a hand up.

In his broken words he said, "We stay here tonight, work comes tomorrow." Then he threw a few heavy blankets towards me and began making his own bed in the back of the truck. When I peered into the dark backside of his truck there was little space left that wasn't eyeball high with boxes and bags. I looked back at the loading platform. Simon saw my glance and spoke up immediately. Although his words were few and cane-garbled, his message was huge, "la, la, la, many bugs and snakes!" That was my cue to sleep standing up if need be. I hadn't tested the option but figured I could sleep standing on my head if it meant dodging the odd snake or two. I found enough room to curl up under cover for the night.

As I lay there with mind whirling in thoughts of the day and what tomorrow might bring, my mind turned to thoughts of snakes curling up next to me in my sleep to warm themselves. It was never so much a fear of snakes, but rather a fear of karma. As a kid, I was fascinated by snakes and reptiles and went on daily adventures to regular haunts where I knew I would find them sunning themselves. I had caught literally thousands of beautiful, harmless snakes and after holding them and looking at them for a while I would let them go again. I did bring home a snake with two heads and a salamander with five legs. But just like all the others I had brought home in earlier years, someone would let them go after I went to sleep at night. There was this one time at summer camp when my older brother stayed in his own cabin. He was deathly afraid of all snakes and I had put several garden snakes in the refrigerator in his cabin. It wasn't long before he came out like a flash, screaming, feet barely touching the ground as he ran. He yelled my name, but I stayed hidden.

Maybe it was that day that I changed from curious to afraid. I could feel my brother's fear as if it were mine. In later years I too found my fear of snakes, and this has been an ongoing problem for someone who goes poking around in mountains and deserts looking for rocks. Oh yes, I have seen those people who show no fear of the deadly types like the snake charmers in the Souks. To me they are just like those who climb sheer rock cliffs for thousands of feet with nothing but a pouch of talc for their fingers; they are taunting fate to come take them away. I love my life and I don't wish to lose it to a small meaningless bite or a slip of the hand. So I slip into slumber curled up in the back of Simon's truck while he snores away the miles of today's journey.

Only moments had passed when I awakened to the light of Jasmina's eyes gazing into mine. My heart leapt into full beat and I was fully awake and rested. It was still night and Simon was sound asleep. Jasmina took my hand and led me to the wall at the edge of the dock where we appeared to walk through the stone. This had a strange "out of body" feeling to it as we walked through several feet of stone. It looked to be dense rock, but walking through it felt as though we were pushing through heavy mud. Was this a dream?

On the other side of the wall Jasmina turned to me and said, "No, not a dream, a security measure. At sunrise we will offload our friend's truck and we will tell him that you are with me. He knows us and he will understand. You were fortunate to find yourself in the hands of such an honorable traveler as Simon. He has supported my village for many years and we trust him endlessly."

As she turned to guide me away, she asked if I was well rested. I told her that it seemed very strange just how well rested I did feel considering the circumstances. She simply smiled. She seemed so much more composed and eloquent than the young rebel girl I remember from years before. People do change, but this was far more than that which most would expect. I could still feel her strength and confidence, but it was tempered with composure and control. Her voice exuded power and calm. Her posture was stoic yet supple. And her beauty could truly stop a heart from beating. One look into Jasmina's deep, brilliant green eyes and the brain went numb. I thought to myself that she must get tired of men not finishing sentences.

We walked along a corridor for a time and emerged into daylight as the early dawn grew brighter, then stepped out into the Medina in the midst of her village. It seemed strange that I couldn't see this village on the horizon yesterday as we approached the storm, but maybe it was already obscured by the darkness. After all, we did turn directly into the approaching storm before dropping out of sight. I had countless questions for Jasmina. First on my list was how did she appear to me in my sleep at the bus station, or was that just me dreaming? It is pretty hard to consider something is real when you only see it in a dream. But the dream felt so real, real enough to get me to drop everything and change the direction of my journey to come here. She spoke before I had a chance to begin my line of questions.

Jasmina inquired with hope in her voice, "You saw my sister; how is she? I trust you have come to help me; I have been calling to you for help. The problems we have are very difficult and urgent, and I feel that you are the only one who can help me bring the solution. There is no time for making this easy for you to understand. You will need to put a great deal of trust in me."

"Whoa, wait, Jasmina, are you sure you've got the right guy here?" I unloaded on her. "As I remember, you never really liked me as a kid. I haven't seen you in ten years, and you and I hardly know each other. That said, what makes you think I am qualified for whatever this thing is? I don't mean to overreact, but you will need to give me some information first. So far this trip, I have been shot, chased, followed, tracked, lost and visited by you in my sleep. Where is this going to go from here?"

We stopped in a cobbled street near the middle of her village. When I turned to face her I could see worry and sadness in her eyes. I felt the sense of urgency that she was trying to convey and asked if there was a good place to talk. The heat of the day would begin to soar soon, and it felt like this was going to take some time. She nodded yes and led me away to her home.

It wasn't long before we were walking through the gates of her garden and into the house, which was large and nicely situated on a small hillside overlooking the village. As we walked into her home, everything changed. It was cool and quiet with the sound of streaming liquid from a water feature in the courtyard. There were birds singing in the garden and shades that prevented the sun from shining into the rooms. The house and garden smelled of jasmine, which grew throughout her garden, the tiny white flowers in full bloom. Jasmina offered me water and directed me into a large room off of the entry where we could sit and talk.

She returned to the room with water in hand and we sat to speak. This moment felt like those few seconds before being launched on a first-time roller coaster ride. I had no idea what to expect, but I could already see that it was going to be something really big. Maybe huge was a better word. We sat in massive carved hardwood chairs much like I have seen in the castles of Ireland. We sat a few feet apart and faced each other. She began by saying thank you for coming. Then she went on to talk about our past. She explained that when we were younger she was only ten years old. It wasn't that she didn't like me; it was that she was jealous of her older sister for our relationship. It bothered her that her sister was able to break with tradition to have a friendship with me. She explained that she felt put out by the growing intensity of the bond between Kadishya and me. It seemed there was no room for her in our friendship.

I sat listening, bursting with the urge to speak. She went on to say that they had both fought over this many times when younger. It had all turned into a great misunderstanding that caused a rift between them. I could tell there was a great deal more to hear so I sat quietly in the massive chair, pressing my fingers into the griffin's heads carved into the arms of the chair. Jasmina admitted that she had only recently realized the dynamics of what this all meant for the three of us. She confided that she needed to speak with Kadishya about this as soon as could be done. Jasmina said that this must wait for there were much greater issues to deal with in a timely manner. There were things that she said must be spoken, but also other things that could only be shown. There seemed to be concern that she do things in the right order as she began to talk about my work. She explained that she had been watching me all of these years tracking down fallen rocks from space. I didn't quite get what she was trying to tell me, but part of me took this at face value based on the visions of her in my dreams. She had spoken to me directly in my dreams more than once. That was weird and something I could not deny, nor could I admit it to anyone else. So her saying she had been watching me all these years somehow seemed plausible. I wanted to ask her why, but sat quietly hoping she would lead to that. Then it came out, the stone I had gotten from Sharif, a piece of which was still in my pocket. She told me that she had sent it to me with her father, Sharif.

Suddenly my mind was filled with dots connecting! Oh man, what the…inside me a voice was screaming to get out. My brain was firing questions at my mouth, but I struggled to remain calm and listened for more answers and connections. Jasmina continued to explain how that stone had unlimited value to her people as well as to the entire world, and that the value was in it being identified by my scientists as the first phase of a much bigger revelation. She told me that her people had decided that I was the key to this entire effort to get that specimen into the hands of scientists. I could feel the fragment in my pocket and there was temptation to pull it out to show her, but I let it lay as Jasmina continued. While I rested there looking into her stunning face and eyes and listened to her silky voice, my mind wandered a bit, wondering how Ali was doing in his quest to get that stone to the museum.

Looking back it seemed that we were tracked the entire

time and I realized that this feeling only ended when I left the bus station to come here. This was the first time I had branched out alone with no plan and found my own way from hither to yon. She then spoke of how the stone being examined would begin a new age for us all and how soon she would need to show me what this would mean to us. We sat there in the cool shade sipping cold water with mint leaves suspended in sweating glasses. A drip of condensed water jerkily ran down the side of my glass and splayed out onto the low table. Back home when water spills if nobody wipes it up it lays there for days, but here in the dry when water is spilled it is gone before one can wipe it up. It was decadently luxurious after many days of parched throat and dehydration to have a glass of cool, quenching liquid sitting in front of me for my thirst.

My mind still wandering as Jasmina spoke, her words had more meaning than she could express. There was no language barrier between us, it was just that there appeared to be much more information behind her words as if there were no words to cover what she was trying to say. How could any rock be as important or life changing as she was trying to say? I do recall when scientists had thought they found fossils in a Martian stone meteorite discovered in Antarctica called Allan Hills 84001. The announcement was like a shot heard 'round the world. That caused a lot of hype and it pushed the price of Martian meteorites through the roof for a while, but then the discovery was disproved and eventually we all went back to searching for that first clue all over again. So how could this stone of hers, an obvious meteorite, be anything that life altering? She had my attention, but I needed her to get to the point. Mina was a nickname I gave her when I first knew her. She didn't like it, but her sister and I liked that it seemed to tick her off so we used it from time to time. I liked it. I have always enjoyed names that suit people better than their formal names. Mina was a pretty name and fit her well where the alternative, Jas, just didn't fit her at all.

Mina smiled at me with a fondness I had never before seen from her in those months I had known her so many years ago. She admitted, "This is enough conversation for today. Tomorrow we must walk into the desert, where I will show you more of what you must see for yourself. Today you can bathe and rest; you are a guest here in my home and tonight we will enjoy a small, quiet dinner together, and if you have questions I will answer them as best I can. If you have any needs you can call my name and I will answer." She stopped and turned to look back at me as she rose from her chair. "Yes," she said, "you may call me Mina if it pleases you." Her eyes flashed back and forth at mine while she leaned into me in a way that made me feel warm throughout.

This was an entirely different person than the girl I remember with the scowl and the curt replies. It was nothing I had done. Could it have been the years? Was I being set up for a big takedown? Was this a performance leading up to asking me for something? My gut told me that this woman was sincere and in earnest but so far things really did not add up. Ok, well, no matter, I was in good hands, having fun, feeling safe, and curious as all get-out about where this was leading. Besides all of the intrigue it was a world-class pleasure to get to look at and listen to Jasmina. In the words of an old friend in the business, "Jasmina was her sister, on steroids."

I couldn't get over how safe it felt to be here with Mina. It was as if the outside world was not there for a time. All of my worries were gone as if all of my work was finished and every loose end was neatly tied up. As each minute clicked by I felt more focused and relaxed. Even the lingering pain of being shot several times seemed to dwindle away. It felt like the guys were well on their way and that everything was good for them too. I knew not what to make of this, but I figured I'd just go with it and see what tomorrow would bring. Looking forward to a nice quiet dinner without distraction sounded really great.

A shower or a long hot bath right now just felt like the perfect way to top off the day. I was led to a guest wing and Mina said it was mine for as long as I needed to remain here. She said that her home was my home and that I would always be welcome to stay here. She sauntered back down the hallway to the main house, and as she walked away, I couldn't help notice the air of confidence in her stride. I could still see that strength in her gait and her demeanor. I wondered if that young girl was still inside her, full of spice and spit. She had tested my mettle many times and it often felt like she had won. Even when she didn't win, she still walked away as though she were the victor. It was as if I had fallen into another level of her intricate plan; I was yet to learn of my ultimate failure and fate. She always seemed to have plans inside of plans, schemes on top of schemes. She was a definitive chess master in the game of life. But now it was as though she had softened her edges ever so slightly. Still the power within her radiated in an aura around her.

Tonight I would keep the questions simple and direct. I

would try to keep things in the moment and take tomorrow as it comes.

When Jasmina called me to dinner, I was still wet from a long hot bath. I had to throw on a shirt and pants and run for the door. I was wearing spare clothes she had told me were in the closet. I could feel the desiccating desert air dry my skin and hair as I ran through the hall. In the main room was a small table with a candle burning, several dishes that smelled amazing, and a shaft of light streaming in from the low-hanging sun. Mina stood with one hand on her chair and gestured for me to take the seat across from her. We sat quietly while she prayed in silence over the meal. It was a simple meal of elegant flavor and aroma, with more water and bread. After we ate, we talked but I made an effort to keep it light. When I asked her how she remembered her nickname she told me that she heard me think it, and we both laughed. Then I asked her to tell me two things. One was "How have you changed so much?" And the other was "Please tell me about this princess status of yours."

She told me that in her culture it was not acceptable for young girls to have men friends. She admitted that she envied her sister's friendship with me, but that she also resented that she could not have this same relationship partly because her sister already had and partly because she was younger and more afraid of doing such a thing and how it might anger the elders. She was very direct and forthright in telling me that for Kadishya our friendship was just that, a deep love of friendship that would last forever. She went on to explain that for her it was different. She admitted that she had a love crush on me and that because of tradition and her sister, there was nothing she could do and so she grew to resent both her sister and me. I was not at all prepared to hear this admission. Here was one of the most beautiful women on Earth telling me that she had a crush on me when we were younger. I felt very uneasy and found it hard to look into her eyes while she peered straight into mine with unwavering intensity. Add to that I was sitting in her husband's family home and quite possibly wearing his old clothes. There was an unlimited mystery behind this woman's eyes, but at this moment she was cutting me open with her words and baring my soul to the world. I felt like back paddling, but I had no idea what to say. Her words, if they were true, were so bold that they took the air from my lungs.

I kept thinking, *how can this stunning creature be telling me these things? She has admitted to loving me. I don't like conceding to having an ego, but right now I am pretty sure that I have one and it's puffed up bigger than life. Part of me worries that she is about to tell me something that will end this moment.*

Jasmina reaches her hand across the table and rested it on top of mine. For a moment when we touched, I saw her as the younger Mina from our past. I blinked my eyes, but the younger Jasmina was still sitting there. "Relax, my rock hunter, you will always be in my heart. I will always love you as I did the first day we met. You will always be my star man." She kept her warm hand on mine and gave me a long compassionate look. "I pray that you will be with me always and forever. I have prayed this for many years. I have known you since before you can remember and have watched you from my heart."

I didn't understand what she was saying, but it felt good. She went on to say that I would understand these things better tomorrow. This all came across as very ethereal, especially coming from someone I had known to be so rigid and grounded like a standing stone.

Jasmina the adult was a complete metamorphosis from Jasmina the child. This lovely woman before me was so eloquent and serene and yet that element of intensity was still there; it was just more controlled, more diplomatically presented in easier doses. The more time in Mina's presence, the more a relaxing calm took hold of my mood. In the finishing moments of our evening, the outside world no longer existed. Jasmina had connected with me in ways I did not understand. I felt a trust in her like no other before and since we really hadn't talked that much or spent much time together, I could not understand where these feelings were coming from. It seemed to be a connection of a more spiritual nature.

As we rose from our chairs to end the evening and head off to our rooms, she put her hand on my arm saying, "Everything will become much clearer for you tomorrow." Mina walked me to my room at the end of the long hall. As we walked past the open windows the full moon was rising above the edge of the sand. In this part of the world the stars appear to touch the Earth as they rise and fall. The moon appeared larger than ever, tinted amber and hanging below us from our vantage on the hill. We stopped at the end of the hall. As we faced each other Mina put her hands on my arms and bowed her head saying, "Rest well tonight, Bryce Monroe Sterling; tomorrow when you wake will be a new day and all of your pain will dispel. Bless you for coming to me." She looked up, nodded with a thin-lipped smile, and turned to leave. I wanted to say something in reply, but I felt frozen in place and just stood there watching her disappear into the moonlit hallway.

That night as I lay on the bed with arms crossed behind my head on the pillow, I tried to think of the plight of my fellow travelers, but it was too easy to clear the mind and fall into a deep sleep. Something about this place took away my worries. Morning arrived, and I rolled over under the covers and bunched up the pillow under the side of my head. I could hear pots or pans clanking down the hall and I smelled the aroma of coffee and cooking. The aroma lifted me out of bed and set me gently on my feet. For me, coffee and Danish in the early morn is the equivalent of throwing gas on a fire. As I made my way toward the sound I began to feel inner warmth. My body felt aglow with well-being. First, I noticed I had no limp from two old leg injuries, my nagging toothache was gone, and the new bullet holes were not hurting. I stopped in the dim morning light streaming in a hallway window and pulled up the shirt sleeve to find that my new battle scars were gone! It's not that they were better or that the pain had gone: it's as though the shots never happened.

I arrived in the area of the sounds and smells to find a stranger busily creating a meal. She was a tiny woman who moved swiftly around the room. Jasmina's voice came from the corner behind me, "This is Magna, she helps me some days. We are having a light breakfast and Magna will join us."

I was so distracted by my newfound health status that all I could muster was to reach up with the left arm to grasp the right and began with, "What the..."

"It is a gift," Mina interrupted. "It is something my

people can do for you. I can feel your pain and I am able to take it away."

Entirely pleased and utterly confused, I dropped into a chair next to Mina and pondered what was just said. Nobody had this ability and yet my body was living proof of what she had said. She stopped me again and said, "Sterling, relax and enjoy this gift. We will enjoy this meal and then your answers will come. When the day is done, you will be able to choose your questions more wisely." Jasmina's ability to put me at ease was indescribable. I sat back in the chair and watched as Magna brought us thick coffee in tiny cups with sweet cream and huge sugar cubes to take away some of the bite in this wonderful morning drink. Quick as a flash she returned with a great silver tray covered with fruits, cheeses, and honey-covered fluffy pastries.

Magna sat with us at the table in the corner of the kitchen. The coffee was strong and bitter as any I've had. The large rectangular cubes of sugar and the fresh, heavy, sweet cream spooned from a cup made the powerful wake-up drink delectable. Nothing was said while we sat there. The room grew lighter as the sun began streaming in through every opening on the rising side of the house. We sat at the table for only minutes and then it was time. As we stood, Magna moved the tray to the other side of the kitchen and returned with a water bottle for me to strap over my shoulder. Mina turned toward me and said that we would be walking into the desert today, that there were a number of things I needed to be shown. Magna was going to stay behind. As we walked out the door, my skin could feel that the heat of the day was already beginning to build.

CHAPTER SIX

The Void

Before long we had woven our way through the tiny village with children playing in the streets and people busily going about their lives. I could hear the playful squeals of the children's voices long after we had cleared the edge of the town. As I stared out into the barren landscape, I thought to myself how magical the sound of children at play was. I remembered how happy it would make me feel after a long time in the field hunting for meteorites to hear the heartwarming sounds of children playing as I marched closer to camp or the village where base camp was set up. Hunting in groups we had all learned about safety in numbers. Over time it was realized that if you went out there with the intention of having fun, then even if nothing was found, it was still so much fun that you would always go back to search again. So many of my helpers and fellow hunters would bring the whole family along and that meant there were always children playing around camp or sitting around the campfire. There were days when coming out of the wilderness you were not quite sure if you were close to base camp until you heard the joyous noise of children at play; it always felt like coming home. As Mina slowed to move alongside of me rather than leading the way, I heard a slight sound of laughter and when I looked she was smiling brightly. She looked into my eyes and let out the slightest laugh as she spoke.

"This is why I admire you so greatly, Sterling; you see the beauty and the joy and humor in everything. I know this will be difficult for you to understand, but I hear your thoughts; I always have. When I watch you and listen to you, I feel love. I can hear your thoughts, my star man. I am not from this world. I hope this will not be too difficult for you, but I have no one else to turn to. In your dreams you saw me?"

"Yes," I said, puzzled.

"That was my doing." She continued the beginning of her reveal, "I needed you to come here now to do this with me. Do you remember the stone wall behind Simon's truck? Do you recall how it felt to walk through that shroud?"

Again, I replied with a blank yes.

"This is how we have kept to ourselves through the millennia. In your eyes the wall is an endless depth of stone. To my people it is a heavy, gray matter of molecules that can be manipulated."

I was about to ask about Mina's references to her people when we came to a halt. Jasmina looked over to me and smiled as she took my hand in hers and told me to look down and watch my step. She gave my hand a light squeeze and stepped ahead pulling me along. Looking down I watched my steps. "What the heck!" blurted out of my mouth completely unrestrained. I was not prepared to see my lower legs sink into the ground. The ground was still there and still had the same opaque color. As we moved further into the rising horizon, we continued to sink lower step by step into the gently sloping ground. Remembering the wall experience I tried to relax.

I could feel that I was going to have a tough time going under. Looking over to Jasmina, she told me to simply breathe and continue forward with her. In an instant we were deep in the ground and obviously walking down a ramp. If I were to try to describe this experience I would say we were walking through thick, cool, gray soup. We could still see each other and could breathe normally. Although it broke all of the rules of modern physics, we were doing this and it felt real. Mina spoke as we walked and told me to keep an open mind, that there were still many more surprises to reveal and that she was certain I was the man to share this with.

Walking for a long distance, maybe miles, we arrived at the bottom of the ramp, but still there was more soup ahead. Here on what felt to be flat ground there was a dim illumination around us. I could see ahead an opening in the soup. It looked like a bubble or Vug similar to what is found in planetary basalt and classically it appeared to be lined with a thin layer of glass. Mina led me to this Vug and stepped inside, turning to offer her hands to lead me inside. Once standing within the Vug, Jasmina raised a hand and we began to move, rapidly accelerating through what should have been solid rock.

So far so crazy, thus far everything I was seeing broke the very rules of life on Earth. My mind was ablaze with unlimited questions. We seemed to travel endlessly through the soup, accelerating continuously. There were no bumps or surges, we were floating through the "Gray" at tremendous speed, but there was no sensation of force and we were standing stationary and comfortable. But it was becoming noticeably brighter. Then, without indication we were out of the gray stone soup and flying with no change of pace into what appeared to be a massive, endless cavern. My eyes could not judge scale, but this was a world below ground. In the far distance I could see massive stone pillars reaching from floor to ceiling; they tapered from broad at the base to narrow in the center and back to broad at the top. They appeared to be miles high. Everything was illuminated with dazzling bright light that emanated from everything. I could not see the end or the sides of this subterranean void. There were humanoids everywhere; they were walking on both top and bottom and many were apparently flying.

Jasmina spoke, "These are my people, we are Terans, we have lived here for many millions of your years. We have lived in harmony with humans on the surface of the Earth. We come from a dead planet that once existed nearby and was destroyed. We terraformed this world after it was surmised that our planet's doom was pending. We call this EarthUnder or New Tera. It spans most of the planet. There are windows against the oceans where our oxygen supply is primarily produced as is yours on the surface of our biospheric shell planet."

"We are humanoid in appearance, but much more evolved than humans. As an example, we use our brains as a community and we share all knowledge communally. We maintain the gravity of this planet, preventing Earth's atmosphere from being scoured away by the solar and cosmic rays. Our mind energy allows us to hold the outer crust suspended

about the planet core. The pillars you are seeing are a man-
ifestation of our thought, which appears as a physical entity.
The strength of this physical energy is much stronger than
the rock they hold, which is part of what makes them visible to your eyes. We communicate without oral speech as
we all are able to communicate through thought. The light
you see is created by sono- and bioluminescence, which is
part of our ecosystem. We live without sunlight. There are
no circadian rhythms here. Our bodies do not oxidize. We
are not ravaged by the damaging rays of direct sunlight. We
age over much longer spans of time. Terans do not manu-
facture because we have no needs that are not met communally. We seldom sleep as we do not have daily cycles and
rest only when it is needed. My people are able to fly with
little effort, but rather through thought. Yes, I can hear your
thoughts, feel what you feel, heal your wounds, watch you
wherever you are. I can call to you when you are at rest, I
can warn you when you are in danger, and I can love you
for all time. Parts of my genetics are inside of you and all
humankind. The 'Gray' or 'Soup,' as you enjoy calling it, is
solid planet crust to humans, but to my kind it is manage-
able and easily manipulated. This has allowed our security
and secrecy through time. Oh yes, we can swim the seas
without breathing and a rare few of us have been genetically
altered in order to exist on the surface.

"Most have no desire to visit the surface, but we have
found that through time our future has become at risk. On
our home world (Tera) we lived this same way. In time, we
realized that the destruction of our home world was coming.
We had the time to prepare and to select a planet to meet
our basic needs, but then we had to adjust certain elements

of that world in order to create a more hospitable place to live. With our minds we were able to perform two major, necessary feats: we adjusted the core and crust to house our population and we used our ability to travel here through thought in an instant by folding the ribbon of space. Everything we have here is as it was on Tera. This is only a small part of the entire image. I understand that you will have countless questions and I will enjoy answering them. Our lives are tied together and always have been. We all rely on the survival of the planet. You may remain here with me for as long as you feel the need, and I will be your guide."

Jasmina went on to describe how her planet was destroyed millions of years earlier by a massive, rogue, black dwarf star, an event beyond Teran control to divert. She shared, in detail, how her race had been facing extinction if they did not move to another home world and that her planet's population went to a number of new worlds, all of which had been conditioned for their arrival. The Earth was one of those chosen planets. They were able to project the approach of the star, but not prevent the cataclysm. The Terans had sufficient time to prepare themselves for the move as well as the worlds they would be moving to. She explained how they used a large part of the brain that still remains dormant in humans to create the energy needed to move through a folded ribbon in space. She described how our scientists have a basic idea of this concept, but parts are far more simple and basic while other aspects of travel through space and time are far more complicated than a human mind can comprehend.

Coming from this woman who had just healed my wounds and had flown us through solid rock at hyper speed with seemingly no inertia, anything she was willing to share I was easily led to believe. She went on to reveal that there were other events out there such as neutron stars or massive, maverick asteroids that would eventually pose a definitive threat. Right now we (Earth) were in the beginnings of a meteor swarm. I knew this to be evident; back in the earlier days of my work chasing new fireballs when there were only a handful of guys doing the same thing for a living, we would often talk about how we were lucky to get one new fall in a year's time. But in the last decade there were more like five to ten per year and in the past year there had been roughly ten to twenty major, ground-shaking fireballs per week. Not all of them were putting inventory on the ground, but then some, like the bolide that blew up over Chelyabinsk, Russia, were doing more damage than we had seen in thousands of years.

Mina interjected, "Some are making way through our dusty atmosphere with tremendous mass and force. Just as Tunguska in 1908 and Sikhote Alin in 1947, Terans have been able to deflect these planet killers. But these events occur without our early detection because they come through wormholes that exist near our sun."

Mina explained how Earth is a fragile ecosystem and that the Teranians live here in a delicate balance. She looked deep into my eyes and said that even man's greatest scientific minds cannot explain such things as gravity or how space is folded or how light is bent.

She expounded without hesitation, "These and many others are things are done by my people through collective thought and the focus of our mental energy. These are efforts that your people will be able to participate in as well in millions of years when your bodies and minds evolve as ours have. We create the gravity that keeps this planet in its balance. The gravity fields we create that allow us to exist here in EarthUnder also maintain the gravitational eco-system that you call your home world, Earth. Luna, Earth's moon, is also an integral component of the Earth's bal-anced ecosystem. We all live in and on the same biosphere: a spaceship if you like the term. We all travel through this protoplanetary disc together: our solar system. And," she went on, "the oceans are our oxygen tanks. Most of the oxygen we all breathe comes from the oceans."

She told me that widely dispersed through the Void, EarthUnder, there are massive windows to the seas and oceans and that the waters are suspended much like the stone above and below us. Jasmina explained that Terans pass through these windows at will and that oxygen flows freely as do all of the other atmospheric gases, which maintain the same bal-ance of atmosphere we enjoy on Earth's surface.

There was so much information coming at me that there was no room in my brain to form a solitary question. The induction into this new world was thrilling. I didn't want Mina to stop. My eyes were filled with stimulation from all the dazzling colors. Nothing here was the same as my world; the light had a strange effect on the eyes, and there were frequent pools of water as clear as window glass. There were no structures or roads and no vehicles, the Vug must have been created for our arrival. Light was everywhere and there was very little shadow. People moved in fluid motion and some walked, but with a similar fluidity. The air was so pure that it burned the lungs and there was a clean taste to it. I could see detail at much greater distance and for as far as my eyes could focus there was the same brilliant light and movement. People were standing on both the floor and ceiling and plants grew in all directions.

Jasmina listened to my reactions and answered questions before I could ask them. As I glanced from one distracting anomaly to the next, she would begin to tell me about what I was seeing. She explained that the gravitational field generated by her people was omnipotent and that one can stand upright or soar from place to place depending on the need anywhere in EarthUnder. She took my hand again, and we began to glide. There was no feeling of inertia and no rush of air watering my eyes, but I could see that we were moving at great speed by the kaleidoscope effect on the surfaces above and below. Soon I could see where she was taking me; a window! This was a surreal treat; I could see from near the top to the bottom of an ocean. I hung there floating next to Mina, my jaw hanging open, breathing in the cool, clean air, and stared at the sunrays glimmering, dancing, and fading to nothing as they sliced their way deeper into the salt sea water. For the first time in the history of mankind, I was witnessing a single ray of light end its existence in the depths of the abyss. Near the surface I could see the shadows of large fish plying the water. At the bottom there were flashes of light from luminescent sea bottom creatures. I could smell the ocean and taste the salty brine on my tongue. Jasmina explained that there are many such connections with all of the oceans and that we all have the same symbiotic relationship with these great bodies of water.

Mina turned to me again as we hung there more than a thousand meters above the ground or whatever it's called, and she told me I could remain here for as long as I wished. Then her expression changed as she continued. "There are other hazards that threaten our planet and soon we will need to talk about those concerns. That is why you have been brought here. You have become our greatest hope for the future, a future that we all hope will last for many more millions of years. So we will remain here if you are willing. As you continue to stay here your body will adapt to our conditions and you will require less rest, less nourishment, and your mental focus will become keener. There are no days or nights here. You may need time to adjust to this, although we find that humans adapt very rapidly to change. Terans are not as adaptive as humans; sudden changes here are nonexistent. I will do all I am able to help you make this transition. Can you think of any questions at this point?"

I told Mina that this would take a great deal of time for me to assimilate. She nodded knowingly and gave me a warm, comforting smile. I did have one question suddenly pop into my mind. "Where are all the machines and buildings?"

Jasmina explained that machines were abandoned by her people many millions of years ago and that what remained on her home world were relics of a former life that were pre-served as monuments for memories of earlier generations. Those material items were left to be destroyed because only living tissue can bridge space via the folded ribbon, and no tangible items can be taken. Only the memories of them remain. But she told me that certain treasured items were cached away in "Paleogarcks" made of nearly indestructible material in hopes that they might survive the cataclysm to be recovered in the future. These were items of tremen-dous historic value from Tera's past much like famous oil paintings or carved marble statues or historic, antiquarian books. She appeared very pleased with my first question as though I had touched on some key issue. She went on to say that in this time they have no need of machinery or structures of any kind. "We all know what everyone is thinking and so there is no deceit, no privacy, no property, no greed or possession, no competition, basically nothing to hide. We all share in the same brain power and so there is nothing to prove or display."

Next Jasmina took me down to the surface below. There I was shown things I haved never dreamed of. There were unusual plants, wildly colorful flowers, and strange, small creatures skittering about, stopping to look up at us. Everything glowed with its own light and unusual coloration. The surface was soft, and warmer than the air. There were plants the likes of which I had never seen. Many of them turned as we walked by as if they too were looking up at us. People walked past us and looked at us, but they all reacted as though they already knew me. There were no expressions of surprise, concern, or curiosity.

Again, I was not keeping up with the first day's briefing. Mina said that they all know everything that she knows. I grinned at Jasmina sheepishly, and thought to myself that this would take me time to get accustomed to; she smiled back and nodded her head. I thought to myself, *Then why have a voice or why use it?* Mina looked at me and said that the vocal cords are vestigial for Terans but they use them for prayers and for singing, so they have not gone into complete dormancy. "Ok," I responded rather cynically, "what do you pray about and who do you pray to?"

"We pray to our ancestors and to the creator," Jasmina

replied with solid confidence and conviction in her unwavering voice. "We pray for all races throughout the universe. We don't pray for specific issues or requests. We chant in prayer as a way to share our good fortune and faith with others and we do so through rhythmic thought and sounds."

The next question demanded an answer, "How long do Terans live?"

"The average Teranian will live three thousand Earth surface years. Some Elders live to be over four thousand years. This is how long our spirits live but we must reincarnate a number of times throughout this span of years. We don't have the same endogenous components as humans. Without having to adapt to the solar and lunar rhythms, all creatures on Tera live extensive life cycles. Those who exist in EarthUnder do not suffer the same senescence as those who inhabit the surface of Earth."

"Are you going to live that long?" I pried.

"No, my family line was genetically specialized generations ago to survive the rigors of Earth's surface atmosphere. There is a cost for living in the light of the sun. The chronobiology of life under the light of the sun and moon dictates that we age much more rapidly than our people of New Tera. We still enjoy being Teran and we have been given additional abilities through our exposure to humankind."

"Are there many others like you on the surface?"

She admitted, "No, very few, and most are part of my family."

I had to ask the hard question, "So you intend man and womankind no harm?"

Mina quips, "If we did mean to harm you, don't you think this would have happened a long time ago?"

"Hmm, so then why do this now?" I inquired, thinking I had her pinned in a verbal chess game.

"Ah, my dear man, that is just exactly why you are here," Mina replied with relief and confidence in her tone. Right now your best researchers are watching a maverick asteroid they call Apophis. Some have predicted that it will make a near Earth pass in 2024 and again, it will pass even closer to Earth in the year 2036. Your people are just beginning to understand how powerful this threat can be. The Terans monitor the balance of all orbiting objects that might threaten this planet at any time in the future. We have helped orchestrate a delicate magnetic balance in this solar system, as have our brothers and sisters on planetary bodies throughout this galaxy and several others across the universe. Over time, my people have grown to feel responsible for the continuation of your species and all other creatures on the surface of Earth. We brought you here. Terans altered the flora and fauna and the environment of the surface several times to accommodate your kind. We altered Man's genetics to help you develop and to help you survive on the surface. Now, sadly, over time we have realized that we must help you survive each other. Man has become Mankind's gravest threat.

"If there were another massive planet killer hurtling toward Earth, then Terans would be forced to leave. Without the time to prepare we would need to move to another planet already prepared for our numbers and we might then be forced to coexist with another population on their world for a time. In doing this we would be left with the grim choice of leaving your race behind. This is a choice that no Teranian ever wishes to make. Terans have a special love for all mankind and in spite of the crimes between you, we see your good and wish to protect you as we will protect our own.

"Your scientists are making plans and building ships in order to travel into space and begin mining minerals from random asteroids and planets in our solar system. They have proposed plans to harness an asteroid and bring it back near Earth and place in an orbit around the moon. Take this to mind, my star man. These planets and planetoids drift and spin in a delicate balance. We, the Terans, maintain that balance with the strength of our minds and millions of years of putting all the pieces in their places. Just as your greatest minds cannot fathom our most basic creation, this planet's gravitational field, they cannot possibly understand what holds all of these planets and planet killers in the stasis your people call the solar system. Terans have patiently observed your people since the beginning of your time on Earth. We have enjoyed your successes and have marveled at your creations, but at the same time there have been wars, competition on a planetary scale, crimes between one another, and crime between entire countries.

"Sadly, it gets much worse, while your people busily go about your lives under the sun, most of your refuse is dumped into the ground, rivers, lakes, oceans, and air. Your scientists and military experiment with atomic bombs and nuclear energy, creating massive amounts of deadly fallout and waste on many areas of the globe. They have exploded and still plan to test these bombs above and below ground as well as beneath the seas. There seems to be little regard for the lives of others and certainly no regard for lives in the future. It seems to my people that yours are not looking far enough into the future. Mankind must ask the question, what of the lives of humankind one thousand years from now or one million years from now?

"You see, my dear Sterling, Terans have no reliance on the existence of Man on Earth, but without my kind, Man will perish in a handful of heartbeats. In this time, Man poses many threats to our survival. The oceans are our oxygen tank. Think of the planet as a spaceship and the oceans are our rebreather; they take in our carbon dioxide and breathe out the oxygen that our lungs require. Just one too many bombs or barges of waste or chemical dumps or accidental spills of oil can kill our oceans. One more fresh water river dies and spills only pollution into the oceans of the world, or the long-term effects of a tragedy such as Fukushima, oceans die and with them so do we. Many times now Man has ignited nuclear bombs below ground or under water and my people are forced to exact a greater surge of our energy to prevent a breakthrough into EarthUnder. This drain on our mental energy force has caused a weakening in other areas of the planet, where resulting catastrophes have then occured.

"You understand what I am saying; I can see it in your eyes and I can hear it in your mind. I need not continue on this bent, but this is why you have been brought here. The small fragment in your pocket represents our only hope. In the time it takes a human to inhale a breath of air my people can depart from EarthUnder and the surface of Earth will be scoured away like the surface of Mars or Mercury. This is not our wish. Our desire is to find a life of harmony with mankind.

"Our hope is that this fragment of meteorite that you have will bring this world to a changed direction. What you possess is a fragment of our sacred Cunene Obelisk.

The obelisk was built using the brain bone of an ancient sea creature, a Drillian named Cunene. Cunene swam the seas of our home world for several billion years. This massive, gentle creature went into extinction, but its brain bone was preserved along with its entire memories and all of the memories of my people down through the millennia. When Tera was destroyed, this was the most treasured artifact placed under the protection of the Garck. Just like you, many of my family have searched the surface of Earth for generations hoping to recover any Paleogarcks that might have survived the cataclysm and then by some miracle found their way to Earth. Our sacred stone is a fragment of Cunene's brain bone and the piece you have is a piece of that powerful, ancient artifact. Your love of the quest is no accident; your passion for the hunt is the result of genetic memory. A part of me is in you. You may recall strange dreams from when you were younger. These were vivid dreams that seemed too colorful to be anything but real, but at your young age you could not understand them. Those were some of our memories. You also have some very keen residual talents. You tend to do things prematurely before they become commonly known, this is because you have a vague sight into the future but it is not perfected in you. When you were young you felt unlimited strength and energy. That too was genetic effect. Your body will adapt quickly to this environment because there is Teran in you. We have watched your genetic line for thousands of years and have waited for you and your time to come. I have loved you for many of your lifetimes, Bryce Monroe. Now in my prime I have seen the culmination of all of the traits that I have admired in every one of your prior lives. You are he, the one we have waited for to bridge the gap between our peoples, and you can do this with the stone.

"Now is as good or bad a time as any to tell you of a great disappointment. Your trusted friend Ali has betrayed that trust. This is something that surprised us as well. It appeared to us that you two were as brothers. Ali has met with your nemesis Laurent and has offered to sell him our stone for the right price. Your other travel friends are safe, as are my family members, but you were all followed aggressively by corrupt competitors trying to take what they believed you to possess. When you changed your mind and walked away from the bus, your pursuers took the long ride north and your ride to us with Simon was unfettered. So, if this is too much, too quickly, I am happy to give you time to rest," Mina offered with kind consideration. "But if you desire more, I can go on with your indoctrination."

I nodded in agreement and simply said, "Yes, more please."

Jasmina went on. "We understand that your scientists will have serious skepticism and we are hoping that your relationships with many in that community will carry weight enough to get them to give extra consideration to what we are about to reveal to your world. The consensus is that once they have had the opportunity to analyze our fragment, they will change their minds on their own about what they feel is a certain reality. Right now the most intelligent minds on Earth do not believe in life elsewhere in the universe, yet many are scrambling to be the first to find evidence. A majority of those researchers figure that the most they will find might be a life form similar to the cockroach and possibly to be in the form of a fossil. What they will find in our fragment will be bone cells far older than this star system and still unmineralized as well as having fusion crust that can be dated for its terrestrial age.

"The Elders feel this may be the key that allows humans to open their minds to further possibilities. Our hope is that through your science experts, we can then approach your governing body for further revelation. Based on our calculations, there is little time for this process and we shall aid you in any way possible to expedite this effort. I do understand that there shall be great danger for you during your journeys on our behalf. But now that you are more informed, you will be more receptive to my thoughts. If you trust me implicitly, I will get you there and I shall be with you in mind, heart, and body. I have been with you for longer than you know and if you allow me, I will never leave your side again. From now forward our souls are one."

How lucky am I? The most beautiful woman in three galaxies is never going to leave my side! I turned to see her looking at me intently and about to burst into laughter. I have just been busted for thinking happy thoughts. Her laughter broke the tension and helped me to get over the embarrassment.

An unavoidable question came to mind, "What comes after I get the fragment into the hands of researchers?"

Jasmina revealed to me that there was no need for a plan beyond this point, but rather there would be a very predictable chain reaction that would transpire. The discovery would be announced, and coming from humans of such reliable credibility, the truth would never find question. Government leaders would want to hear more and would find a way to the source of the material. At that time I would then play the role of ambassador for a time while the transition took place. The idea was to turn things around with Teranian help wherever possible. But the fear of potential abandonment would be necessary to force the change, and since it would take less than the blink of an eye for this to occur, there would be a great deal of motivation for all surface dwellers to respond to the need for change. I could not imagine how the entire global population would react to the news that we are not alone. This is a question that everyone ponders at times. It's been the source of thousands of books and other publications, the plot of thousands of films, the fabric of myth, legend, and storytelling through the ages. All of that speculation will end. The only part of all this that might be easily accepted is the thought of coexisting. That would be a moot point since it has already gone on since the beginning of time.

We have cohabited this planet for ages without mankind knowing about it. This brought other questions to mind. I turned again to gaze into the lovely green eyes that shone even brighter here in the luminescent glow of every living thing in EarthUnder. I asked Mina if the Terans had anything to do with the dinosaurs.

She replied swiftly, "We had everything to do with the dinosaurs; every creature on Earth was brought here from other planets. We could not always fold space. In our early ages of experimentation with the utilization of space ribbons, our earliest efforts six hundred million years ago were partial failures, only transplanting single-cell organisms. But with time Teranians perfected distance travel, populating many planets with life forms saved and transferred from dying worlds. Later in time when our doom became more clearly apparent, we began to modify some of the worlds more suitable for our kind to inhabit. I know from your education that you are familiar with the fossil record and the explosions of life and later extinctions of certain species; this was designed and orchestrated by our efforts. A piece to this puzzle for your history books might interest you. Your paleontologists find many species of dinosaurs in fossilized remains, but they are no longer living while other creatures that appear in the same fossil formations are still present on Earth today. It is assumed that the giant lizards and many small species were driven into extinction. The fact is that some did die off for various reasons, but many were moved elsewhere to planets more suitable for their anatomy or lifecycle. Many of our early efforts were flawed, lacking proper planning and preparation. Over time my people in their wisdom have learned to be far less invasive. We have learned that in an effort to maintain balance it is better to make small nudges than to push and shove to make things work, Compri?"

My heart leaps. The word fills me with warm, comforting, distant memories. I should have expected that Mina would know that word and how Kadishya had used it back then. It felt good to hear it used again. It seemed to flow into the moment. I was absorbing a great deal of new and exciting information and it was an appropriate word for her to use. The word had reminded me of the surface and all I had to eventually return to. For now I wanted to hear more about Jasmina's home world Tera and EarthUnder.

As Jasmina revealed more about the history of her people, questions that have boggled the minds of brilliant men and women for centuries were being answered. This experience was connecting the cosmic dots! Her descriptions and explanations painted vivid images in my mind.

I could feel the excitement her ancestors must have felt being able to do all these amazing things. I needed to ask Mina more about this "brain bone"; so far this made little sense to my caveman brain. Again she showed me with her eloquent eyes that she was listening in on my thoughts. It occurred to me at this moment that her abilities would be very helpful in the race to get this specimen into the hands of the right group of scientists.

Mina nodded knowingly, answering, "This giant, gentle, sea creature was much like the gray whale found here on Earth, but far larger and able to live for great spans of time. They were a magnificent creature that swam in our ocean and lived a life much as your whales do here. The Drillians' large brain afforded them great intelligence and power. We learned how to control and develop our brain power from the Drillians. Not only were they able to perform massive displays of mental power, they were able to clearly communicate with all species of our world including the Terans.

"Now, this part may be difficult for you, my Bryce Monroe Sterling; in your culture and in recent years you have developed the ability to store memory into crystals such as the silicon wafers in your computers. Billions of years ago the Drillians outgrew the memory capacity of their massive brains. You see, they were unable to forget anything. The massive brain was as a light that burns always; they could not erase or prioritize memory—it was always right there in the foreground. The end of a Drillian's life came in the instant the brain could hold no more information. This would take many millions of your years, but it was tragic to the Drillians to lose one of their ancient companions. Over the millennia Drillians evolved, developing the brain bone. This was a large, heavy, silicified mass above their brain that acted much like what your people would consider to be a biological supercomputer with great quantities of memory. Within this bone they would store literally every memory, including those of others and what memories could be recalled of their predecessors. In more recent times their memories included all those of the Teranians as well. In the last millennium of our time on Tera a small comet had fallen into our ocean. This was assumed to be a harmless event, but locked within its icy nucleus was a rabid bacterium that spread throughout the Drillians, killing every one. We were devastated by the loss of our mentors, the Drillian. Not only had they taught us much of what we live by, but they were so intricately involved in our lives that their memories were a complete chronology of our own lives for many millions of years. When the corpse of the oldest Drillian Cunene was located, the bones were preserved in a memorial obelisk. We discovered in touching the brain bone that all of those memories were accessible by our minds and we learned that by touching this bone our current memories were also stored within the Drillian brain bone much like memory is stored in a silicon wafer.

"Sadly, when we folded space and jumped to this new world, only living tissue could be transferred. As I told you before, this bone obelisk was stored inside a Paleogarck chamber. The Garck was never found, but somehow a large fragment of the brain bone of our oldest and wisest Drillian, Cunene, survived the millions of years drifting through the vacuum of space. It also endured the fiery fall at cosmic velocity through Earth's atmosphere to come to rest where we found it many years later after many miles of searching deep in the desert above. Although this meteorite is only a symbol to our people, we now realize it holds great hope for us all. Just the structure of the matrix will convince your scientists to research further. If they can find a way to tap into our memories, even a few glimpses, then much of the process will complete itself long before we reveal our existence. This thing we are trying to do doesn't need to take a great deal of time, but we know that it will take some time for your people to acclimate to what they are about to discover. There is far more for us to share, my star hunter, but first I feel compelled to ask if you need to rest."

It was hard to choose. I was feeling pretty wiped out, but the excitement of this flood of information was so stimulating that I wanted more. Jasmina could see that I wanted more, but that my eyes were showing fatigue. She suggested that we find a piece of soft ground and take rest. This sounded decadently good to me. We came to a place that looked inviting and reclined for a time. What seemed like moments later, I woke from a deep, refreshing sleep. I couldn't recall closing my eyes, nor falling off to sleep, but awakening, I felt renewed and energized.

We walked for a bit, stopping to watch strange little creatures darting across a shallow pool. As we strolled by patches of flowers resembling bulbs, they turned to follow our movement and changed color as we passed. I could make out tiny flying objects flitting from plant to plant. They appeared to be fairies. They weren't birds and they weren't insects. They appeared to be tiny humanoids with the wings of a dragonfly. I couldn't tell for sure; my eyes were causing me to question. It might have been my still sleep-filled eyes, but as we moved through the area the lumens closest to us appeared to intensify. Mina explained that what I was seeing was an attraction between all living things in her world, and when a humanoid passes, the tension of that attraction intensifies, creating a passing illumination.

Mina continued with my orientation: "At a distance your eyes will soon notice a pulsing that is the flow of life in EarthUnder. There are many anomalies in our world that will seem different to you, for now, but in time you will grow to find them natural."

She pointed and smiled at something slowly moving alongside our path. It was a huge, flat, segmented worm moving at the speed of a snail. It was mostly chartreuse in color with stemmed eyes and measured roughly three feet in width and maybe nine feet long when extended. It, too, seemed to notice us as we passed. I looked towards Mina and she nodded to my question about her ability to communicate with the worm.

There was life all around us and now that my eyes were acclimating to this new light source, I was beginning to see that this cavernous Void we were traversing truly was of unlimited dimension. I could not see an end, only a distant haze of the same tapered pillars identical to the one closest to our position. There were vines twisting up and down the pillars and all manner of plant life covering much of the pillar surface flowing out onto the forest floor of this massive cavern. I asked Mina how she was able to heal my body so well—not just the scars were gone but all of my old injuries and battle scars as well as the pain from them. She described it as a way of communicating with the cells in the body, getting them to continue with their unfinished work. She explained that in Earthling bodies the cells are on constant overload fighting the damaging effects of human life on Earth's surface.

Mina went on to say that because of the rapid aging process and the damaging effects of the sun's rays, our bodies are decaying at a surprisingly rapid rate compared to the body of a Teranian. Because of what the cells of a human must endure, they never quite finish the job of healing any one injury. A human body's ability to heal becomes stretched too thin, and the cells never get back to healing any injury completely.

"While you slept, I took over for your body's cells, allowed many of them to take full rest and encouraged others to finish their jobs mending all of your past injuries. It is not magic and not medicine; it is pure thought and mental energy which inspires the community of cells in one's body to respond and comply. Basically, your body is now one hundred percent of the body you were born with." Mina finished her comments with a gentle, caring, hand on my shoulder.

I asked her about being shot and could she have stopped that from happening. Her explanation did make sense. Jasmina did say she was watching this event unfold. But that sometimes even tragedy plays a role in which path destiny takes. She knew the gun shots would play an integral part in getting me to find my way here. She did say that the odd wound locations were her doing. As Mina spoke I was growing more familiar with her greater depth of understanding, her wisdom, and a strangely different scale of emotions. She immediately picked up on this and told me that Terans have a powerful range of emotions, far more intense than humans and at the same time more controlled.

She went on to say that Terans cannot see the future, but they can see the present if they wish and they can predict the future based on present human behavior.

"In the case of your shooter, I simply made his elbow slip when he pulled the trigger. Yes, Bryce Monroe Sterling, I allowed this evil man to shoot at you, but I never would have allowed it to be more that a scratch."

"Four scratches," I replied sarcastically.

She smiled again, understanding my angst and forgiving my sarcasm. Her smiles were so alluring that I found myself doing and saying things just to get another one.

I was about to ask Mina to tell me more about aging. Questions were now firing away in my awakening brain. Just then Jasmina took my hand and led me soaring high into the air. We arrived at a random point where we came to an instant halt and she released our hands. We drifted there looking at each other. Mina grabbed my shoulders and gave me a spin. As I spun, she bumped my lower leg, which started me spinning in two directions. Then the spinning ceased as suddenly as it started. She told me that this was my freedom of movement. I could move with a thought and halt with a thought. She had stopped my movement with her brain and said that I would eventually be able to do the same. She told me that my body would absorb the abilities of the Teranians.

For now, it was time to begin our journey across the Void. Jasmina had heard me thinking about how large this cavernous subterranean world might be and decided to give me a sample view. She told me to stay with her and to think of forward motion and to simply relax my body and to mentally insist that my body remain with hers. She included that when it came time to stop, she would take care of that for now. Off we went soaring side by side at unimaginable velocity. I could see our speed by the blur of everything around us. There seemed to be no friction or feeling of cutting through the air. It was as if we were motionless and the world around us was moving. We halted abruptly, but with no feeling of slowing or inertia. Mina moved out in front of me as we floated there thousands of feet above the surface below. She told me that our travel had just traversed a continent and an ocean, approximately seven thousand surface miles. She went on to explain how the physics doctrine I was taught in school was not nearly complete or accurate, that I would want to open my mind to new standards. That this was going to be difficult for many in my culture to fathom and accept, but then again it might be exhilarating for some. I asked her where we were.

"We are directly below Montana," was Mina's reply. It struck me funny that I have good friends in Big Sky Country. Mina smiled and commented how much she enjoyed my ability to maintain a network of dear friends all over the planet. "This is one of your most endearing traits and has been in your line for many generations, that and your love for adventure and travel."

Mina asked me to look around at the environment here. She pointed out that there were great waves of movement below. We were so high that I wasn't able to make out what I was seeing, but I could see pulsing, brilliant waves of color change and rapid changes in direction. We slowly lowered closer to what appeared to be the bottom, but along the way Mina put her hands on me again and turned until the moving floor was now above us. Nothing changed, nothing felt different, and yet the moving floor was now the roof of the world. As we drew closer I recognized that the moving mass was an endless herd of bison. I felt puzzled, but then Jasmina said that the Terans had begun to preserve species that humans were driving into extinction, that it was a simple solution and easy for them to perform. Since they had brought these creatures here in the first place, they felt it was required that they preserve the species that had done well here for so long. Mina told me that there were preserves throughout EarthUnder where surface creatures were being held in repose. Eventually they would be returned to the surface to infuse with the population above. She explained that this effort applied to every creature big and small. Thoughts came to mind of wondrous creatures I had never seen such as mammoths or my favorite predator, saber-toothed cats.

The possibilities seemed limitless. This inspired a flurry of questions from my geology background. I wanted explanations for earthquakes, tsunami, volcanoes, plate tectonics, the truth about planet cores, and the origin of our moon. The questions were now pouring into my mind. I could see Jasmina acknowledging each word as they came to mind. Mina would continue to reveal the truth about these queries. But I felt the first place to start was to continue to learn about Teranian age. Mina told me that although Terans live for approximately three thousand human years, it would take a great deal of time to explain the complexities of everything that influences the difference between our span and theirs. As I began to ask the next question, she replied that her own life span would be nine hundred years. Her family line was genetically directed many years ago. Alterations to DNA were imposed in order for her family members to spend ample time on the surface living human lives. They were tasked with searching for ancient, treasured relics from her home world. Mina and her family line would eventually represent her race to humans as liaisons helping humans with the transition into a new age of awareness. Jasmina explained that there was a cost for her ability to survive under the sun. She went on to say that this was a great honor and that she had learned to admire the delicate nature of human life and the intricacies of each individual personality. She shared that in time she recognized that humans were limited in many traits compared to Terans. She revealed that human beings were as keenly emotional and often even more complicated in their emotional considerations than any Teran. She admitted that this one aspect had puzzled her for all of her time in life thus far.

Jasmina smiled as she expressed joy and amazement observing man- and womankind's love and attachment to one another. She also shared how difficult it was for any of her kind to understand the irony among humans to love so deeply and yet to be able to exact such cruelty and hatred upon others. She had a forlorn expression in her eyes as she spoke of the broad spectrum of our emotional tendencies from the highest pinnacles of love and bliss to the lowest levels of deceit and abuse between humans. Her forehead wrinkled and her lovely emerald eyes watered to a cascade of tears as she spoke of all the killing through the centuries. No matter how much they had the capacity to understand, all Terans found it extremely difficult to witness human cruelty and killing. Jasmina recovered from the sadness of our conversation to lead me in one more direction. She wanted me to see one more feature of her environment. Jasmina told me that from here below the North America continent, we were going to move to a location below what humans refer to as Central America. Immediately we were flying again and the view was changing swiftly; colors, contour, movement, everything we could see as we passed appeared to change.

In what seemed like only a few minutes I could see ahead that we were approaching a brilliant glowing feature of light that from this great distance resembled a sunset streaming through the smoke of burning fall foliage. The closer we drew, the brighter and warmer the colors of this apparent sunset grew. Side by side we flew through Jasmina's magical world. Soon we slowed to a drift as I glared up and down at a feature beyond comprehension. Welling up from one surface to the other stretched a column of molten rock: magma! Mina went to work helping me to understand what I was seeing.

"This is Colima," she said, pointing to the column with her hand outstretched. "This is a volcano named by your people. It is one of many throughout the planet. Volcanoes are destructive and yet they are necessary for both our races. In addition to their participation in building continents and islands, they have helped produce the dusty atmosphere which blocks out deadly cosmic rays and protects living creatures on the surface of Earth. At the same time these columns of molten rock provide Terans with a waste disposal system. Our gravity and bio system forces inward pressure that creates this magma, so we must control its flow and guide the molten material to the surface where it can vent and cool. The Earth's core is still molten and throughout time that magma finds new ways to break through to relieve itself. So when this begins, we guide it to the surface, which prevents magma from filling the Void we call home."

As I listened to Mina's voice I watched, entranced by the column of fire. In this area I could see literally millions of Terans busily coming and going. I couldn't see what they were doing, but there was a symphony of motion around us as bodies flew by from every direction. Mina told me that these people were doing cleaning and maintenance and helping with the mind focus that kept this molten pillar restrained in place and prepared for the next eruption. This was all so new and strange and yet it made sense. We hovered here watching the movements and the undulating tornado of molten mantle outstretched from below us to above. Jasmina shared with me that when this planet was young there was only a single massive continent that Earthling scientists refer to as Pangaea. She said that her past home world was similar to Earth with only one continent and the remaining globe being covered with ocean. This continent was broken into smaller continents and those were enlarged in the process of continent building and developing this shell-planet underworld of New Tera. She smiled again as she said that the Earth is an ongoing work in progress which has taken many millions of years and will continue for many millions more. She said that the Earth is a living, breathing orb that requires constant maintenance.

I looked at her with a puzzled glance of doubt and question. Mina looked out into the glow of the magma and said, "Think of it this way, Bryce Monroe, if the planet should die, we all die with it." The clarity of her words stabbed into my thoughts with absolute finality and icy truth. A wave of fear made me shudder with concern for our future. This was Jasmina's message and her mission. I began to put together why I was allowed to witness all of this. This wasn't just some mystical attraction or fortunate happenstance. She and I were chosen for this connection and this task. Being a human from the surface, this was my tour of her world in an effort to show me what was at risk of being ended and lost forever. She was showing me that the delicate balance of our biosphere was far more tentative than humans cared to believe and that any number of potential ends were pending and out of Teranian ability to control or prevent.

Mina gestured for us to leave this place. We took a wide swing around the lava tube and rocketed off through New Tera. I could see countless changes in the terrain as we moved through various regions. There were varying concentrations of Terans and animals as well as areas that appeared to be forested with massive trees and other areas that might pass for endless lawn or farmland. There were bodies of water throughout the land and countless windows into the oceans. One sight I repeatedly hoped to witness was whales swimming past one of the windows and it was in my mind to ask Mina to show this to me if it were ever possible. Then it occurred to my endlessly curious mind whether I might be able to reach out and touch one swimming by.

Mina answered my thoughts, "Yes, my star man, someday you may swim with the whales and they may want to touch you also." I grinned in utter satisfaction.

As we cruised through the Void, Mina told me that we were going back to her home if I wished or she could show me how rest is taken here in New Tera. She could tell that I was ready for a break. Soon we were back where we had entered New Tera. I could see the Vug we had used to come through Earth's crust. There we settled on the surface below. We walked for a short distance and stopped. There was no apparent reason for stopping in this particular spot, but Mina sat on the ground and reached up for me to lower myself as well. As we sat, small creatures scurried out from where we would settle. Mina said that when one needs to rest, it is done in this manner. I thought I had already experienced this aspect of life in her world.

She whispered, "You lie back so that your head touches the ground." As we lay there an apparent static energy began to glow between our heads and the surface we were touching. She called this an accelerated awareness of the spirit. My body felt an energizing glow and my skin felt a sensation of tiny pinpricks and fiery heat at the point of each prick. As we remained prone, inner warmth began to develop and grow. I felt heavy as though I couldn't move no matter how hard I tried. In what seemed like seconds the sensations had ended suddenly, and I craved more.

Mina stood and looked down at me. She took a deep breath and reached down to help me rise. As I rose I felt powerful and energized. I looked at Jasmina in amazement. This beat the heck out of a full night's sleep. This was what had occurred earlier when I needed sleep. Jasmina told me that this would be enough rest for me to go on for several days, but since I had no idea of time as it passed, I could only trust my gut to tell me when I would need rest again. We walked for some time watching as Terans went about their work around us. Coming to the base of a pillar, we both leaned against it to watch others go by while we talked. It seemed surreal to me that these people and my own people looked so similar and yet they were so different, so advanced, evolved, and powerful. They were calm, quiet, and seemed to be very happy.

Mina stopped my thinking with her words, "It is not as you see it to be. What you see here is the world we support. It is as a room in your home, neat, quiet, everything where you want it, everything where you put it. This is how we keep our part of this and other worlds. But all is not perfect in the universe. Many of your people's concerns are founded in reality. Your people have seen alien visitors. They have seen many unexplained anomalies. There is a dark side to the universe beyond this planet. Much of what is a danger to us all, we Terans work hard to protect against. There are outsiders who would take this planet for their own, but we make it appear as though this planet is rapidly dying. Part of this façade takes the form of the deserts above. To outsiders, deserts near the equator and polar ice caps denote planetary decay gone out of control. We have generated this appearance to deceive some of the worst of the marauders that have come here over time. There have been other less evolved species who have visited this world many times, but typically they are driven off by our energy and influence.

"There is one danger that is even more hazardous than the dark side of humans, the dark side of Terans. It is not an immediate concern, but this is something I must share with you so that you will always trust that I share everything with you. Before we left to come here, there was a rebellion on Tera. Many Terans grew to abuse their power. They began to feel that they were superior to others of their own race. They created a religion that justified all of their evil actions. They would travel to other worlds and rob those worlds of all their valuable resources. Anything considered rare in that world became coveted by our dark ones and was taken to a place that they modified to be their treasure trove. This treasure planet became an obsession for the dark ones. As they began to fight amongst themselves over their precious bounty, the rest of our race recognized that there would someday need to be a break between our kinds. When we departed Tera, the dark ones were abandoned to live out their last moments on Tera. We blocked their ability to jump from Tera as the planet destroyer black dwarf star made its final approach. We have maintained a vigil since those days, many millions of years ago. There is no confirmation of their demise. Our concern has always kept us on guard, keeping watch over the space surrounding our solar system. We make certain that the dark ones keep their distance from our worlds, not just this planet, but the worlds of Terans who traveled to the other bio-formed Teran shell planets throughout the universe.

"It has been so long since those turbulent times that many planets believe that the dark ones (Teranor) vanished with Tera when the dwarf star disrupted our home world. We here of EarthUnder do not share this confidence with our sister planets. We remain in constant vigil and so even if we succeed in persuading mankind to change their destructive ways, there will always remain this threat concern. One of our greatest concerns has been that our corrupted brothers and sisters might direct an unstoppable event our way from some distant point in space in retribution for our desertion of their spirits on Tera. So even if you and I succeed, Bryce Monroe Sterling, in saving Earth from immediate demise, we may someday have to leave this world for another. We can take the whole of mankind with us, but not unless they understand and agree to join us."

As Mina spoke, we sat on two humps rising up from the surface, and she reached out to place a small peanut-shaped object in my hand. She had another in her hand, which she put in her mouth and began to chew. When I asked what it was she said it was our meal for the day, a blend of pro-biotic ingredients containing tetrameric protein, fiber, and concentrated carbohydrates. In a survival situation, one of these meal pods can sustain a human for as many as thirty days on Earth's surface. I popped the meal pod into my mouth showing all the faith and trust I could muster. As I bit down for the first time it had the viscosity of well-used chewing gum and a flavor similar to raspberries and meadow foam honey. As I chewed the pleasant meal pod, it slowly dissolved away to nothing. Jasmina told me that this would give me strength and energy while maintaining all of my body's physiological requirements. She noted that my physical well-being would allow me to more efficiently assimilate further orientation into her world. She also included that it would not be much longer before we would be leaving Tera to move back to the surface of Earth, where we would embark on our journey.

Mina leaned over and picked up some sphagnum from the earth below, pushed it into the pool next to us, and then squeezed the water into her mouth as she tilted her head back to catch the falling stream of water. She then offered the mossy sponge to me for a drink from the pond. As I hesitated, she assured me that water gets no more pure than this. In all my travels over the planet through the years, I have always been leery of drinking the local water. I have been sick from waterborne critters so many times that I always hesitate as those painful memories race through my mind. Again, I acted on trust and allowed myself to mirror Mina's actions.

My mother always enjoyed the taste of really pure water. In fact the town where I grew up had wonderful, pure, clean water and Mom always told us that this was why we lived in that town. She used to describe how our water came from a deep well and that the water was pressed through a thin seam in Columbia Basalt two thousand feet below the surface. Mom was a school teacher by career, but her education was hydrogeology and her passion was the arts. I grew up in a home filled with music, family antiques, and Mom's art collection on the walls. As I tasted the refreshing, cold water from the pond, it was as if I were back there in time listening to Mom preach her water words.

Jasmina crinkled a small reassuring smile of authority as she told me, "This is the same water that comes from your well at home, filtered by the same rock."

It felt good to hear her say this. A fond memory of my childhood brought back by something from this new world was helping me to feel more at home here deep in the belly of my own planet.

As we sat I asked Mina about other destructive powers that represent danger to humans such as earthquakes. She explained that planet Earth is always growing, both from the roughly one hundred tons of debris that falls through the atmosphere each day, most of which is dust, and also because the Earth is expanding from within. She told me that the Terans control this movement we call plate tectonics.

That even though they work to slow the movement and struggle to stop continental shifts as soon as possible, a small amount of destructive energy does escape their grasp. She then explained that things would be far more violent if the Terans weren't here to maintain the planet's movement. She reminded me that this is a living planet and that they can control much of Earth's volatility but they cannot stop it. All that Earth does is an integral part of the biosphere we call home.

Jasmina took my hand and led me up into the air again. This time we flew to a window into one of the oceans. We hovered near the bottom edge of the massive opening into the Brine. Once we drew within a few yards of the water I could feel the energy that was holding the water in place. I could hear the sounds of the sea as if I were in the water. Facing the window I could see little else but the wall of water since the window must be thousands of yards high and even wider. There were no fish visible, but at the bottom I could see hundreds of steel drums covered with sediment. Mina explained to me that this was Man's idea for nuclear waste disposal. These were ordinary steel drums filled with concrete and waste material from nuclear power plants and nuclear bomb manufacturing. I could see that the steel was rusting away.

Mina was trying to show me the human "out of sight, out of mind" approach to pollution problems. This was one of many examples of what she had talked about earlier. The list was endless: oil drilling, mining, water drilling, asphalt and concrete roads and parking lots, burning waste, dumping waste in the oceans and landfills, hiding it in salt mines. Ignoring the energy of our life-giving sun, Man has dammed our glorious rivers for hydroelectric power. Gas-powered automobiles on asphalt roads and jets in the upper atmosphere burn fuel producing deadly gases and belching them into the air. Burning fields and forests, draining virtually all of our waste into rivers, oceans, and the ground; all are deadly practices. She could have listed many more examples, but she knew I understood the message. She told me how she needed to communicate with the world leaders of my people that this must all stop immediately in order to save the planet for us all. She added that it would be much easier for Earthlings to save this planet than to grow accustomed to a new and fairly hostile alternative home world.

Mina cast deep into my mind with her beautiful eyes and said quite clearly, "Your birds are dropping from the sky. You are eating fish that are filled with the poison you dump into your waters. Your fruit and vegetables are filled with toxins and dioxins and you spray them with poisons to kill the insects that attack them for their own nourishment. The flesh of the animals you eat is tainted with toxins and hormones, and the air you breathe is causing cancer. From outside your civilization this appears to be a global death wish. We can help Mankind but only if they choose to change their destructive direction. The end result of the human course is an end for the Terans as well, but we do not choose to go with the humans any further down that path of self-destruction. This is what needs to be conveyed to your current global leaders. Terans do not have leaders. When you speak to one of us you communicate with us all. I am merely chosen to do this task, as are you, Bryce Monroe Sterling. Together we must start this change."

She pointed to the wall of sea water in front of us. "Your scientists call this part of the ocean dead. There is not enough oxygen remaining here to support life. This is an infection that will spread until the oceans of this world roll over and die. If that comes to be, then we all will die. Scientists used to believe that an ice age would take millions of years to return. I tell you that a global ice age only takes three of your years to occur. Your scientists believe that the oceans can heal themselves while Man keeps using them as toilets. I tell you that one day the breathable air will simply fade away and in just one of your twenty-four-hour days. I know this is hard for you to hear, so try to understand how hard it has been for my people to watch. Your people must come to realize that the end is near and if it comes to another planetary move, the ones who have fallen into darkness will be left behind to expire. This will be hard for many to accept, but it will be done regardless of emotional reaction. This will all be revealed to your leaders as we make our attempt to communicate our concerns about our coexistence here. After that it will be up to your people to decide how we move forward to save this planet. Either way this goes will be difficult for us all to complete. For now I would like you to meet some Terans. Then, we will move back to the surface after you and I discuss our approach to the next phase."

We remained there with the sea window behind us and watched as several individuals approached from various directions. Soon there were several dozen Terans standing in front of us. They all wore robes with bare feet. Mina told me that the robes were for my cultural benefit since Terans find no need for clothing. This group of representatives appeared to have the same diversity that one would find in a group of humans. They did not show the same smiling face that I had grown accustomed to seeing during the time with Jasmina. They were calm and studied me with obvious intensity.

Mina introduced me to them and many of them nodded knowingly as if they already knew who I was and why I was there. One of the older looking men moved forward to face us. Mina told me that this was Talleyrand, one of the eldest of their kind. Talleyrand looked at both of us, back and forth. He reached out to take my hand and put one above and below mine as he gave me his blessing. He looked into Jasmina's eyes for an extended time and I could see that they were speaking to each other. The others nodded several times in unison and smiled as a group while this took place. Talleyrand looked back at me, welcomed me to his world, and wished that I find ultimate success in our endeavor. He bade us farewell as he turned to rejoin the rest of the group.

Just as he met the front of the group another individual came forward from the group. As he approached, I recognized him. My spine tingled. It was me! Now, this was my idea of weird. The closer he came, the more I felt that this had to be some kind of trick. He too stopped to take my hand. Mina introduced us and told me that this was my twin. She wanted me to know that part of my genetic line had come from Teran strain and that throughout time there had been uncanny parallels between members of his line and mine. She thought I might enjoy knowing this phenomenon existed. She could see that I was a bit put off by meeting myself. It did feel strange knowing that I actually had a real live doppelganger. She told me that beyond appearance there was very little similarity. Then Jasmina told me as she waved her hand across the group that these Terans would be there to help us in many special ways, and not just this group, but that they would lead if the strength of others was ever needed during our quest. There was a strong sense of security in the air, knowing that these and others would be helping to keep us on task and safe from harm. They all moved forward to encircle us with arms outstretched; it felt to me that this had created a special bond of familiarity and friendship between us all. A moment later they all moved off, and blended into the colorful forest around us. I turned back to look again at the barrels of waste resting there on the other side of the window next to us. My thoughts grew heavy with the importance of our pending mission to save the world.

CHAPTER SEVEN

The Tube

The main goal had always been to live a simple life gathering rocks and traveling to unfamiliar corners of this big blue marble. Now, after half a lifetime of learning how big the planet really is, I am put to task helping a group of aliens save the planet from its pending doom. My simple life had just rocketed to the opposite end of the simplicity spectrum. There was no choosing to be done. I had to help make this all happen immediately. With confidence and conviction I began to rehearse in my mind how we would make this project come together. The first hurdle to cover was getting to the Natural History Museum.

Mina in reply said, "I will get us there." She detailed how there is no need to return to the surface until we get where we are going next. This was a priceless asset since no adversary on the surface can predict where we will appear and we can avoid any hazards along the way. So the plan would be to position ourselves as close as possible to the museum and make arrangements for a meeting. Once we met with the science team, we would need to remain close to respond to their reaction. I don't want to say too much, but rather allow the specimen to impress the right people. Then when they come running with a flurry of inquiries, we can give specifics. The idea should be to put together a small group of scientists and government officials to bring to New Tera for an orientation similar to mine.

I heard once in a seminar that to complete a large task the best way to begin is with small slow steps. There remained a sense of urgency, but we will want to take it slow. We needed to build a network of believers who can educate others. Jasmina said it was time for us to begin. I checked my pocket to make certain the stone was still there and glanced one last time at the dead water holding down the rusting barrels of nuclear waste. As we began to rise and move on, I surveyed all of the colorful life moving around us. When we drew closer to the ceiling of this world beneath, I could see trees and other brilliant plant life growing down from the top as well as animals and people standing there as if wearing gravity boots. The top and sides of this cavernous world were as actively populated as the floor.

We used the Vug once more and I soon learned why. Mina asked me if I would enjoy crossing through an ocean rather than under it. She could tell instantly that I was all for it when I replied, "Heck, yeah!" I was surprised; we didn't head for a window and instead turned to a side wall and into the Gray. Before long we emerged into the ocean. Jasmina said this was our Atlantic Ocean. She explained that the sea creatures can sense our approach and move away from the path of a Teran traveler so there are no concerns for collision with creatures. She also pointed out that this deep underwater, there were few creatures and no human mechanized vessels. We shot through thousands of miles of ocean in minutes. I marveled at our movement and what a gift this was to be able to traverse the planet this way, and how it lowered the risk while making our way to the museum. Mina told me that the Vug would carry us through stone again and come to rest in a dark abandoned tunnel, part of the London subway system. We would check into rooms at a hotel near Heathrow airport and then immediately take the Tube to the Museum. Our hope was to meet with one of the meteorite collection curators, to show them the fragment of brain bone meteorite and get them interested enough to rush the making of a thin section.

We were at the point in our journey where things needed to fall together flawlessly. But I could see too many things wrong with going back to the surface. If any scientist were to get a view of this stone with a microscope, the excitement would build rapidly. Someone needed to be there on this day for that to get started. As people begin to realize what we had brought here, the din of curiosity would be an endless flood of needles pricking at the skin of Man's limited knowledge. No human could imagine where all this might go. There was no idea of how the people would accept or deny the truth of what we were about to bring into the light of this sun-scorched planet I call home. I knew where to take this stone, whom to talk to and whom to trust with invaluable scientific research material. I had zero clue of what to expect in response to a specimen so beyond the boundaries of this physical world.

The Vug made its way through the Gray to an opening. There was light and movement showing the direction to the Tube. As we made our way towards the light I could hear the familiar roar of the Tube. When we drew closer to my "former" world, I struggled to get my head around the fact that I was an alien. It was already beyond imagination that I had been chosen for this mission, but learning that this had been planned many years before my time, and that DNA stuff, and then meeting the body double, it was a lot to comprehend. Why was I the one? Jasmina splashed ahead through the pooled water of our temporary parking spot.

"Not one," she said; "there are many like you within the Teranian population. This is a byproduct of DNA culmination and sequencing techniques. Your mental processes are uniquely yours alone as is your overall personality, and combined with your terrestrial DNA and your birth and growth development here on the surface of Earth. You are our best hope for the success of this endeavor."

I stumbled, saying, "Whoa, way to make me feel special, Mina," just as we stepped into the illuminated portion of this side shaft. Jasmina turned to make a gesture behind us. I could only guess that she had activated some sort of barrier to hide the Vug.

"Yes," she said, "it is secure." We continued out into the subway. I felt embarrassed for my world, much like the feeling from a messy desk, bedroom, or house when surprised by visitors. The flavor of the air was a thick blend of diesel fumes, cigarette smoke, concrete, stagnant water, and essence of human. One could feel the air on the tongue: a syrup of aromatic signature that morphed from moment to moment and place to place. How quickly I had forgotten the subtle nuances of my world. Maybe I had learned to ignore them and being away opened my eyes to all they had denied. I began to notice how the surface light had no vibrancy or color. My world seemed stark and lifeless except for the roar of noises and the movement of people and machines. As we walked out of the Tube and onto the gauntlet of streets and structures, Mina reminded me that she too had lived her life here as if to comfort and remind me that I was not alone. She took hold of my hand as we wove our way through the crowds of pedestrians moving about their selfish lives. I could feel her strength in the warm glow of her hand wrapped around mine.

We only had to cross the bustling street and walk halfway down the building to get to the main entrance. There we would ask a docent to call down to the catacombs below this majestic storehouse of historic treasures to ask one of the curators to come to the reception desk and escort us to the laboratory. Since I had been here many times, there would be no need for ceremony. Anyone in the department of mineralogy would assume the reason for the visit. As we waited in the great entry hall, Jasmina began to show a concerned look in her eyes. She stepped very close to me and asked that I break the stone again. She wanted me to keep the larger fragment and let the scientists do their work on a much smaller piece. Her suggestion was that we hold back material for the sake of posterity. This made sense, as a probe session and thin section would not require much material for what we were trying to accomplish. As long as they had a convincing amount of fusion crust in order to establish authenticity of origin, the rest could be held back for a plethora of reasons. My instincts told me that there was a deeper, more specific concern in her eyes.

Mina responded to my thoughts: "Ah, that's the Teran in you coming through. Your feeling for what you see in my eyes is correct. Later, when we can, I will share with you my worry." I felt a twinge of discomfort listening to Mina refer to the alien blood coursing through my veins. I felt like a decaffeinated brand of human; I still looked like a human or a Teran but I wasn't all there. Mina shot me a look I hadn't seen since we were kids, and I got the message immediately.

As we waited, we slowly gravitated out of the flow of traffic coming into the museum and stood next to the wall, where we labored to break the fragment again. A small, perfect piece broke free, and this piece had a very nice representative section of glossy, bubbled, black fusion crust on one surface. This piece was just what was needed to get things started. A few minutes later we noticed an official-looking person wearing a lab smock with an ID badge walking briskly towards us from the far end of the great, main hall of the museum. She was dwarfed by the distance and the height of the walls on both sides. This building looked as though it was built by giants for giants. We were greeted with handshakes and guided to a marble staircase behind the security kiosk that took us below street level several floors down to the mineral department and the meteorite collections room. There we met with several other researchers and students who were busily working on labeling parts of the collection. I reacted as the proverbial "kid in the candy store." Laid out on various work surfaces were countless world-renowned specimens, many of which I had seen photographed in books I had read through until the pages fell out. These people were in the midst of a large project reorganizing the collection and labeling pieces before moving them to new drawers.

Our arrival seemed to instigate an impromptu break for everyone. Many moved off to get a bite to eat and coffee or tea. We remained there in the room with a small group of interested onlookers that moved to a small workstation with a microscope. The fragment was placed under the microscope and everyone took a turn looking at the new arrival. One would have thought we had brought in a new-born baby the way everyone ogled the fragment under magnification. Immediately several people noticed the bonelike structure of the matrix and others commented on the lustrous, thick fusion crust. This was the first of many steps that we hoped would lead to the inevitable outcome we were there to instigate. I told Vanessa, the head curator, to please pay close attention to the extraterrestrial age of this specimen. Beyond that, I knew all of the other standards were soon to be broken or seriously violated. Mina stood back and watched as everyone took a turn at the microscope. The curator promised us that a thin section would be started the next day and should be finished quickly. I felt the question before it came. Vanessa queried, "Where is the rest of the stone?"

I replied that the main mass was with Mina's people. As usual, any answer would have been accepted as long as there was a chance to obtain more for research. There are set guidelines implemented for classifying meteorites, and a piece would have to be donated for a repository research sample. I knew this could be taken care of later, but for now it was critical to get people to see this stone up close and to get them to start probing the matrix. Once scientists have seen this specimen in cross-polarized light under magnification and have compared the matrix to a terrestrial standard in a microprobe, an endless list of questions will arise.

I could feel the sense of urgency emanating from Mina.

It seemed there wasn't much time to get from the research phase to the part where world leaders would come forward with concerns, inquiries, and action. We needed to turn the world around now, not later. If Jasmina and I couldn't make it happen, then something more dramatic and cataclysmic would need to be done and soon. The hope was that a great deal of this sales job would be done by the scientists. When Vanessa finished her turn at the microscope, she stood up and stepped out of the anxious group crowding the work station. You could hear the comments as normally calm and reserved research nerds finished their turn at the view. The excitement grew exponentially as comments flew and suggestions were made. I could hear the wheels turning in their heads. This specimen made no sense to anyor.e.

Vanessa pulled us away from the group and asked us to explain this joke. She had the half look in her eyes of someone asking a dire question while hoping it was an impossible, almost unforgivable prank. I leaned into her suggestive grip on my arm and replied that this was very serious business. She lowered her face to look deeper into my eyes over the rim of her glasses as if this was her way of seeing into the truth of my expression. She pulled the gloves from her hands as she moved swiftly back to the microscope. A few clever words disbanded the group and people went back to their projects.

Vanessa took another peek through the scope, carefully took the sample from the stage, placed it in a Teflon specimen bag, and labeled it for the technician that would start the thin section. A small crumb was still under the microscope, which she bagged separately. Vanessa looked at us through the bag as she stared closely at the tiny crumb. She told us that she couldn't wait for the technician to finish the section and that she had time reserved on equipment that night and the crumb would be examined by her through the night. This was a good sign that its special, unique characteristics had gotten their attention. The curator urged us to stay close to the museum and to call her when we got settled as she might have questions for us.

We climbed the stone stairs again to leave the historic building, but just before reaching the ground floor flight of steps Mina grabbed my arm as she stared into the steps with the far-off look of a dreamer. "Laurent is here," she whispered with acute intensity. "He has many men and they are in and around this building! There is something else; I cannot see what it is but it is not good. The Elders are calling to me, but I cannot hear them clearly. We must make our way to the Vug; it will help amplify their thoughts."

Hanging from the walls of the stairway at each landing was a thick plush curtain. Jasmina pulled me behind the curtain next to us, took a firm hold of my arm, and pulled me into the stone wall. Here we were again in the soup. I found myself growing more comfortable with moving through stone as a ghost. It felt much safer than walking the streets and corridors of a city on the surface. Knowing that we were being hunted made the cool, dark dank of the Gray that much more comfortable. I felt something also; I felt fear and concern in Mina's grip on my hand. As we drifted through the Gray, I could feel her energy more than ever before. I could not hear her thoughts, but I could feel them changing and I could sense the level of her emotion. My strong, fearless little Jasmina trembled.

In seconds, we reached the Vug. Inside the Vug there

was an air of comfort and security like a warm campfire on a cold winter night. We lay against the side and slipped down into the cradle of its egg-shaped form. I didn't ask any questions. Mina began explaining what she had seen and felt. While she was talking to me, she was explaining to the Elders and others in our watch group what had transpired. Somehow our pursuers knew where we would emerge and they had been in position, preparing to intercept us. She had sensed the presence of a number of bandits which she had tracked before when they were after me. She recognized several of them specifically but there was one she did not and there was something about this individual that caused her to feel alarm and dread.

Suddenly, Talleyrand appeared in the Vug. He sat across from us and silently listened to Mina speak of her concerns. When she finished, Talleyrand reassured us that we were safe. He had sent a pair of our doppelgangers off in the direction of the airport to our hotel room there. There was something else he hadn't covered yet and I could feel it wasn't pleasant information. I tried to imagine how this could get much worse, but then it really did. Talleyrand divulged a long-held secret that had been kept from Jasmina and her family: that the Teranor had found their way to Earth and were infiltrating humankind with their own genetic line. Somehow, the dark ones had mastered the ability to shield their thoughts from the Terans. The Elders felt that the Teranor were plotting to instigate a conflict between our two races that would result in our self-destruction through a minimal effort by the Teranor. Our encounter with one of them confirmed for the Teran Elders that this was plausible. Our mission was now a dangerous race. There were so many clocks ticking to the same destructive end, and any one of those clocks could be the first to run out of time. Talleyrand assured us that he would bring unlimited support to our aid as needed. As he faded away Mina called him back. She asked him why his image was so dim in the museum and why their thoughts were blanked in a shroud of darkness. He replied that this was how it was confirmed to be the dark ones. We were being isolated, jammed basically. The Teran's power comes from the power of thought. Disrupt their communal thought and you break their strength. The Teranor were using a rudimentary military strategy; divide and conquer. Talleyrand was gone and we slumped there in our Vug, staring and thinking.

Now the questions began to ignite in my mind. The first question was how would we call Vanessa to leave our phone number? Mina told me to visualize myself calling the museum to speak to Vanessa and she would take care of the rest. I could hear the phone ringing and the voice mail greeting. When the machine beeped, I spoke, leaving my business number, and ended the call. Mina told me I would hear the ring if she should call. We lay there for hours thinking and talking. Now Jasmina was as full of inquiry as I was. Our concerns and fears felt as if on the same page. We both had issues with the unknown, and it seemed that Terans did feel stronger emotions than humans. Claus Laurent was not my only adversary in this business of recovering space rocks, but I didn't wish to share with Mina how many jerks there really were out there who would do anything to trip me up. The only silver lining to this cloud was knowing that they were all trying to beat each other out as well.

While I lay there pondering my own thoughts, Mina was

asking questions of her community. She shared with me that many things made better sense now, and that because she was of the surface Terans, she had been left out of some parts of the communal knowledge as a precaution in the case that the Elder's suspicions were correct. Turns out that for as long as the Terans had prepared a genetic line for this day, so had the Teranor, and the Teranor had mastered mind isolation to prevent being discovered. The most recent concern for all was that there might be Teranor disguised within the Teranian population in EarthUnder. I began to understand how I could feel Mina's fear. She was feeling the emotions of an entire race of people. She was recalling their ancient past and the nightmare her people lived with prior to their jump to our world. She was responding to the paranoia developed over millions of years of concern that this day might be realized. This was all flooding into her thoughts while we lay there trying to figure out what to do next.

Just then the Vug filled with the rattling clang of a telephone ringing. Mina gestured to me to respond to the sound. I said hello and Vanessa replied without hesitation. "Hello, Bryce, are you sitting down?" Vanessa inquired.

"Yep, " I replied in brief slang.

"Well, again you have brought us a unique, exciting, yet puzzling goody." Vanessa continued with the conservative air of a true nerd scientist. "So far there is no way to tell what this is. It breaks all the standards and it will require a lot more tests before we can even hint at what it might be. Still, it is so unusual that I have already made some calls to other institutions and I got several emeritus curators out of bed to come take a look. I've never done that before, so I am truly hoping that I haven't shot myself in the foot. What you have here appears to be a piece of biological material, not fossilized, not of this Earth, and definitely covered with fusion crust. Would you mind please telling me, my dear Mr. Sterling, what do you know about this specimen?!"

Vanessa has always had this powerful, magical way of getting right to the point—a delightful personality with a huge, infectious smile and a gentle spirit, the kind of person that everybody enjoys spending time with. I love working with this woman. But when the scientist in her comes to the surface, she turns into a tigress and will go for the throat to get her job done. Her passion for the study of meteorites is matched by my passion for finding them.

"Oh, by the way, a friend of yours dropped by today and he is here now enjoying time in the lab with me; say hello," Vanessa deferred as she handed the phone over to Claus Laurent.

"Hello, Mr. Sterling." The slimy voice of a "snake in the grass," my nemesis, Laurent, slithered through the air and into my brain. "This is quite an interesting specimen you have brought to Vanessa." I said nothing as we sat there listening to the oozing voice of the miry serpent bounce off the surface of the Vug. I glanced at Mina; her face grimaced in terror and tears as the voice hissed into our ears.

All I could say was, "Laurent, what goes around comes around, and you'll get yours." Mina ended the call before any more words could be exchanged. She knew I had no desire to speak with the snake.

Jasmina exclaimed in utter surprise "My Bryce, this is the Teranor; I saw him when he spoke. He is a dark one from our past; he is not human and he is pure evil! He cannot see us; we are shielded by the Vug but we must leave this place."

It was hard for me to consider leaving material behind, but our instincts were right and the extra material still in my pocket would allow us to venture on. In a whirl of thoughts I could think of several other people to go to for help with this first phase. I figured that Vanessa was lost and we needed to get as far away from here as we could. The thought occurred that most of the big name institutions would be monitored, so the same scenario might occur just like today. Mina was deep in thought while I ran through the list of researchers and locations in my mind to come up with just the right person for the job. We both lay there connecting the dots, hers from the past and mine for the near future. This encounter was a rush of information for us both. It was difficult for me to see Jasmina so rattled. She had always been so calm and collected that this reaction to a voice in thin air gave me reason to worry.

CHAPTER EIGHT

Endeavor

A name popped into my head: Gary in Hawaii. Nobody goes to Hawaii except for vacations and the team members in the lab there were specifically working on the search for evidence of life elsewhere in the cosmos, so they would have the right equipment and the right frame of mind. My concern was that the bad guys would show up there when we did. Mina suggested that we travel to a number of destinations first to throw off any possible tracking. We made up a list of institutions starting with Houston and Washington, D.C., then New York followed by Vienna and then Frankfurt before making the long run to a small volcanic Island in the Pacific Ocean.

The hope was to disperse any efforts to find us so thin that we could have plenty of time with Gary and crew in Hawaii. Without hesitation we were on our way to Houston. The plan was that we would make brief appearances at each location to throw off the dogs. We had to keep our travel slow enough that the Teranors didn't figure out our strategy. I asked Mina to tell me what she could about Ali's status. She shook her head as she said, "Nothing, I think he is being shielded by the dark ones. If they are doing this, then they have him."

There is no way my long trusted friend has turned on me. If anything, they have him, but not the stone. Ali is more of a brother than my own siblings. I will wait to hear his story of what transpired. If anyone can outsmart an entire alien race, it is my road warrior buddy Ali Baba.

The Vug began to carry Mina and me into the Gray once again. This time we were going to go slow and take days between stops on the surface. We wanted our followers to think we were using surface transportation. As far as we knew the Teranor had no clue about my knowledge of the Terans and their world below. And Mina had no clue about how many Teranor there might be on the surface.

We cruised through the Gray and out into the Void. Mina suggested that we spend some time looking around various areas of her world while on this leg of our voyage. We needed to pass time for at least a day and so I agreed that this would be interesting for me. She said that we needed to spend time with the Elder group I had met earlier, but she wanted to wait until later for some considerations to be sorted out. I am sure that Mina needed time to come to terms with information and knowledge that had been kept from her for many years. She seemed to be dealing with this pretty well. We slowly lowered as the Vug took us across the landscape of New Tera. The terrain ahead was covered with dense forest. The trees were far greater in size and mass than any tree on the surface of Earth. Each tree appeared to be its own ecosystem with brilliant birds resting on branches and bat-like creatures hanging below them. There were animals grazing at the base of the trees; a mixture of creatures from other parts of the universe blended with animals from the surface of this globe. There were countless little creatures crawling through the forest floor and my favorites, the tiny fairies, flitting about everywhere.

Mina told me that the fairies were Mizlets, a tiny, winged humanoid from a planet on the other side of the galaxy. She told me that they are reasonably harmless and hardworking but if threatened or angered, they will defend themselves in such great numbers that they can suffocate their target. They are very easy to coexist with, but much like honey bees it is best to avoid making them angry. From behind the roughly hundred-foot-diameter base of the tree closest to us stepped a giant deer. This deer was huge, its antlers bigger than a large car. I looked in shock at this majestic beast as Mina told me that the last of these deer were hunted and farmed into extinction by early man. The tree was coated with brilliant colored beards of moss woven through by vines wrapping up and around the truck. Every tree we could see from where we were located had a similar individual environment with living movement everywhere.

We soared over rivers and lakes, waterfalls and beaches. There were no snow-covered mountains but there were countless rocky cliffs stretching the many thousands of feet from bottom to top of this world. We toured over thousands of miles of varied terrain; as we moved along, the scenery changed just as it does on the surface of the Earth but with wildly different content. After having been back on the surface for a day, returning to EarthUnder felt much more comfortable and familiar. We had no direction and no plan while we were stalling, and I had no idea of what to ask to see. Jasmina suggested that we go somewhere fun on the surface, someplace neither of us had ever seen and a place where people go just for fun.

"I've got it," burst out of my mouth with pure impulse. "Let's lie on a beach in Bora Bora for a couple of days!"

We dipped the Vug into a pool of fresh water to take a long drink and off we flew through more of Mina's world. I could see in the far distance another window into an ocean. Without slowing we shot through the window and into the deep sea water. Again, we were breaking the rules of physics that I had grown up with. As density changed from rock to thin air and then to water and deep ocean pressure, we soared along at the same steady, incredible speed. There seemed to be no distortion other than the blur caused by our speed of travel. Before long we were moving upward as we continued to travel the globe under water. I could feel and smell changes as we moved closer to the equator and into warmer thermocline. As abruptly as we had shot through the window into the salt sea water, we came to rest in the Gray.

We stepped out of the Vug, out of a sheer lava cliff and onto a snowy white sand beach with palm trees and a soft, warm, sea breeze that carried the aroma of sugar and salt. The sea water gently rolling onto the beach disappeared into the snowy sand, and the sun flickered on our faces through the breeze-shaken palm fronds. This was my idea of Paradise: nothing to do, nowhere to go, blue sky, warm air, warm water, and not a soul for miles. Mina had chosen an uninhabited island many miles from anything, where we could rest and play without worry. As we stripped off our clothes, I slipped Kadishya's coin pendant over my head and stashed it in a pocket of my pants, making sure to button down the cover flap over this pocket. Laughing like children at play, we raced for the translucent, shimmering blue water. We swam and played in the water for what seemed like hours. I did my best rendition of a crawl stroke while Jasmina seemed to swim like a mermaid with fluid motion and little apparent effort. After a time we went back to the beach and lay in the sun to dry off. The sand was fluffy under the waving palm trees, their fronds rattling in the slight breeze.

We lay there stretched out on the warm, clean, white coral sand and we talked. Mina lay on her side facing me, and I lay on my front side with arms crossed under my turned head facing her. Mina asked me about dreams. She wanted to know if, when I was younger, I had experienced any dreams of other lives. As soon as she asked the question, memories came to mind of dreams I had that seemed real. They were dreams of flying, of swimming endlessly, of hunting with stone implements. "Yes," I recalled dreams that felt like memories from past lives. But the strongest memories were of dreams where I remembered looking into eyes just like hers. It seemed to strengthen the importance of these dream memories to have her ask about them. She lay there with her head dipping into the sand, one eye closed to block out the bright sun while the other studied my face as I looked at hers.

We both had patches of sand grains stuck to our faces. As our bodies dried we could feel the tightening of salt-soaked skin in the sunlight. Mina explained that a certain number of our memories are ghosts from our genetic past. That even before we can walk or talk as infants we have these dreams which emanate from our past lives. She went on to say that when I think of these memories or when I have the dreams, she can see them, and that she can recall those events from my past.

"Your memories of looking into my eyes are the memories of me watching you," she exclaimed. "Until now I was never allowed to intervene, only watch. Now, only in this time I am allowed to reveal myself and to change your fate. You remember dreams of flying effortlessly and swimming endlessly without the need to breathe?" As I nodded my head yes, I felt grains of sand fall free from their grip on my skin.

"Those are memories of things you have done and can still do today," she continued. "Although you are not a Teranian, much of who you are comes from our line. We are both made like this so that it is easier for us to do certain tasks, easier for us to communicate, to feel the other near, and to transition between our worlds. It is my hope that in the future, I will be able to help you develop your instincts and abilities beyond human limits. Many Teran abilities are the result of problems overcome through evolution over millions of years. These are gifts of time and survival. They are not easily assimilated by younger races of humanoids, and therefore it was decided that you would be prepared over many generations. Sadly, now between man's status as stewards of this planet and the revelation that Teranor are present, we no longer have the luxury of time to make the transition easy for the rest of your kind. You and I will do all we can to turn the current self-destructive direction that man has taken. And soon we Terans will need to reveal ourselves to your people. In the next two days while we are here enjoying this time alone, we need to develop your trust in me. You must try to extinguish any doubts you may have of me. First, let me show you something that will require your trust."

Jasmina rose to her feet blocking the sun from my face, her perfectly flawless, muscled body framed in youthful glowing skin surrounded by the day. Mina reached down to take my hand and pulled me to my feet. She wrapped her lissome arm around me as she led me back to the shore. We stood looking out across the water as it lapped over our toes and around our ankles begging us to enter. We continued until the water was waist deep. Jasmina stood in front of me and gave me that deep look that I have seen in so many dreams. Just then I could hear her voice in my head. Her words were clear and strong in my mind. She asked me to trust her actions and to let go of my impulses.

We dove together, arms locked, into the water and swam deeper and deeper. I mirrored Mina's movements as she thrust her legs together as one like a dolphin. Our speed increased far beyond my ability and soon we were so deep I could feel the pressure of the deep blue squeezing my chest. My skin began to tingle with the sting of oxygen debt, my throat bursting for a breath. Jasmina continued into the deep with me in tow as my body began to convulse for air. She stopped to face me again; I heard her speak softly, telling me to let go of fear and doubt and to accept this change. Again she reminded me to use my dreams.

I felt the warmth of her body as she put her hands on my shoulders, wrapped one leg around me, and pressed her lips against mine. I closed my eyes as my body filled with excitement from the intimate contact of her touch. Suddenly, in a flash of light and memory, I realized that the need to breathe had gone. We were drifting there in water so deep that the light of day was dimmed to a simple glimmer overhead. I could hear the siren song of millions of sea creatures chirping and clicking. I could feel the dream. I felt the power of the moment. The strength and endless ability I had felt in those childhood dreams were real memories.

We had remained here for an impossible amount of time when Jasmina began to swim off. I followed her, but with difficulty. She looked back at me and told me to stop trying to swim, to relax my arms and wiggle as I had in my dreams. As I mastered the rhythm of her kicks, I began to gain on the lovely princess. It felt comfortable and familiar: swimming endlessly without breathing. The farther we went, the more powerful I felt, until every stroke felt stronger than the last. We swirled around each other and moved side by side challenging each other's speed. After what seemed like hours in the deep, chasing schools of fish, we moved into the shallows of a lagoon within our paradise island. There we practiced jumping out of the water to see who could jump the highest. It felt as though we had fins and tails. As I tread water, watching Mina's jump, I thought to myself "humanoids with arms and legs made better swimmers than fish."

Mina came to the surface grinning as water drained from her open mouth. She blew the last of the water from her lips and said, "Yes, humanoids do make better swimmers. In fact," she said, "we are able to outswim most of the predatory fish in the seas."

She told me I did very well for a first time swimming, but that I would need more practice to build confidence in this new gift. I had to agree, it was quite a gift. We swam to shore and walked over to our clothes. This was another aspect of Terans that would take some practice: getting comfortable with nudity. Swimming in the buff made perfect sense, but then walking alone on the sand with this perfectly gorgeous naked woman was going to take some time to grow accustomed to.

Once we were dressed again, it was time to make a shelter for the night. I found a great place to build a fire and began to gather dry wood for the night. We had logs to lean against and a beautiful view of the sunset. My hope was to give Mina a small taste of the pleasure and joy I have had here on Earth's surface. It was no easy trick, but in time the fire started crackling away and we settled down on palm fronds against a log and spoke as we watched the sun slowly lower to the edge of the horizon. After our star vanished behind the curve of the Earth, the air cooled so more wood was committed to the fire. We visited by firelight exchanging views, ideas, and favorite things from our pasts as well as concerns for our future. We lay back, resting our heads on the log to watch the star show dancing in the sky above. I asked Mina if she knew where Tera used to be. She pointed into the sand between us. Her home world was once located in another galaxy that was below the southern hemisphere. She seemed saddened by my inquiry. I reached over to take her hand in mine, smiled, and told her how fortunate I felt to have her in my world. We sat there a while longer to enjoy the warmth of the firelight, then retired to the Vug for the night. I didn't know if Mina needed rest or sleep, but as soon as we settled into the Vug I was out for the count.

Sleep that night was filled with brilliant renditions of my old dreams. I woke thinking they must have been inspired by the long undersea swim we had taken. Mina was awake and sitting by our fire pit. I walked out of the Vug; without her there to assist me it was much more difficult to climb through the thin veil of rock between the Vug and the outside air. I figured it must be that everything was easier with Mina there to empower me. As I walked over to sit on the log she was leaning against, she handed me a coconut filled with fresh water and a nutrition pod from New Tera. She looked rested, but then she always looked ready for anything. Whether it was the magic of the Vug or being in Mina's presence or the limited time in New Tera, I felt a magical well-being. I was feeling a strength I'd never felt before.

Mina appeared deep in thought as I looked over to her. She had the long-distance gaze of someone staring into a campfire as though last night's fire was still burning. It felt right to leave her alone for a bit so I walked out onto the beach and turned to face the sunrise. The thought occurred to me: what a beautiful experience to wake up with early morning light coming in the sunrise side of your home. Then in the evening the long rays of the setting sun pour in the windows and doors of the sunset side. The bonus would be getting to watch the sun and moon traverse the sky north and south with the changing of the seasons. I stood there in a daydream glaring through the palm trunks at the golden globe climbing into the day and thought of so much beauty that would end if our mission should fail. Some of the simplest aspects of life on Earth carry with them the most beauty: a single snowflake, a grain of sand, a drop of water, a leaf, a flower, a wave breaking on the shore, or a wisp of wind in the trees. I stood reflecting on the

Earth's endless beauty and all that would be lost. Memories and visions streamed through my mind's eye and faded into a wash like rain falling onto the sea. Jasmina walked past me and curled her arms around my neck. She whispered into one ear my favorite things: a campfire, a warm sandy beach, watching the sun set and rise. While we stood there together as one, watching, the dawn light intensified. She spoke of her thoughts. She said that in all of my lives she had admired the continuity of my favorite things. She went on to describe how she watched me live many prior lives. In those lives there were moments of reflection while enjoying my favorite things. These were the moments when she would most intimately connect with the man she could only observe, guide, and protect. She had watched me live those lives over and over: the victories and failures, the mistakes and lessons, the loves and lives lost. She had felt my joys and pains for generations until now, now I am the one, the one she had waited for.

As we stood in the cool morning sand, it occurred to me how much it must have hurt her to watch me befriend her sister those years ago. She whispered, "It had to be this path we have both taken. We are here now and we are the culmination of those years. Time takes its path and as creatures of time we must honor its direction. It is our time now to inspire a planetary change in direction."

Enveloped in Mina's comforting embrace I could feel her powerful strength and from her words I could hear her tenacity. We were already on our way to the goal as Earth spun under foot and time roared forward. Even resting here on our island refuge we were moving forward at the speed of time, and every movement was a step along our path to the end. I drew energy from Jasmina's strength to combat the onslaught of fear. Fear is the life killer, I shall not lay down in fear.

Jasmina asked me to focus my thoughts. She coached me as we watched the day brighten to the east. She wanted me to think with my mind as if I were a "dark one" to anticipate what they might try in order to intercept our efforts. She told me that my human side was more receptive to the thoughts of deceptive action. From our limited exposure, thus far, to the Teranor, she suspected they had mastered a shielding ability that prevented her from seeing them or hearing their thoughts. She wondered if Laurent was a hybrid like me, only cultivated by Teranor to counter our mission. That would mean that there were a measurable number of Teranors here on the planet, possibly even some who had infiltrated New Tera. I told her that I knew they would try to anticipate our movement to other institutions and that our appearances at the planned locations needed to be brief and cursory. Beyond that we might need to draw from the powers of her people. She said that her people were far more powerful than the Teranor, but the powers were millions of years untested and their abilities would need to rely on my human contribution.

I stood there with the warming sunlight soaking into my face and listening to Mina's mentoring. Her reference to my contribution made no sense in the big picture. She reminded me that Terans share every thought and hide nothing. To deceive was beyond her natural ability. Digesting this train of thought I pondered several things that didn't add up, knowing she would hear my thoughts: thoughts about Kadishya and both of their missing husbands, thoughts about the Teranor and how they had suppressed their presence, thoughts about her Elders and what they might know that she didn't. I could see the shock in her face as she reacted to my thoughts. I had opened questions she would never have considered plausible. We walked out onto the open beach and sat "crisscross applesauce" knee to knee and discussed possibilities. There were several advantages in our movements. We had the Vug, the elements of surprise and deviation. We still had a piece of the brain bone meteorite. And we still had a plethora of allies here on the surface and below as well.

Today we would make the journey to Houston and tomorrow we would then hop over to Washington, D.C. I told Mina that we didn't need to meet with anyone as long as we were seen in the area by someone I knew. This would be enough to throw the dogs off the scent. Not knowing who would be waiting for us meant difficulty planning our moves. I did know that once we were in Houston I would call Vanessa to make sure she was safe. We were enjoying these final minutes of solitude together on the shores of Paradise. Soon it was time to head out to our next destination. As we walked to the cliff that held the Vug I couldn't help wishing we could remain. The world had a morbid feel as we walked into the stone face of the cliff. This would never again be the world I thought I knew. So much had changed so suddenly that my brain burned with feelings of doubt and a paucity of courage.

Soon we were under way through the Gray and into the ocean. Before long we were passing into the Gulf of Mexico, according to Mina. As we shot towards Houston, Mina asked me to watch the sea floor here as we slowed. She told me that this portion of the gulf was a rapidly growing dead zone. I could see that everything was black or gray and there were no fish at all. She went on to say that the Gulf had been a nursery for multiple species of the world's tuna and sailfish as well as many other species for millennia, and its destruction had only begun in the past seventy years. Thinking in geologic terms, this wasn't even a partial blink. Mina looked at the shock on my face and she nodded as she reminded me that the Earth needs not Man but Man needs the Earth. The shock of this scene inspired a greater sense of urgency in my conscious thought. Eventually we cruised beyond the black waters of the Gulf and into the Gray of the land below Texas. From there it was minutes to Houston. We came to a halt and stepped out of the Vug onto the shaded concrete staircase of a sports arena.

Across from the Vug I found vending machines and a phone to use. First, I called a friend at NASA/Johnson Space Center to let him know we were in town for a visit. I told him we would be in to visit the lab in a few hours and he said that would work fine and to look for him in his office. Then, I called Vanessa at the Natural History Museum in London to check up on her. Vanessa surprised me when she answered the phone at her desk. The tension stretching bones to the breaking point let go when I heard her cheerful voice vibrate through the earpiece. Vanessa said she was fine, but that she had some unfortunate news; the crumb she had used in the ion probe had somehow mysteriously vanished without a trace. But she had gotten great gobs of information from that tiny fragment that made no sense at all.

It tickled, listening to her pleasant British verbiage. As she began to explain, her words of the specimen making no sense, she interrupted herself to say she had forgotten about the piece she sent off to the tech for thin sectioning. She had gotten the slide back and was beginning to look at it with the Scanning Electron Microscope. She just started asking me if I had any idea of what I had when the phone clicked and the voice of Laurent interrupted our call, "So, hello, Mr. Bryce Monroe Sterling, you are in Houston now; ha, where will you go next?"

I looked at Mina but she already knew what was happening. We ran for the Vug and left immediately. Mina showed intense concern; I reached over to put a hand on her shoulder and reminded her that this was just what I expected. From what I saw they were playing right into our hands. I didn't think the Teranor had any magic on their side. It was a simple connection through a bugged phone in Vanessa's office.

Now I worried about Vanessa again because he learned she had another piece. I knew I couldn't reach her on her cell phone because the lab and her office were so far below ground. But the cafeteria was in a solarium on the top floor of the museum. I had joined curators there for lunch several times. What I needed to do was to guess when she might go there for dinner and call her to speak or leave a message telling her to get the heck out of there with the slide.

We would now travel to Washington, D.C., to make another appearance, but we needed to lag enough to make it look like we took surface transportation again. The thinking was that after visiting Vienna we could shoot over to Hawaii to see Gary and the diversion would provide us with two to three days and nights before we would need to run again.

In college, I had enjoyed a few terms of Karate lessons. The teacher was an ethereal philosopher who shared his ideas with regard to self-awareness, personal improvement, and the responsibility that comes with power over others. I asked him once after a class of sparring how he handled conflict with his ability to take down an opponent. He gave me a very cool look and said, "Always remember that no matter how advanced you are in this martial art, it's impossible to outrun a bullet." In encounters with bad guys, I would always hear the instructor's voice reminding me to avoid conflict.

Mina took us back to the Void to meet with her Elders. We had some time and she felt a need to confer with them. When the Vug came to rest on the floor of New Tera, the Elders were waiting there for our arrival. Mina asked me to stay by her side as she moved out of the Vug. Her posture was rigid, and her voice was hard and sharp, cutting through the air like a battle blade. She expounded with surprising volume in the faces of the attentive group of Terans. "What have I not been told!" she screamed with a growl in her candied voice.

As the closest Elder began to reply, Jasmina interrupted with temper and concise accusation. The power of my little Mina was expanding as fire from the mouth of a dragon. "I am questioning my trust in our people right now! There are things that have been kept from me! How can you expect an entire race of humans to trust me if I cannot trust my Elders?"

In her current, succinct fashion, she demanded to know everything. And she demanded that all speech be in audible words for my benefit and edification. Again, I was feeling more faith in my savior than ever. Mina was winning my conviction. I felt her strength coursing through my veins. Standing there next to her while she raged gave me a part of her strength or so it felt. My gut told me I should never piss this woman off. Here we stood waiting for answers.

The Elders looked down, which gave me a bad feeling. The nearest Elder began again, "Jasmina, we are saddened for having done this, but our actions were purely involved with Teran security. We have known of the Teranor threat for some time. They have been performing a silent invasion. We are far more powerful than they suspect, but a conflict could endanger the people of Earth, and our hope is to once again eliminate their threat. But they have deceit on their side and they are armed with their own genetically altered human/Teranor population. We have tried to monitor their efforts, but our work can only be performed by the people of your line. Please, Jasmina, believe us when we tell you that the less you knew the better. We will answer your questions, but it is better that we do all we can to assist you on your quest. As both of you know well from your own life memories, fear kills. We all know that fear and panic could cause a global meltdown of the society on this planet. Therefore, we have chosen to keep the knowledge of specific threats from both our populations. Elders have known for millennia that the Teranor were coming. We have lost many planets to their invasion over millions of years. Our colonies are only half what they once were, and those lost worlds are now populated by the dark ones or they are dead globes of rock and ash. I am feeling a question that you and your sister have pondered for ages and I must address this with you now. Both of your husbands have been lost to us during their journeys to our outer colonies. We have confirmed that they are expired, but sharing this with you might have revealed the threat. We know this is going to make your next move difficult, but you have been chosen for your array of strengths and we hope you will endure. As you know we have mastered interstellar travel folding the ribbon of space. Now the Teranor have devised a method for corrupting our mental technique and thus for now, we are trapped on this planet. This we believe is why they are making such a relentless effort to stop you in your mission."

The Elder explained further, "This information we felt might lessen your effectiveness and we chose to keep it from both of you. In recent time we have revisited the prospect of using wormholes to travel but our minds are still not able to control the turbulent chaos that resides within a wormhole. We were spoiled by the ease with which we were able to utilize the fourth dimension ribbon and fold the space between our worlds. Now it is known that we have lost the option to move elsewhere and thus we have lost the ability to communicate with many of our colonies. This compounds the sense of urgency that we try to reverse man's destructive direction. We have yet to learn what the Teranor intend, but we must assume it is nothing benevolent. They maintain the embodiment of pure evil and we must act accordingly. There is one more subject that I am required to reveal to you at this time. In the years of our concern over this matter, we Elders chose to build an army of soldiers to defend our world against Teranor offense. They will only be utilized if a need is recognized and will be assimilated into the population once this threat is diminished. Jasmina, you and Bryce can trust that any other information is either an oversight or is negligible. Our knowledge is yours."

The Elder gazed intensely into Mina's deep green eyes, which returned a sullen glare. Their eyes appeared to illuminate for a time, after which Mina stepped back, slumping into my arms. He glanced at me and said that now she knew all things. She leaned into me as though she had lost her strength, then stood erect and walked back towards the Vug, leaving me behind feeling almost abandoned. I had no idea what to think of her actions, but I could see a distant look in her eyes as if she was out of her body.

Jasmina walked to a nearby tree where she turned and leaned against the trunk, staring off into the Void, deep in thought. I stood there helpless to do anything. She recovered from her daze and came over to me. Jasmina grabbed my arm and led me back to the Vug. Soon we were on our way apparently to the surface, but in an indirect path at an odd angle. When we came to a halt and walked out of the Gray, we were in a spectacular, lush, boreal forest of apsen, jack pine and spruce trees. We stood in front of a beautiful, rustic, moss-covered log cabin with a bench out front next to a stone-rimmed fire pit. Mina settled on the bench, and I sat next to her and put a foot up on one of the rocks. It was obvious nobody had been here in a long time. The cabin was intact, but it was showing the years. A few aspen and pine trees had died and fallen onto the open ground around the cabin, but had not been touched or cleared. There was a small creek gurgling in the woods just beyond the tree line. From where we sat I could see there was a light opening in the distant trees that seemed to be better illuminated than the rest of the forest around us. We sat there for a time and then Mina spoke. "I feel violated," she started; "it is hard to know what to believe. I don't understand how or why all of this information was kept from me. It feels like the foundations of my world have been taken away."

In my limited wisdom I gave her a sober glance and asked her to think of how I felt having learned that my life was a blended slurry of lies and reality, that there were many other versions of me, that I was planned generations ago, that I was led to this point in my life. "So, welcome to the club," I retorted. "It must be hard to learn that your husband is gone forever."

Mina looked at me and said, "Please, he wasn't a husband; he was a figurehead with title who gave me position here on the surface. That is why we are in this place, my Bryce Monroe. You and I spent a great amount of time here in your past lives on Earth. We spent many hours looking into the fires here in this sanctuary. Out through that illuminated cleft in the forest screen of trees is a rock pinnacle where you and I spent the best parts of our days watching sunrises and sunsets. My thinking was that by bringing you here we could dispel any questions you might have about my so-called husband or how I feel about you. We used to dream of making this our home."

We walked through the meadow, out of the woods, following the light to the edge of the trees where the rocks extended far out beyond the tree line. I remember this place; it was in many of my dreams, and there, in those dreams, was Mina, her lovely eyes smiling back at me. The memory of this place enveloped my senses. Over the years the smell of campfire smoke had always brought the ghostly images of this place to mind. It wasn't a dream—it was a distant memory. While we were zoned out on our island paradise, this was the place I was seeing in the memories brought back by the fire and the sunset.

In the sunrise all I could see was Jasmina's glowing aura. I turned to Mina, pulled her into my arms, and melted into her embrace. The love I felt for her filled every cell in my body. Holding her in my arms felt like I had lost the most important love of my life and found her again. It was a reunion of all the senses, and it was a feeling of such overwhelming importance that I felt my entire being struggling with concern over ever losing her again. Mina gazed at me with sadness in her eyes as she listened to my thoughts and memories of our time together. I understood that she was feeling the sadness of the same loss, but for her it was a clear memory from a prior time.

We were here, together again, working through the confusion of memory and emotion, a mixture of sadness and joy that blended into tears of agony and ecstasy. There was pain and pleasure in this time of ours together as we worked through what was past and what was yet to come. There was a palpable energy between us above strength and beyond time. Our connection was somehow timeless. Mina revealed that she had known me and loved me for generations, and that every version of my prior self was evident in the man before her now. I couldn't get my head around this. Many of the new revelations were hard to accept, and the concept of actually being "born again" was beyond difficult. On top of that, this gorgeous woman has stood by and watched me come and go for many lives. It must be dreadful to know that she must live through this cycle again and again. How can she and her people be so tenacious as to wait for this time, my time to save the world and their own kind? Mina put her hand on my shoulder as she assured me that the result would be worth the wait. While we gathered wood for a fire, she talked about living each day to the best of one's ability rather than dwelling on the long-term goal.

I cleared out the fire pit and built a small structure of kindling in the pit. Jasmina went to the cabin for tinder, a flint and strike plate stashed by the powder-blue paint–peeled front door. As we both moved about our duties I could see this as a memory image from the past. We had done the same thing many times before this day. It felt uncommonly safe here with Mina in our idyllic hideout. The fire grew; we sat on the bench and stared into the flames.

Mina could feel my sense of security and she explained that she had maintained a shroud around this refuge for countless years in order to protect it from any approach. She told me that because of the energy she had always devoted to protecting this preserve, that for any human, Teran, or Teranor, this place did not exist and could never be detected. She detailed that even her Elders had no idea of the existence of this safe house. This comment stopped everything. Jasmina felt my heart race and saw the flash of concern in my eyes. She was telling me that not all things were shared communally with all Terans. We were both frozen in motion for a moment when she gave me a reassuring expression and explained that this was one of the genetic gifts given to her family line. "This is a protection mechanism that the Elders felt would benefit their surface guardians," Mina explained. Her brief explanation helped bring my heart rate back to normal. Talleyrand had explained to Jasmina that this was an ability shared by the Elders as well to protect their kind from worry or panic. He had told her that some things are better left unknown or unspoken. I could feel myself relaxing as I realized that this trait makes the Terans seem even more human.

We picked a few handfuls of chamomile from the ground around us and made some tea in an iron pot over the fire. Mina brought a chest from the cabin that held food pods for us to enjoy. Either these pods tasted better with age or I was getting more accustomed to their flavor. I had no idea of how old these pods were, but the chest had a thick coating of dust on the hand-hewn hinged lid. She explained that the small food cache box is lined with metal charged with Tesla energy that can preserve biological material endlessly. Jasmina told me that all things have a characteristic energy. Tesla discovered that this logarithm of energy in cells can be aligned to strengthen and protect cells. Using his process of charging certain metals, he learned how to protect cells from decay.

Mina described our longtime friend, "He was an exceptionally clever human who was deeply tuned to the power of Earth's inherent life forces. Had his theories been more widely accepted and studied, humankind would have taken quantum leaps forward in technology and intellectual evolution. You knew and admired him in your last time here. He made this chest as a gift for us. He was your dearest friend. The two of you spent many of your days together discussing his ideas and puzzling over how to turn the perpetual movement of water on Earth into the energy needed to power his inventions. The movement of water was your idea. In all of your lives, water has always been at the center of your focus and passion. Your influence in our choosing this place was the sound of the stream bubbling nearby and our view at the cliff from the top of the waterfall."

Jasmina continued, "The waterfall has always been your favorite place of meditation. When I can't find you, I always know to look for you at the top of the falls. It is there that you always travel the globe in your mind's eye. It is as though the falling water carries you out of body. You were emotionally crushed when Nikola passed and after that, it seemed that the two of you kept in contact during your time at the falls. For me this was a powerful lesson in how attached humans can become. This bond between friends is something that Terans have lost or possibly never possessed. We feel love deeply, but friendships seem to escape our societal structure. I have watched you enjoy countless close friendships throughout your many lives and I have learned from them. But parts of the friendship dynamic escape my comprehension and understanding. It is an exciting and endearing aspect of humans, and it is a facet of life that I feel Terans would benefit from."

Woven together in conversation, comfort, and reflection, we sat by the fire enjoying our hot, relaxing tea. Chewing bits of our pods, we both stared into the flickering yellow flames of burning branches gathered nearby. My mind turned to the simple subject of how accelerating atoms created the flames that consumed the wood and produced radiant heat that comforted us as the sun set in the silent stand of trembling aspens near the falls. The last rays of the sun sailed through our opening and illuminated the mist that rose from the crest of the falls in the lone break of the tree line. Everything around us seemed to dance a symphony of movement in cosmic, melodic synchronicity with the passing of time. The long late-day shadows reached our fire pit as I sat there leaning against Jasmina. I peered into the glowing embers of our diminishing heat source, pondering all of the new information that had flooded my brain in recent days.

Jasmina put her hand on my knee and her arm around my shoulder and stopped my thoughts for a moment to say, "This is not a dream, your memories and all you have learned recently are real. It will take time for you to adjust to all the new information, but with time you will adapt to this new age. I am here to help you accept even that which you don't understand. I will do all I can to help you trust what is real. Often it is difficult to distinguish a dream from a memory."

My eyes widened as the flame's hypnotic dance put me in the place between wake and sleep. I watched myself standing next to Tesla alongside the stream behind the cabin. We talked endlessly about the perpetual motion of water as Tesla argued his idea of harnessing a river to produce power enough to light cities and suggested his idea of powering towers that might allow us to communicate wirelessly across oceans. I remember that my stand was all about the power of the oceans and the pull of the moon and the sun. I countered his idea with my own concerns over changing the course of a stream and how that would affect fish migrations and water temperatures. My idea was that rather than putting water wheels in the rivers and under glorious waterfalls such as our own here in the glen, we should use the ocean tides to power massive turbines to produce an inexhaustible power source. As the fire crackled,

I came out of my waking dream. Mina was there to assure me that this was a memory of a real, past time.

While we sat there on the bench I recalled the memory just like it was yesterday. Nikola and I stood there throwing blades of grass onto the water and watching them gently float away to the falls. In that moment we were both inspired by the relentless power of flowing water. His thoughts were always about how he could tap into that resource of power before it emptied out into the sea. My thoughts were always more about the wonder of how through the cycle of life this supply of clear, cool, flowing beverage was eternally gurgling past our little cabin in the wood. In my mind, this was a gift to all living things. I was not concerned with where the water was going, but rather where it was coming from. Nikola saw it as a challenge to be controlled and used for a greater good. Now he is not here to see the cost of his conviction. Nikola Tesla was the only friend ever allowed into our sanctuary. We found him wandering in the woods after he had gone through a rough time in his life. He was bitter and emotionally lost. We had taken him in only to save his life, but those days grew into a lifelong friendship like no other, and as we spent more time together he became more and more inspired. Our times at the sanctuary were good for all of us. Jasmina was there and I can remember her face in the memories as if it were right now. She has not changed at all. I remember now a common thread in recent and distant memory. She was always there, the same lovely, strong, wise, confident, beautiful woman.

This time by the fire was a powerful awakening. Now, in this age, I felt it would have crushed Nikola to know what his creations have done to change the world he knew. If he could see the many thousands of power transformers that lay at the bottom of rivers below his dams, leaching toxins into the rivers, rendering the fish deadly for consumption, he might never have built a dam. If he could see the rivers filling with silt and the water temperatures and mercury levels rising, he might have stopped. If he could see the reservoirs filling with weeds and the salmon runs cut off from their spawning grounds, he might have agreed with me. If he could see now that we are finally building windmills and solar panels and turbines underwater in the oceans, then he might never have built his first hydro plant at Niagara Falls.

Jasmina leaned over to bump her shoulder into mine. I smiled while looking up from the fire to see her there beside me quietly waiting while I reflected on fireside thoughts. There was something magical about the thoughts and ideas that came out of time spent peering into the glow of firelight. The sunlight was almost gone now and dark would soon take its place in the air. The birds and bugs were racing to their evening resting places, so the air in the glen was filled with a flurry of motion in the smoky sunlight. Mina suggested that we go inside while there was still some light to prepare the cabin for the night.

As we walked into the main room, I could see flames glimmering through the bubbly, uneven glass plates of the front window. There were candles in every room that had stood there for years waiting for our return. The bedding was folded and sealed in a sea chest at the foot of the hand-hewn log bed. The books in a cabinet were all old classics from the 1800s to early 1900s. The kitchen had cast iron cookery and the water system was a "one of a kind" unit that looked familiar. It was a hand-carved gutter that ran along a trestle from the stream to and through the cabin out the front wall and then back into the kitchen and back to the stream. There was a coffer gate near the stream to allow the flow to the house. Over the sink and at another sink in front of the cabin were spigots where the water could be turned on to drink, or to wash or cook with. I remember that we had kept a fish bowl on the window sill above the kitchen sink and whenever either of us noticed a small fish or aquatic insect drifting through our water line, we would catch it and keep it for a time in our aquarium. We would name them as part of our little woodland family.

I turned to Mina with surprise in my face. She noticed my expression and asked what was up. "Caesar," I said as Mina's curious expression crinkled into a tearful smile. I remembered that I had named my favorite fish Caesar and Mina's was named Cleopatra! The fish bowl was still there, turned upside down on the shelf above the window, where it had remained empty for nearly 100 years. The inside of our cabin after dark was like a scrapbook of memories and a three-dimensional photo journal of the past lives lived here in our paradisiacal refuge. Every turn produced shocking, awakening flashes of past memory.

As Mina started a small fire in the rock and mortar fireplace, she watched me move through the maze of memorabilia from our past lives. Over the mantel was a rough-framed, charcoal drawing of Mina and me. Jasmina had drawn this portrait of us together in another lifetime many years ago. The drawing was nearly the quality of a photograph. As I touched some items and looked at others, a flood of images poured into my mind. It came to mind that this vestige of solitude was located well north of Lake Superior.

There were details I began to anticipate. I ran my hand across the mantelpiece over the fireplace. I knew that my hand would reach a notch in the wood where I used to lean my bamboo fly-fishing rod on days when I wanted to wax the line or tie up a new leader for the next morning. There were figures we had burned into the wood with a glowing fire iron. Some were messages we left for the other to figure out, and I could remember what each of them meant.

I stood behind the wooden chairs in front of the fireplace and closed my eyes for a moment to see if I could recall what the attic looked like. Climbing the ladder and peering in, everything was just as I remembered it from past lives. While looking around I wondered if the memories could be sorted out, or were the years and lives a blurred blend with little or no chronology. Then again, what did it matter? I was happy to be here, now, with this lovely woman who seemed to have loved me eternally. I wondered if I had made any of those mistakes that tend to drive people off, any that might have driven Jasmina away. As I returned to the main floor, Mina was standing there facing me with her hands fisted at her sides, and she instantly answered my pondering thought. "Oh yes, you have made plenty of mistakes! I have always found it easy to forgive you your silly shortcomings. In your own curt words, 'you have stepped in it more than your fair share,'" she said with a kind but sarcastic smile. "In fact, you have a gift for blowing it and for getting yourself into troublesome situations that are often not necessary. But these things are part of who you are and I can never get enough of the man you have always been."

So now it was time to rest for the night; tomorrow we would need to head out on our next leg of the journey.

I wondered if Jasmina needed the rest; I certainly did. I needed time to shut down and allow all of this to soak into my mind for a night. Both of us would rather stay here in safety and solitude. But there were important things that had to be done and we had to remain on task in order to stay ahead of our pursuers. Things seemed easier when I thought we were just up against human hunters, but the Teranor have really added a new twist that seems ridiculously beyond my control. How is it that wherever we go they are there waiting for our arrival? I'd like to hear more from Mina about the safety and secrecy of this hideout. I am wondering if whatever she is doing to shield our refuge can be applied to our final destination. As I fell off to sleep my dreams were intensely vibrant and colorful, filled with images of the past and plans for the immediate future. For the first time my dreams seemed to build a road map and make contingency plans for nearly any scenario that might transpire. When we woke it was as if I had been programmed with everything that ran through my dreams last night. I awakened with firm confidence in our ability to complete the task ahead. Fear had faded off into the distance, and determination had taken over my forward thought.

Mina was already up and moving about in the kitchen. She was making lemon grass tea from nature's garden with a touch of honey from an earthenware pot. It was delicious as ever and gave us a kick of quick energy for the morning. Beyond the meadow the rising sun was slicing through the tree line with golden sheets of brilliant, dawning daylight. All things flying were hard at it, flashing through the veils of diffused glow over the grass and flowers of the clearing. The morning mist lay like a blanket in the still, dawn air. The drizzle of heat streamed upward from the fire pit, punching a shaft of rising tepid air through the beads of mist hanging over last night's outdoor fire. Two deer were feeding along the tree line near the opening by the falls. There had always been a game trail just inside the trees that crossed the stream near the falls, and whitetail deer often came out into the opening during the early morning and late evening hours to feed and sometimes bed down in the grass. As always they would take turns feeding and watching for danger. The image of the deer was like a photograph in my mind. Jasmina stood next to me with her hand hanging from my shoulder as we watched the morning movement of a new day beginning. We had done this before.

Today we would journey to the U.S. National Museum in D.C. We both knew this would be a very quick stop to make a brief appearance and then we would move on to Vienna. We stopped the Vug in the walls of the Library of Congress and caught a cab to the museum. We walked in the front door, signed in at the visitor registry desk, called down to the curator's office, where we left a message, and then we immediately left the building and caught another cab back to the library. We clasped hands as we climbed out of the taxicab and walked back into the library. Once inside the entry foyer we walked up to the mezzanine, made our way around to the side, and stepped into the heavy stone wall and into our waiting Vug. We had agreed that based on our past close calls with pursuers that this should be enough of an appearance to draw attention.

From here it was off to Vienna for our last decoy visit before we headed for Hawaii. While traveling across the planet, I asked Mina a few questions about the technology behind the Vug. My query was why when we could step through stone was the Vug needed for travel. Jasmina responded that this was a very good question.

Mina explained with eloquence, "The Vug is a scrubber; it protects living tissue from radiation saturation. We can traverse Earth, but there is naturally occurring radiation throughout the planet. Our biological tissue absorbs this radiation during travel through the Gray. The Vug is designed for long-distance travel and protects our bodies from absorbing that radiation. Over time, the Terans have incorporated additional technology into the Vugs for our convenience and ease of travel. The atoms we impact on the leading edge of the Vug are absorbed by the Vug and immediately replaced behind our path of travel. This way there is no displacement of material or impact inertia. This allows us to pass through soil, stone, or water without causing any structural disruption." I asked her if she knew how much the Teranor might know about our thoughts and movements. Her reply was completely unsettling. She admitted, "I don't know this answer."

Her response gave us both intense cause for concern. This made her more human to me. The playing field had just become more level. We were going to have to lean on each other and act on instinct. Suddenly my gut feelings held more value than ever before. As we sped along I thought ahead to what we might encounter. In my mind, I was pondering the possibility of Teranor being posted at every center for meteorite study in order to stop us from our planned effort. Could there be traps waiting for us everywhere? How could we trust that we would not be face to face with Teranor anywhere we went? How could I know whom I was dealing with and how would we get the word out to the people of Earth? As I stood thinking, Mina glanced at me and said, "I hear your thoughts and I have the same concerns."

"Oh no, really?" I squealed with embarrassment and questioned, "You always hear what I think?"

"Yes," she replied. "One of the things I admire most about you is that you always seem to think the right thoughts at the right time. And so often I agree with your feelings." She went on to say, "I trust your gut feel on this as well."

The next stop would hopefully cause enough confusion to give us time with Gary. We would have to make a bigger appearance in Vienna, something that would get our pursuers to take notice of our direction. Maybe we could get into the probe room and fire up the equipment with some bogus specimens that we could leave behind on the stages so the Teranor would be left puzzled.

"Mina," I inquired with reservation, "in your years of searching for meteorites, have you stashed any unusual specimens that we might use to install in the probe and leave behind?"

Mina answered with a "yes" as she waved her hand to change our direction. In minutes we came to a halt and stepped out of the Vug and onto the desert hardpan. Next to us was a massive stone cavern that rose out of the desert floor like a giant cornucopia of black sun-baked rock. We walked into the vacant cave, our footsteps echoing into the depth of the darkness. Mina closed her eyes for a moment, and great wooden cases appeared along the sides of the cave. "These are my finds from all of the years of searches for stones from the sky. You tell me what you wish to use and I will retrieve it."

Stunned, I recovered from my daze to reply, "Ok, can you find us five different individuals of planetary basalt? They can be from Mars or the moon or any other planetary body in our solar system." Mina returned with a sack full of priceless research specimens, pieces of exactly what we needed. It was agonizing to do the unthinkable, but we took a rock from the floor of the cave and proceeded to break fragments from each of the glorious, fusion-crusted, fresh-fallen stones. I could see at a glance that Jasmina had brought mare basalt and a regolith breccia from Luna, our moon, and a Shergottite and two Nakhlites from Mars. This was a perfect cross-section of samples for the plan. As we walked out of the opening of this dry, cool, "mouth of the desert," I stopped for a glance back into the cave. Mina responded by telling me that the cave was nearly full and that they would all be mine if I wished. This was a generous gesture, but I reminded her that one cannot eat rocks. We both laughed a bit as we stepped into the Gray and then the Vug. With us, we carried five perfect decoy specimens that should confuse anyone who would find them in the stages of the probe in the lab in Vienna. What we needed to do now was get to Vienna, find our way into the lab, get into the probe room when nobody was in there, load specimens into the stages, and begin to fire up the ion microprobe (called SHRIMP for Sensitive High Resolution Ion Micro Probe). The hope was that by us making a false stand here at the SHRIMP and hastily leaving behind these specimens, the Teranor might be thrown off our trail for a couple of days while we make the run for Hawaii.

We dropped through the Gray and into the Void and began to traverse the planet from below the surface. As we rocketed through the distance there appeared to be a massive gathering of Terans below.

"We are asked to stop for a moment," Mina informed me. The Vug looped around in a half circle. It began to lower us into what must be the center of the gathering. At the core of the sea of bodies stood a number of Elders, their silver hair and yellow skin shining in the fluorescent light like a full moon in a star-filled night sky. The younger Terans appeared in varying shades of azure to violet. The Vug came to rest in the midst of the Elders. We stepped out of the Vug, which then rose above us a few meters. There were no words spoken, only intense eye contacts. I could feel a flow of energy passing through me and could hear a low susurration. I could only hear the whispers, not the actual words. It had to be something of critical importance to our mission for this many Terans to get involved. Soon everything became silent and still, and the Vug lowered to take us away. As we sped through the Void Jasmina shared a few things with me.

"First," she started, "we have been given a number of powerful gifts to aid us in our plight. My people have rallied to assist us in any way they are able. Both you and I can now see the Teranor. The Elders have given us the ability to see a red halo around the Teranor, and we now have the ability to repel them if it is needed. We are both shielded now and our movements cannot be seen or tracked. We have the ability to appear and disappear at will in the presence of humans and Teranor. We have both also been given destructive power: we can stop, maim, or kill anything with a look or a hand gesture. There are many millions of Terans who are watching us now and sending us their power and energy. There are other abilities that will emerge as needed; suffice it to say that my people feel that we must not fail this quest."

There were lines in Mina's face I had never noticed before. She had the look of deliberate intent. The perpetual smile in her eyes was gone. Her movement was less melodic and more rigid. She stared ahead as if she was looking directly into the future at exactly what was coming. I on the other hand had no clue of what was next. But I knew to expect just about anything; after all, we were buzzing around in a bubble underground, flying through solid rock, with no propulsion system, no steering wheel, and no brakes. Mina's briefing of our commune with her people seemed to suggest that we were preparing to do battle. Well, the bad guys did always have guns so it felt good to have something to work with. Deep down inside I could feel the urge to try out the new powers. I kept thinking how cool it would be to simply wave my hand and send someone flying. As we sped along I looked over at Mina to see that she had the same smile on her face that I had on mine. We must have been thinking the same thing. It felt powerful knowing that we had options, that we didn't always have to run, couldn't outrun the bullets. Mina nodded without a glance in my direction as if to agree with what I was thinking.

Soon we would rise through the Gray and make our way to the Natural History Museum in Vienna. We would need to make several appearances and somehow leave in a huff that would force us to leave these specimens behind. It occurred to me that as soon as we made an appearance the Teranor would figure out that we were now shielded. It wouldn't take them long to go on high alert from surmising that they could no longer track our movements. It felt strange to me that the bad guys were all on my side of the two worlds—above and below. Then again, I have always said that the only thing I fear in life is my fellow man. It would be interesting to see who glowed red. "Mina, what if we get back to the surface and virtually everyone has a red aura?" Mina shot me a look like I was eighteen again. Her serious demeanor implied that we were in for some difficult encounters ahead.

In minutes we were rising to the Karl-Renner Ring, which encircles the inner core of old Vienna. Jasmina placed the Vug just inside the stone wall at the base of the Parliament building near the Vienna Natural History Museum. We stepped out of the Vug and the stone wall and onto the steps at the outside base of the magnificent marble structure of the Parliament. Grand architectural structures surrounded us: the Rathaus and the Hofburg as well as the Staatsoper and the Natural History Museum. As I looked around and walked with Mina, I could recall being here with her many times in the past. Mina looked down as she smiled as if to say "yes, many times." We were walking along the ring when a group of people came right for us. I was looking for red, but saw none. They were busy talking as they approached.

Mina stopped me by the hand and we stood as they advanced. Like children playing "chicken" in a school yard, we stood our ground while the group grew nearer. In an instant they strolled through us! Not between us, through us. I felt the strange wringing sensation as they walked directly through our bodies. It was as if water had been soaked up by a towel and then wrung out again. There was the slightest pulling sensation as they passed through the other side as if they were almost stuck inside us. We had held hands while this occurred and there seemed to be a tug at our clasped hands as if we were delicately pulled apart. This was part of our shield; we were ghosts. This was fun stuff! We had to stand there for a bit while I wrapped my head around what had just taken place. Mina seemed as amused by this new ability as I was. I wondered if this meant that bullets could fly right through us as well. That would be a huge benefit. Turned out she was amused by my thinking.

Mina interrupted my thoughts with, "Yes, Bryce, bullets can go right through us now without damage, but only when we are in this state of being. We did this in order to walk out of the walls of Parliament and to try on our new abilities. We will most assuredly see red when we begin to move through the museum. It might be a good plan to cover some ground within the museum to see how many Teranor we might encounter before we make our first appearance. We will want to make our presence known eventually, and when we leave it must be under duress in order to convince those after us that we had hoped to complete our mission here. If we don't see red, then we will need to remain here until the Teranor begin to close in on us."

Things are going to get dicey; I am sure that Mina is thinking the same as I am: what tricks do the Teranor have and can we counter them? Soon we arrive at the museum and walk through the marble walls into the great hall filled with arches hanging over grand marble stairways leading to various wings of the museum. Wading through rooms filled with dinosaurs and taxidermy, butterflies and minerals, we made our way to the meteorite display. It was rewarding to see specimens on display that came from my efforts. I was distracted by the specimens while Mina was watching for red. Totally distracted I called out, "Come on, Mina, check out the great rocks! Nobody can see us anyway. Just look at these killer specimens!"

Mina settled down and joined me in enjoying the displays. We made our way around the entire exhibit before going to the reception desk to ask for the curator of the meteorite collection. We both went into the restrooms and turned opaque again before leaving our respective rooms. As we came together and walked across the rotunda, I could see the curator was just arriving from outside the museum. We could see from the distance that he had no aura of red and I hailed him with a raised hand to stop him before he moved on to the lab. We could see the surprised expression on Kilian's face as he stopped.

After a happy greeting we followed him to his office and pulled the glorious array of specimens out of hiding to lay on his desk. Kilian, the curator, seemed calm until we began to remove the wrapping from each fragment. His response was a long-winded "oh" with the reveal of each individual specimen. There was little doubt that we had his attention as he pulled a hand lens from the lanyard hanging around his neck and gloves from the desk drawer. He could recognize from across the desk what we had brought for his enjoyment. As he pored over each piece he asked us what we were hoping to do with these specimens. I replied that our hope was to have them identified and classified. I told Kilian that we held the main masses of each; we knew the location of each find, the name of the finder, and the weights of each piece. Kilian was delighted to hear that all of these large repository specimens were to be donated to the museum for research and classification. Then we pushed the envelope as far as we could by asking if he might be able to get time on the SHRIMP for a cursory look while we were there visiting. I knew this would be a stretch, but really all we wanted was for the specimens to make it into the probe room before we were forced to flee the onslaught of Teranor.

Kilian's response was a very wry, squinting look. He rubbed his beard and sighed with a deep breath, then sat back in his high-backed leather office chair. With a heavy Austrian accent, Kilian agreed that this could be done. He admitted that he had time reserved on the probe for that night and this was why he had come back to the museum so late in the day. Kilian asked for some time to prepare the stages and offered to set us up with a meal in the cafeteria. This sounded great to me; the tables in part of the dining area were set around a balcony just below the domed pinnacle in the roof of the museum, and the view from these tables was spectacular looking down through each floor of the museum through the rotunda.

A docent arrived in Kilian's office to guide us up to the cafeteria; Kilian gave her his card and asked her to make certain that our meal was charged to his account. As we left the office the curator was busily gathering up the specimens onto a tray to carry them off to the lab. We took a freight elevator to the top floor with our docent guide, who left us on our own at a reserved table in my favorite spot. We were sitting for only a moment when a server came to offer us a beverage. As we waited Mina reached across the table to clasp my hands and asked me if I recalled the last time we were here. It caught me off guard, but her question opened my mind and in a flash I could see us sitting here in another time. The moment held weight. I began to recall details when the server returned with ginger tea for us both.

As I stirred honey into the cup, I glanced through the bars of the ancient handrail to stare into the past in recollection of those memories. Putting the piping hot beverage to lip, I noticed the dreaded red aura moving through the entry foyer on the ground floor. Deep in subconscious thought I had known that as soon as we parted company, our curator friend would do what any researcher would do: call his cronies to have them join him in the lab for the excitement. This was purely innocent on his part, but the call drew the Teranor like flies to a kill. We both knew it would transpire something like this, but I thought that I would at least get to enjoy this one cup of tea. Mina told me to relax and enjoy. It was her thinking that they would head for the lab.

As we sat there sipping tea, a stream of men with red auras moved into the museum. Jasmina reminded me that we needed to be seen. We had to make a brief appearance and then run. This was going to be the dicey part. The freight elevator was a dedicated elevator. It would not stop at additional floors. It would only take its fare to the floor requested and then move on to the next waiting passenger or freight. Mina said that we should step out of the elevator, be seen by the Teranor, retreat back into the elevator, and hopefully the doors would close before we were apprehended. Then we would ghost and step through the back wall of the elevator shaft and move off. This all sounded good to me, but I felt we needed to somehow make certain that Kilian and the others were safe. Mina heard my concern and against better judgment she agreed.

We got to the ground floor and stepped out into the back of the foyer. As we revealed ourselves, a surprising number of men in red started towards us; we backed into the elevator and agonized as the doors slowly closed. There were loud bangs as we rose through the building's floors. Deep dents appeared on our side of the doors, which showed us that these men would not hesitate to shoot us. As we passed the next floor Mina took my hand and we jumped through the wall into a hallway that led to stairs and down to the laboratory. Ghosting as we walked, there was nobody in the hall. When we arrived, the lab is empty: no researchers and no meteorite specimens. We moved through the building from room to room, walking through walls as we went. There were no more gunshots, but we weren't finding Kilian. We ran back to the entry foyer to see Teranor frantically searching from room to room. It was obvious that our ghosting was working effectively. But where were the researchers? Mina closed her eyes in concentration. She flashed them open and exclaimed in a whisper, "I've found them." She grabbed my hand and led me down the marble stairs. In a room below ground we found the small group of researchers busily polishing small pieces of our stones in preparation for the SHRIMP. They were completely oblivious. When we walked into the room we learned that Kilian had left the main pieces in the probe room, and they were gone, taken by the Teranor. Apparently they had no interest in revealing themselves to the researchers and causing more trouble, so once they had obtained our specimens, they backed out.

The scientists were safe; we left them to their devices. We stepped back into the hall and began to make our way back to the Vug. Walking together through the halls of the museum three Teranor came around the corner at the end of the hall we were in. We had stopped ghosting, and they screamed at us to halt. As one of them began to draw his weapon, Mina quickly raised her arm; with a pulsing gesture of her hand, the three Teranor were thrust with tremendous force against the wall behind them and fell limp to the floor. We ghosted again and worked our way to the front of the museum and on towards the Vug. This ghosting phase is no way to live, but it is a great way to remain safe. Moving through the ring we could see the Parliament building coming into view. From our vantage point we could see a number of Teranor in front of the marble steps.

As we stopped, Talleyrand appeared in front of us holding his hands out to stop us where we stood. "The Teranor have located your Vug. They have yet to learn of your new abilities. They will try to stop you from leaving the city. It will help you if they believe they have trapped you here. We have sent decoys to several areas of the city to carry out the deception while you continue on your journey. We have left another Vug under a split willow tree on the east bank of the Danube where it flows into the Black Sea. You are shielded so the Teranor will not track your movement. You can swim to the Vug. We intend to keep the Teranor busy here in Vienna. You must get to the Vug and continue your journey."

Talleyrand put a hand on his chest and the other flat in our direction, wishing us farewell. We began the walk through Vienna's streets to the Danube River, where we would soon see if I could swim underwater for approximately nine hundred miles. Ghosting and moving along at a brisk pace, we stepped out of the Ring. Mina and I began to fade into the shadows of the surrounding buildings when our Vug erupted in a massive fireball of destructive energy, blowing a gaping hole into the face of the wall below the Parliament building. We turned to look back at the sight to see that the damage had been miraculously selective and only red-haloed bodies lay on the ground. No humans appeared to have been injured, only Teranor. I looked for a smile of reassurance from Mina, but she looked ahead of our direction with deliberate intent and little emotion. We threaded our way through narrow cobbled streets lined with ancient architecture, historic buildings dating back many hundreds of years. Any other trip here might have been to enjoy the history of this beautiful part of the world; instead we were here to save its history from an abrupt end. Soon we arrived at the banks of the River Danube, where we stepped into the mud along the river's edge.

Jasmina stopped to prepare me for this next leg of our effort, saying, "This portion of our travel will be strange for you; we will be under the water for many miles and swimming very swiftly. You will not be able to see in this water, and when we encounter obstacles such as river traffic we will ghost right through the hulls as if they are not there. We will keep our hands together as we both move on instinct. You won't need me for this, but I will stay by your side regardless and we shall remain hand in hand. It will take some time for you to adapt to our speed. You have within you all of the tools needed to do this; you only need to trust my words. In time you may find that you enjoy this ability as do I. My dear Bryce, in your own words from another time and place, 'trust, enjoy and relax.'"

Ghosting and shielded, we lowered into the muck and drifted through the river bank sediment until we emerged under the river in the murky, cool currents of the Danube. One could hear the whining grind of engines churning as they motored behind watercraft pushing their masters up and down the waterway. Hesitating for a brief pause, it was easy to feel our pending direction as the river made its way to the Black Sea. I heard Mina's voice in my head speaking to me more clearly than face to face. It was not her voice in my head; it was her mind in mine. The words were felt, not heard. She told me to hold fast and swim with all my might. Eyes open or closed there was nothing to be seen as we tore through water like a hummingbird tears through air. Two hearts pounded out a beat in unison as if one.

Our fingers locked in an unbreakable weave, we soared side by side, arms making slight rudder motions to guide direction. As I relaxed, the sensation of moving faster manifested itself. Mina confirmed that the more I let go, the quicker we accelerated. The sound soaking into my bones of passing ships blended into a symphonic drone of hums and whirrs. We traversed close to half the length and were bearing down on the mouth of the river. When we walked out of the waterway there was nothing to see but lush trees. We covered over nine hundred river miles in a handful of heartbeats, or so it seemed. This was an activity I would very much like to try again and again in clearer water. Mina giggled at my thoughts. She seemed to know exactly where the Vug was waiting. A few short steps from the river and we were standing outside our new transport.

CHAPTER NINE

Capture

leaned over and poked my head through the skin-like outer film of our new Vug. It felt different inside. As I leaned back with a questioning expression on my face, Jasmina explained that the Vugs all had a different feel.

"It's just like an automobile," she compared; "every car has a different feel and a different smell, right?" This simply raised more questions for me about her world and how things that are nearly intangible can also have personalities and character traits. Jasmina stepped into the Vug and turned towards me, where I was still positioned outside; her eyes were like the South Pacific Ocean after a tempest. As she reached out, her strong yet supple hand fingering for my grip, I felt a slamming strike throughout my body like lightning blasting down from the heavens. Something had hit me. As the daylight melted into darkness, there was no way to move. Frozen by shock, mind melting into blur, body wracked with sudden screams of agony, bars of iron breaking my view of Jasmina's face, cringing with panic, I was caught by her, tears bursting from her crying eyes as darkness prevailed.

When I awakened, Elders were surrounding me with hands over my body. I could not move; pain radiated through me as the sound waves of my agonizing screams reverberated through the air. There was a sickening taste of iron and the sting of pain from my last memory. Warmth began to flood through all of me as the Elders lowered their hands onto my skin. Lying there beneath the illumination of their efforts, I could sense that something was very wrong. Taking inventory of my physical self, it was easy to surmise that I could not move or speak. I could think, smell, and taste, but I couldn't open my eyelids or turn my eyes. I could see those around me, but it was a mental image. Then I heard Mina's voice calmly begin to offer comfort and explanation for what had transpired.

Mina spoke with tears in her voice, "My dear Bryce Monroe Sterling, I nearly lost you. You were seized by an ancient artifact known as a Catchkill. The Teranor had set these traps in the obvious departure points, hoping to catch us and halt our progress. The Catchkill cages were designed during our medieval time to capture and destroy adversaries. This is an ancient technology that Terans abandoned long ago, but which has been brought here by the Teranor. The Catchkillers are a despicable device that encapsulate the target in iron-like bars while three razor-sharp tubes pierce the body and drain its life fluids. In your case the spikes penetrated your heart and spine. When the spikes shoot through the victim, a core sample is ejected out onto the ground from the hollow center of each spike. A DNA sample is used to program each Catchkiller and the ejected core material can then be used to confirm a kill or to program additional tech later.

"Tags were also implemented on our home world, millions of ages ago, but Teranor tags cannot survive in the Earth atmosphere, which is extremely fortunate for you. Tags divulge your location, then dissolve your flesh in a matter of minutes, preventing escape or salvation. We were shielded and ghosting but when we stopped ghosting to step into the Vug, the Catchkill was triggered and it took you. You were instantly caged and penetrated. The Elders are bringing you back, my Bryce. I have learned that I must teach you how to ghost on pure instinct to prevent this from ever occurring again.

"The Catchkill tells us that the Teranor have brought their tools of war with them and that they will kill without hesitation to stop us or anyone else who interferes with their designs. There are a number of additional forms of self-preservation that I must teach you now that you have been put into the path of harm. You will be motionless for a while longer while the Elders repair the damage done to your body. They are giving you a new spine and heart. Please remain calm and listen to my voice while you rest here; it's not long now before we depart for our next destination. The Teranor must have gotten your DNA from the specimens we left in Vienna. I will do all in my power to protect you, my Bryce."

I lay there on the forest floor of the Void with the hum of chanting Elders hovering over me and all things around us glowing with a pulsing phosphorescent illumination and a humming vibration emanating from the ground beneath me. There was a sensation of greater strength in my heart as I listened to its slow rhythmic pound drumming in my inner ears. As I lay listening to Mina's tender, affectionate voice, I saw the face that haunted my waking hours and slumbering dreams for lifetimes. Somehow I had lived this moment many times before. Lying there in my own silent reflection, I realized that for once this would not end in goodbye. Jasmina continued to explain that the Teranor would not hesitate to take my life to stop our effort. She told me that the Terans would continue to innovate ways to protect us. Mina's voice calmly whispered as the Elders seemed to be completing the process of repairing the damage done by the Teranor death trap.

"Will I be sore?" I inquired.

Mina's reply was hard to hear, "Bryce, everybody reacts differently to this process. You were gone when the Elders began to save you. Damage was complicated and your anatomy is not similar to Teran. You and I shall know the answers soon enough. The hope is that you recover swiftly and that you will feel better than ever. You will have me by your side sharing a great deal of my life energy to help you make the transition into this new age for your body."

Finishing the healing ritual, the Elders rose up while reciting a few words I didn't understand; then they moved off, leaving Jasmina and me there alone. I felt a hold releasing throughout my body as muscles began to relax and twitch back to life. A finger moved first, responding to the touch of Mina's hand curling under mine. Her touch ignited a spark of joy and comfort in my nervous system. The feel of Mina's finger under and around mine sent a chill up and down my new spine. When I moved to sit up the effort was smooth as fluid. The healing had done its intended service and I felt strong and filled with vigor. As I stood in one supple motion, feeling not so much as a glint of pain or resistance, a broad smile replaced my worried grimace. We slipped our fingers together and held fast, experiencing touch as if for the first time. Every sensation pulsed new and stronger through my senses. The blinding fog of life gone past had faded from clouding my senses, and every detail now held a new sensation.

"I feel" were my first words. Mina blinked as her eyes watered; she looked to the forest floor and leaned to press her forehead against mine while she whimpered a small, cheerful laugh. We stood there for a time enjoying the nearness and touch. Calm replaced the chill of fear and worry. Mina led me into the forest for a walk through New Tera. A glow surrounded us as we moved. People walked by us making eye contact and smiling as we passed. I could hear the muffled voices of everyone around us. Looking down at my torso there were no scars from the three spikes that had shafted my body. I felt where they were but only as a faint recollection. With each intake of air into the lungs, I drew greater strength. The questions begged for answers to the point of distraction. Mina could feel my craving for explanation of what had transpired in our last moments on the surface. "Mina, did I die up there? Please tell me exactly what happened."

Jasmina gestured for me to sit on a nearby log. She paused for a time as a solemn expression washed over her face. She finally replied, "The hollowed tubes spit core samples of your tissue out onto the ground where they could be potentially recovered so that your DNA could be used to create clones. I cleared the area to prevent that potential threat. It was beyond difficult for me to return to that site knowing that you were here suffering. After you were taken I pulled you and the cage into the Vug and put you in stasis to bring you here, hoping that the Elders could save you. You passed before I could get you to the Elders."

"My Bryce, you are stronger than any of us had surmised; your body is fragile, but your will to live is immense, a nearly limitless spirit. You were brought back from dead. Sadly, a number of your doubles have been lost during our time coming here. From now on, rather than shielding our movement, the Terans will be shielding our bodies. A large percentage of the Teran population will be directly focused on you and me to protect us from harm. We know now from this last encounter that the Teranor have deliberate intent, and we will not allow them to harm you. My people are prepared to fight to protect our world. You and I will remain here in the Void while you adapt to your new body, but soon we will continue our journey."

I began to recognize the strength in Mina that I had seen or sensed in our earlier time when I was just a kid traveling the globe for the first time. The wall I felt as a younger man was still there as an integral facet of this powerful woman, always on guard and ever prepared for a challenge. Yet how did she find the strength and courage to return to the location of my capture and face ultimately fearful odds just to recover parts of me left lying there in the dirt? In this new world, I have learned that the importance of the unknown is far beyond the scope of my comprehension.

Both Earth and the EarthUnder world of New Tera were integral parts of this shell planet, a world that I barely understood, filled with new threats beyond my wildest imagination. I sat here immersed in a cloud of thought with Mina standing in view listening to my mind storming about. The fine line between worry and preparation for pending doom was as slim as the line between two shades of the same color. We had to prepare for dangers I could not possibly forecast. Jasmina volunteered that there was a way around this issue of my concern over the unknown.

She explained in detail, "The Elders can meld with your mind and immerse your brain in our history so that you will then know the risks and dangers involved with confronting the Teranor. This process can eliminate the questions, but the knowledge may overwhelm your conscious thought with too much information. Are you willing to take that risk? The Elders can expand the capacity of your hippocampus to assimilate our memories. This way you can be prepared for any threat from our past. We Terans don't really know the extent of your capacity to learn and adapt. You, Bryce Monroe, may surprise us all; that is my greatest hope. Well, are you willing?"

I replied, "Mina, you already know my answer, yes of course I will. I'll do anything to make myself better equipped to defend our world. Let's do this." Mina led me back to the gathering place where the Elders had repaired my body. They were already waiting there for us. It appeared there was no need to explain our return; they were already preparing for our arrival. As we walked their way, one of them came to meet us and took my arm to lead me to the center of the group. Mina stood there where I left her and watched as the Elders encircled me. My body floated in suspension above the ground, level with their heads, as they leaned into me. I heard their whispering voices in my head as I began to experience mass awareness. They helped me to open my mind. The pounding of heart beats resonated in my head as I floated within the circle of Elders, absorbing their collective memories. I began to hear the voices clearly and see crystalline images, memories of countless lives. Tears flowed as I felt the memories. Soon, process completed, the Elders lowered me to my feet. I could feel the power of unlimited recollection. They told me that now I would respond on pure impulse whenever needed. That I didn't need to consciously recall memories, but they were all there at my call. Mina gestured me to follow as she moved through the forest. She bent down to pick a few nutrition pods and handed them to me.

Jasmina held back as she announced, "We leave soon for our next destination. Do you feel ready for this?" Her face showed her concern.

My reply brought a smile back to her ocean eyes. "Yeah, I feel better than ever and ready to roll. If this is what reincarnation feels like, I'll take one a day!"

As we wove our way through massive trees and gin-clear waterways, moss covered the forest floor with a spongy layer that sprang under foot. Creatures of unimaginable variety wandered aimlessly as we made our way to the Vug. Before arriving we were met by a large number of Terans wanting to wish us well on our next leg. As they reached out to touch us in farewell, I heard them clearly speaking to us with advice and suggestions. I found myself able to reply to each suggestion and request rapidly, clearly, and without hesitation. I could see now that speaking out of mouth is clearly overrated and cumbersome. This new mode of communication was delightfully efficient. As well as being able to speak and hear cerebrally, you could feel the love and kindness and concern of each individual as they touched you and spoke. As Mina and I moved off in the Vug, I pondered that if the Terans had this much power and strength, then how much evil capability the Teranor must possess. Calm washed over my thoughts as I began to see in mind the history of the Teranor and the limitations caused by their own evil nature. A voice in me spoke to say, "We can do this, we can win this conflict and turn this into good for both our peoples."

CHAPTER TEN

Gary's Lab

As we traveled once again through the Void, we were flying towards the Pacific islands of Hawaii. I told Mina that we must find Gary at his home rather than meeting him at the lab. Now we were going to be trying to exercise stealth and keep our location unknown. Frankfurt never happened after Vienna, but we hoped it would work as a diversion. Somehow, the Teranor always knew where we were going next. It would be difficult convincing Gary of what we were trying to accomplish, but easy to shock him into listening after he looked at our small treasure from space. An intense researcher, Gary came from a practical application background and he was actively working to find evidence of life elsewhere in the Universe, so he already had an open mind. What was going to be difficult for him was to have someone like me simply hand it to him. Still, once he saw a thin section of this piece, he would willingly fire the shot heard 'round the world. Once his announcement was made, fervor will rise up from the ranks of research scientists that we are not alone, and from there our process would begin.

This would be only the first step of many, but an announcement like this coming from a most reliable source would turn the heads of many if not most political leaders, and then the trend would take on a life of its own. Eventually, a reveal would have to take place, but that would be a long way off, if we could wait that long. Earth's condition is at a precipice and the planet needs saving immediately. Actually, no, Mankind needs saving; the Earth will survive no matter what but Man will be scoured from the surface as will the Terans. Our brain bone meteorite shall be the seed of new life on Earth, a chance for us all to begin again by changing the direction of our destructive endeavors.

Reaching for the priceless treasure, I felt it still there in my pocket. When we meet with Gary we would have him cut it in two, one for the university lab and one for him to work with in his private lab at home. I had visited his home many times in past years. When times were tough and grant money had dried up, Gary built a small but fairly complete geophysics laboratory in his garage, where he could continue his research if things ever ended at the university. It turned out to be extremely handy for weekends and for friends who needed lab time but had run out of grant funds. These guys had been sharing grant money for years to keep each other employed, and whenever one person had landed big dollars, it was time for payback or else make contributions to the communal "secret lab" in Gary's garage. This was where we needed to land. Gary would take us in earnest and he would expedite the effort, based on my personal request.

Soon we arrived under the island, where we could see the classic active volcanos, their towers of magma rising

from floor to ceiling in the Void. The thought occurred
that once humans understood the existence of EarthUnder,
everyone would want to see this. Ghosting, we stepped
out of the Vug and walked up to Gary's door. It was late
night and the hope was that our potential host would not
be pulling an all-nighter at the university. I couldn't help
feeling increased apprehension with the memories in mind
of that last time I rode in a Vug. It used to be that I saw
snakes and scorpions everywhere; now it's Catchkills. The
wait at Gary's door felt like an eternity. Sure enough, he
came to the door, wide-eyed and yelling, reached out to give
his usual hug, and begged us, "come in." After introducing
Jasmina to Gary, I began to explain our surprise visit. We
sat in the dining room while Gary made tea.

"Gary," I started, "we have brought you a small fragment of a very unusual meteorite. Our hope is that you can
take a quick look at it. I can't tell you what we have gone
through to get this specimen into your hands."

Gary leaped into action, grabbing a microscope and lugging it into the house to set up on the dining room table. I
took the meteorite out of my pocket and set it on a napkin
next to the base of the microscope. He sat at the microscope and began to adjust the focus and zoom on the scope.
Gary pulled gloves from his pocket and set the specimen
on the stage of the microscope. His reaction to the view
through the eyepieces was immediate and ecstatic, "What
have you got here? Look at the frothy fusion crust on this
baby!" he mused. "Wow, the matrix of this specimen is very
weird! I have never seen anything like this," Gary went on;
"What do you think this is?"

"Oh, we know what it is, but we need you to confirm it,"

I explained. I had to continue on to warn him of the danger of working on this specimen. "Gary, a number of very bad individuals are after us to keep this specimen from being revealed. The road thus far has been a hazardous journey trying to lead the dogs off our trail in order to arrive here untethered by pursuers. We need to get the word out to the scientific community of just what this material is. It's my feeling that you are the right man for the job. For now you will really need to keep this material to yourself, and all of your work should be done here at home and under cover. The bad guys will stop at nothing to halt our effort to present this stone to the world."

Gary interrupted, "Eww, I like this, very cloak and dagger."

I replied with, "Man, you have absolutely no idea! Also, Gary, may we stay here with you? Someone needs to keep an eye out while you're buried in the lab."

"Ok," said Gary, now with just a slight glint of scowl on his face; "Wow, man, this sounds like pretty serious stuff."

"Well, you take a good look at the specimen and then you tell me how important all of this might be," I replied.

Gary talked about how puzzling the stone appeared to be. He told us that he had been looking for something exciting to work on and that he was well rested and inspired to stay up that night and begin the work. "Bryce, you and Jasmina can cut the specimen while I prep a slide for the Scanning Electron Microscope. I just got in a new automatic polishing unit that will give us a half-micron finish lickity-split. Then we'll carbon coat the slide and put it in the SEM; after that we'll begin to know what we are looking at. This is going to be really fun. Thank you, Bryce and Jasmina, for bringing excitement into my life!"

I countered rather wryly, "Don't thank us yet, old buddy."

Gary is a long-time friend and one of the most enthusiastic people I have ever known. He is a jolly old soul who loves what he does with a passion. Gary is not tall, but he is extremely fit and brims with excess energy. He enjoys a challenge and he lives life to the fullest. He is a brilliant scientist, a bright, shining academic celebrity. When he jumps into a project he becomes a research pit-bull; he goes for the throat and will not let go until he achieves his goal. He's a fun-loving friend who loves living where there are so many activities to participate in. His most important trait: Gary is extremely open minded when it comes to the modern-day space race of trying to be the first to find concrete evidence of life elsewhere in the universe. This is my ace in the hole. I am counting on Gary finding his holy grail in our new stone. And when he does, he is the ideal guy to get the word out and to have it accepted as scientific fact.

Mina was listening to my thoughts and I could see she was pleased with my confidence in Gary's idiosyncrasies.

Soon we were hard at work doing our duties in the secret laboratory of one of the planet's greatest meteoriticists. The diamond blade of the trim saw cut through the specimen like our Vug through the Gray. Gary had asked that we cut the long way and try to cut through part of the fusion crust. He wanted to see a cross section of the glass formed by fusion during the fall. Gary seemed interested in how thick the crust was, and he wanted to see the bubbles in the crust. Then after the curing agent did its job, which took no time at all since the batch was mixed "hot," it was time to cut the thin section. This was Gary's responsibility since it is easy to break the glass slide. So Gary made the cut, which was perfect, and then he hooked it up in the new sequential polishing unit.

We stood there listening to the polisher run through the series of grits. There was a unique mechanical hum that changed tone as each grit pressed into the slide. In a surprisingly short time we were moving on to the carbon coater. From there the finished slide was mounted into the SEM. A thin section can take six months to have made. This night was a dream come to life. Our premier scientist/host sat down at the huge computer monitor connected to the SEM as we stood behind and watched over his shoulder. Gary's reaction was an unusually extended silence. Time dragged by as Gary pored over our treasure and moved back to look several times at the smoked glass fusion crust and then back to the porous matrix. After a long pause Gary pushed his wheeled chair back from the work center and continued looking at the final view for some time longer before he turned around, still sitting in his chair, and looked up at us standing there, but he said nothing. The expression on his face told everything, a painful expression of angst melded with a look of finality and closure. We said nothing but Mina and I were talking to each other with quiet thought.

After a long and somewhat painful silence filled with looks of dubious questioning and doubt, the first words from Gary came out like a scolding in grade school, "Bryce, what have you and your cohort done?" We stood silent and waited for Gary to elaborate. Nothing came forth, as though we needed to drag a reaction out of him. Finally Gary exploded with his classic enthusiasm and asked again what we had done here. I had to ask him to clarify. "Bryce, this is not a meteorite. This is a bone fragment." Gary exclaimed, "My basic education was biology before I specialized in meteoritics, and that education dictates that this is a fragment of bone."

"Yes," I agreed with his assessment, "but it is a bone from space that fell as a meteorite and has the fusion crust to prove it."

"I know this," retorted Gary. He continued, "Bryce, you and Jasmina have changed history."

"Yeah, Gary, but this piece of bone is literally billions of years old and it comes from another planet that I can tell you all about in future days. For now, the less you know the better to protect you from harm. There are those who do not wish this information to get out there. Mina and I have entrusted you with knowledge that we have not been able to share with anyone else. From now on we will do all we can to protect you, but you will be in danger. One of the most important issues is that you keep silent until you have good evidence and then release all the information you can to as many colleagues as possible. Once the public learns of this first discovery, we will begin the process of revealing more information to the population of the planet. The biggest concern is that our pursuers will work hard to sabotage our efforts.

"Gary, you will need to open that wonderful mind of yours to let this in. What you have here is a piece of bone from Mina's people's world far away and long ago. Just like the silicon wafer in your computer has memory stored in it, this fragment of ancient bone stores the thoughts, memories, and history of her people and the days on her world. There's more to tell you, but for now you should do what you can to convince yourself of its authenticity using the technology at your disposal. We would like to remain here while you do the probe work. We'll stay out of your way and do all we can to assist you. Our desire is to protect you from approach by those who wish to stop us. We also feel that the initial release of data should not be tagged with your name; let people digest the information for some time before you validate it with your research notes."

I could hear Gary's thoughts; he was in total agreement. Right now all he wanted was the chance to be first to do the identification of our specimen. His enthusiasm was barely contained. He was already firing up a stage on the micro-probe to analyze the specimen. As the probe was charging, Gary started to speak loudly from across his laboratory. He told us that any announcements he would make, he would send out as a blast notice to every member of the Meteoritical Society.

Gary surmised in his own unique style, "People are going to freak when they read about this! You're right, Bryce; this will be the shot heard 'round the world!" We all settled in for a night of black tea and hours of probe work. This really felt like it was going to work. We got here without a hitch and got Gary to buy off on the project with limited time spent convincing him of our plan. Now we needed enough data to convince others that our researcher had not lost his marbles.

While I helped our resident genius set up the probe, Mina walked around the house inside and out to secure the property by generating a shield of her energy over the house and garage. Our resident genius began to look like the proverbial wizard as he worked the keyboard and watched the three screens splayed out before him. After he stared at the screens for a time Gary looked at me beyond the screens and asked, "Bryce, do you know how old the material really is?"

"Yep, Gary, I know, pretty cool, eh?"

Gary and I enjoyed a shared smile as we both realized together the importance of our work here tonight. In a heartbeat we were changing the direction of the world after billions of years of formation and millions of years of evolution. And it would all get its chance beginning here in a garage lab in Paradise. Two worlds would eventually join to be one and everything was going to change.

Later I would tell Gary about the forces of evil that had come to the Earth to stop the Terans. I didn't want to tell him too much; it was of primary importance that he remained on task. A bark of unfettered enthusiasm blew out of his throat as he laughed and screamed at the ceiling as if to call out a cheer to the stars above. His mood changed from that of a focused scientist to one of a child on Christmas morning. For Gary every bit of data was an unopened gift with colorful wrapping, and he was tearing away the paper as fast as a child at the base of the glistening tree. This was validating a lifetime of wondering and laboring on the questions: Are we all there is? and Where do we come from? Telling him what I had already seen was going to blow his mind. I couldn't wait to show him in person.

Mina walked back into the lab and settled in next to us in view of the computer screens. Gary shot a piercing glance in Mina's direction; it seemed a look of question and doubt. I know Gary well, he questions everything. His inclination to ask the hard question is one of many reasons why he is respected in the community and why we came here. My gut told me that this would be our best chance for a solid start, and of course the garage lab was a huge motivator. No doubt that the look was based on the data we were getting from the specimen, which was showing ages well beyond the formation of our protoplanetary disc. The thing is that the rocks don't lie. I got up from the workstation and moved over to Jasmina. We sat on the sofa and began to talk in silence.

"Mina," I started, "would it be possible to take Gary for a ride in the Vug, maybe even to the Void?"

Jasmina squirmed in her seat as she thought about my words. Her reply was abrupt: "I had expected this."

She told me that she had asked the Elders about this while I was mending from the Catchkill. The Elders had agreed that this would eventually come to pass and therefore it was going to be acceptable to begin this process with key people at first. I told Mina that my thinking was that we might need to do more to protect Gary than just leaving him here after word got out about his data. She could feel my concern and told me that there was no need to ask. Mina understood the vulnerability of an unsuspecting human to the Teranor. It was easy to assume that Gary would willingly accept an invitation to see the underworld of New Tera. I could hardly wait for him to experience the Vug. Mina then informed me that she had moved the Vug to the entryway just inside the front door. Gary's probe was an older unit, but it was dedicated and had only the one work station, so the data was proprietary. He announced that tonight's data would be ready to print and email at close to 6 a.m., which was in just one hour.

Gary rubbed his hands together briskly to get the blood flowing after all of the hours at the keyboard giving commands to the probe. We could tell by his movements and mood that he was pleased, if not puzzled, by the results of his initial probe inquiry. He trotted off to the kitchen, grabbed a bottle of papaya juice, and returned with glasses for each of us. We toasted to a successful night's run and we started the morning with a shot of the nectar.

As we waited for the computer to produce the data needed to broadcast throughout the meteorite community, we sat at the table listening to the birds outside calling up the dawning sun.

It's one of those things that many ignore or take for granted, but it has always struck me odd that birds around the world sing their lungs out each morning and every night. Countless mornings I have awakened before dawn and lay in bed to listen to the birds greet the day. At night in the summer the robins sit on the crest of my roof and sing to the setting sun. In Canada the loons perform this same ritual as the mated pairs slowly ply the territorial waters of their home lakes. Dawn and sunset their haunting call echoes through the arboreal, wilderness forest. Here in Paradise the birds are loud and raucous and scream their songs as if each day is a party.

I asked Gary if he would like to take a little trip to another world; he lit up like the birds outside and jumped up from the table to dance around in what must be a local victory dance. He whooped and jumped twirling in the air as if he had just found buried treasure. He stopped mid-leap and asked, "how and...and...and when?"

I replied, "It's called a Vug, and right after we shoot the data off to everyone."

Suddenly a feeling of urgency washed over me. Mina

noticed my mood change as I glanced nervously at my watch. I grabbed her by the wrist and pulled her towards the house, telling Gary we'd be back in a few minutes.

Gary replied, "No problem," a tone of acceptant patience in his voice. Gary was busy at the controls of his work station and he knew where we were headed. Gary had ended many all-night work sessions with this same climb.

I raced to lead Mina to a place she had never been to see a thing she had likely never seen. We climbed flights of stairs past spare rooms and bedrooms to a door at the top of the last step. I turned the lock, swung open the heavy, over-sized door, and out onto the lanai we stepped. Gary had built this "widow's walk" around the peak of his home's roof for times like this. From his rooftop one could watch the sun rise out of the Pacific at dawn and hiss its final glimmering rays back into the ocean each evening.

The sunrise would be bloodied by the refraction of light through a haze of vog hanging in the island air. Vog is a combination of the words volcanic, smog, and fog, and it is a local form of air pollution caused by the reaction of volcanic gases and particles with moisture, oxygen, and sunlight. Long before our first glimpse of the sun's boiling body, the sky began to turn a rainbow of colored illumi-nation: midnight blue overhead to the faintest pale yellow that floated on the ocean horizon intensified in a morph of radiant color. Spouting whales blew puffs of disappearing mist into the panorama of constant change. The nervous surface of sea water blended a reflection of the sky into a rugged pallid twin. The changing view washed the memory of each color away as the next tone replaced the last.

Our eyes watered from a reluctance to blink for fear

of missing an instant of the spectacle before us. The view was framed by the lush, green vegetation and dew-soaked cliffs of this island habitat. As the sun began to reveal itself from behind the watery screen, its rays instantly found our faces, and the cool night air was dried and heated before it touched our skin. We closed our eyes and stood there hand in hand, facing the arrival of today's solar cycle. We could almost feel our skin sizzle like frying bacon in the island sun as the rays of light burned through our dusty planet's atmosphere. After the globe rose fully into the morning air it reached a low-lying ceiling of mist and volcanic ash hanging just above the horizon, and the sun changed into a red burning bubble of blinding light obscured by the mist. For a time everything reflected a hue of the sun's morning glow. Mina leaned against my side as I wrapped my arm around her. Our minds morphed together in a collocation of memories recalling countless mornings, watching the day begin in a silent roar of planets orbiting around our sun.

Gary, hard at work in his lab, knew where we were and what we were doing. Never in all of my days spent visiting his home here in the Pacific Islands had I allowed a morning or evening to pass without climbing to this vantage to witness life on the grandest scale coming and going as the planets spin their paths through space. Witnessing this phenomenal event is an endless reminder of how small I am. It's hard to know when to break off and leave the view. Once the sun is full in the morning sky, the birds go nearly quiet and begin their busy day of foraging and survival. They'll return to their perches again this evening to call out the ending of another daylight cycle.

As the weight of the day began to hang in the air,

we climbed back down to the garage to find Gary there standing in front of the printer waiting while hard copies were produced. He was printing multiple copies: one for his vault, one to mail off to a neutral recipient, one for Mina and me, one for Gary to tear up at his desk in future days, and one for each of his research team to do the same. When we got close enough to hear his voice over the machines running in the lab, he told us that he had already sent a copy to everyone.

Gary went on to say, "I figure that within two to three days government officials the world over will learn about this reveal." It was time to get the heck out of Dodge. There was nothing we needed to do in preparation for the next leg of our journey; in fact, we hadn't spent any time making plans beyond this point. We needed to get the word out any way possible and keep Gary safe. When I asked Gary if he was ready to take a trip, he jumped up from his desk and burst out a retortive "am I ever!"

We left the lab and walked into the house. As we walked across the living room floor Mina threw an arm around each of us and pushed us hard towards the front door. "Teranor!" she screamed with horror in her voice.

She could see their red nimbus through the leaves of the trees outside the front window. She pushed us into the Vug. Immediately we began to sink through the floor and into the Gray. Mina had set up a shield around Gary's house to protect us all from Teranor approach, but at a glance she could see that they were trying to get through her shield. As we sank into the Gray there came a rumbling wave of shock through the Vug and the ground surrounding us.

Mina spoke, "I believe that Gary's house has been destroyed."

Gary didn't seem to hear what Mina had said. He was so taken by the moment that the house no longer mattered. The shock of what transpired had kept me from introducing our new passenger to what he was going to experience. Gary was entranced, so anything we might have said would have been wasted words. There wasn't much to say; he was going to see it all first hand, and with his science mind he might never wish to leave. If Mina was right and the house was gone, then Gary had no place left to return to. We traveled through the Gray as usual and when we dropped out into the Void a gasp of amazement blurted from the mouth of our guest. He blinked and rubbed his eyes as if the view would change. He mumbled, but the words made no sense. Gary was baffled beyond his own ability to rationalize what he was seeing.

"Gary," I started his orientation, "these people terra-formed our planet. Actually, it's their planet, maintained by them with gravity that is created and maintained by them. We owe them for our existence on this globe; they brought us here. There is a great deal more that will amaze you, man. I don't want to spoil the surprises for you, and there is a lot I have yet to learn for myself. This is the Void, it traverses the entire planet, a world beneath our world, Mina's world, EarthUnder. What do you think?" Gary looked at me, closed his eyes, and shook his head; he had no words.

We sailed through the Void over masses of people and animals between rivers of humanoid forms flying through the air. As we moved along I noticed something that I hadn't recognized before. When flying people change the direction of flight, they circle around one of the columns as if they were roundabouts, and all of the movement is counterclockwise around these columns. This must be their form of traffic control—I had missed this before. No doubt that through time more and more things will reveal themselves as I grow less numb from the newness of this strange world. Gary was seeing the phosphorescent light and color of this world for his first time.

When I could see the lights reflecting in his eyes, I knew what he was feeling and thinking. Gary would have more questions than I, and I felt it would be important that he have his brain filled with answers just as I had. To Gary, information was the greatest gift that one person could give another. Gary had given the world a number of technical journals and large books as his gift to mankind. He was a generous person who believed in sharing any discovery no matter how small, for the benefit of the greater good. Gary looked at me again as we passed one of the fumaroles feeding a volcano above and he spoke, "My house and lab are a very small price to pay for all of this."

This was classic Gary, never a self-centered bone in his body. He would never look back in regret as long as his life was full of adventure and discovery, as this existence promised to provide. And since the brain bone represented the ultimate universal form of information sharing, like a living historic library, he already knew that he would commit the rest of his life to protect it. He smiled a clever narrow smirk as he lifted the samples and the thin section from the pocket of his colorful bird-covered Hawaiian shirt. I saw him as the ideal curator of our world's greatest store of knowledge: a bright mind willing to share and preserve the history and knowledge of all our peoples since the beginning of time. Somehow I knew that once here Gary would never want to leave. I guess it was just as well that he had little to go back to. The time would come when our worlds will communicate openly, and he would be there, ready to share all that he can.

Mina had a more serious expression on her face as we traveled through the Void. I listened to her thoughts; she was concerned with how quickly the Teranor had found our location and descended upon the lab. She knew they had devices and technology beyond her knowledge and she feared they might catch up with us somewhere and stop our progress. I could see in our shared memory some of the terrible tools and weapons they had manufactured over time. Everything seemed destructive in design. Nothing appeared to be built to produce, but rather all to take or destroy. The list and inventory of devices seemed endless. I could understand the expression on Jasmina's face.

I questioned Gary hopefully, "Do you think we got the word out? Is there any chance that those emails were blocked?"

Gary replied with glee, "Not a chance, I felt the importance of this information so I sent out a pulse mail that went into the cloud and will continue to resend until everyone gets it. I also sent it to several thousand random friends, acquaintances, politicians, and religious leaders around the planet. I sent several hard copies through the vacuum tube to a dozen different labs around the island and I brought this."

He held up a memory stick on which he had downloaded all of our probe work as well as pictures from the SEM and a few pictures under reflected light. I gave Gary a huge shoulder hug as we both laughed in relief. His guts were screaming at him like mine do with me at times. Mina could see that we were all on the same page. In her mind the resilience of humans was going to be a priceless asset in the quest to survive the invasion of the Teranors.

We were all happily blitzing along enjoying the view. Mina announced that we would soon meet with the Elders, and that millions of her people were going to join them in a gathering to greet us and to applaud our first success. I could hear Jasmina communicating with the Elders. The Elders had made it impossible for the Teranor to invade the Void, but a conflict with them on the surface could be devastating to us all, Earthling and Teranian alike, especially considering the wicked devices used by the dark ones. I asked Gary to let me see the specimen for a few minutes. He handed me the bag from his pocket with everything in it. I gave the hard copy of our work to Mina and I sat on the floor of the Vug to hold the thin section up into the Teran light to see what I can see using a hand lens I had picked up in Gary's lab. I was peering through the lens at the structure of the brain bone when we began to lower to the gathering below. A breathy "oh wow" came from our guest as he looked through the bottom of the Vug at the masses below. I knew just how he felt seeing this for his first time.

CHAPTER ELEVEN

Flade

The Vug came to a halt just above the surface of the Void and we stepped out. The Elders encircled us in several rows and were surrounded by an ocean of humanoids all watching us as we moved out of the Vug. Just then Gary began to collapse in convulsions as he fell to his knees, his face, neck, and arms turning a bright red. Horror swept over me as I looked at Mina and back at Gary several times searching for an answer to this behavior. Mina screamed out at the top of her lungs, "He's a Flade!"

His eyes filled with blood and his body swelled as he contorted in a crumpled form at our feet. Then, as if a machine, he raised up to eye level and began to glow with the same aura we saw surrounding Teranor on the surface. I realized what we were witnessing, but the Elders had known much earlier than I and they had not flinched. Gary was a human bomb, a drone made to destroy the core of these people. He had won our trust and infiltrated this world. One of the Elders stepped forward and touched the ticking bomb that suspended in front of us all. As he touched Gary's face with his hands the process appeared to stop. Gary's writhing and twisting ceased and the nimbus faded. His eyes cleared and the grimace dissolved from his lifeless face as his body straightened and stood upright floating just above the floor. The light of life returned to his eyes and he whimpered in a slight squeal of pain and remorse. Gary looked into my eyes with a sadness of regret and confused emotion. The Elder shot into the air above and disappeared in the Gray above us all. The remaining Elders began to explain that a Flade was a body used for infiltration and demolition. "They are hard to spot until they are set to detonate," a voice came from the group explaining some of what we had just seen.

Mina explained, "Flades are drones made from average humanoids or animals. The iron in their blood platelets is bonded with a high explosive and fluid memory is installed in the blood that gives the self-destruct command and concentrates the blood for priming and detonation. Micro biobots were most likely installed into Gary's brain to control his actions and to force him to go along with the conspiracy. He had no control of himself during this ordeal, and for the most part he knew not what he was doing. It is all remotely controlled and independent of usual conscious functions. We have lost the Elder who sacrificed his life to save Gary. His memory is ours now and we shall keep him in our thoughts and prayers. There is severe damage to Gary, but we will repair him and give him better health with which to function. Gary also harbored a serious cancer, which was removed by the Elder who has gone."

Mina and I moved away from the center of the masses as the Elders went to work healing our new guest. Jasmina told me this was extremely close even for the Terans. She continued to clarify for me, "The Elders suspected this might be a possibility, so they were entirely prepared for the potential of a trick like this."

My mind turned to the work we had done. Obviously all the work was a decoy and the emails were never sent. But we were there; I watched the work done. I had the thin section and the memory stick in my pocket. Mina had the hard copy. Could it be that in spite of the bio-bots, Gary was able to perform independent functions and did he actually send off those emails? We would soon learn from Gary once his mind and body were cleared of the infiltration of Teranor technology.

Mina looked at me as I worried, "If they got to one of my best friends like this, then nobody on the surface is safe and nobody can be trusted. This would explain why so many of my competitors are jerks and why Claus Laurent is such a royal pain in the ass."

I could see the red around Laurent in my mind's eye. The guy had come close to offing me several times or at least paid some dirty dog to take me out, and all for a few lousy rocks. Well, that was then, now these stones held a great deal more importance, which explains why he had been so relentless in his pursuit of me. And now I understood why this stone was always referred to as the sacred Touchstone; it was able to impart the endless memory of these people in a single touch. I was feeling anxious to speak with Gary. A humming chant came from his direction and I could hear Gary cry out; it sounded painful. We both floated overhead to see what was being done to our friend.

The Elders were finished with the work and Gary lay there on a bed of moss. One of the Elders gestured for us to come. We moved down to their level and listened to what was said. We were told he would be perfectly healed following a brief rest while their energy aligned the cells in his body and brain. He handed us a strange, clustered, wire-like construction that looked something like an octopus. It appeared to be part mechanical and part biological. Along each wire and at the terminal end of each was a group of tiny, finger-shaped formations. The Elder told us that this was new tech that was hardwired into his core and connected to pretty much everything inside him. He didn't feel the pain, but his body reacted with simulated pain to resist the complete removal of this contraption. "Now he is clear of all outside manipulation. He may stand alone in this world," said the Elder as he gently hinted a smile and began to move off. Mina and I thanked him for his contribution and for the sacrifice made by the Elders. He simply raised his hand as he moved away as if to say, "What is done, is done."

Moments later a wave of energy soared through all of us as it moved across the terrain and sifted through everything in this world below. Jasmina told me this was the life force of the Elder who sacrificed his term to save the others of us who stood encircling Gary as he began detonation. She told me that the Elder's energy was in all of us now and that he would continue to live on in each of us. "His conscious thought will become part of the memory within the brain bone; only his body is gone from our world," Mina explained, "as will we all someday."

We walked for some time to find our calm and to talk about what should be done now. Eventually we would need to talk with Gary about what might be salvaged from our work in his lab. Fortunately, we still held the fragments and the thin section as well as a hard copy of our findings. For now the immediate priority was security. If the Teranor were able to get this close, then what other hazards were closing in on us? In my mind, I could see a myriad of horrible contraptions developed for capture, torture, and killing. Based on this most recent event, the Teranor were able to incorporate both biological and mechanical technology into their arsenal of weaponry. It gave me a sickening feeling to think of them, up there, devising their next plan of attack. What nasty artifact will they implement next and where will it rear its ugly head?

As we strolled amongst the giant trees, Mina's people filtered off into the distance. Many of them came by us to silently touch our shoulders in a gesture of support. From a distance we could see that Gary was standing now and speaking with the Elders. He seemed immersed in the conversation so we left him there to get his fill of answers while we enjoyed some time to ourselves walking and watching as the creatures around us went about their subsistence. What we learned from Gary might determine where we went from here. This may be what the Elders were working on right now. It was good to see my old friend standing there, and I knew he was ecstatic about his new lease on life and the opportunity to learn everything about this new world we had brought him into. When we arrived back at the center of the gathering, we were made aware that Gary had been enlightened by the Elders. They felt that his mind could handle the answers and they gave him the gift of an enlarged memory as well. Gary was enabled to answer his own questions. He seemed very calm and collected.

"Hello there, Gary," I greeted him with a reassuring grin, "Welcome to your new life. They removed everything bad from your body and brain, including a nasty little cancer you had been lugging around in your pancreas. You were quite a prize there, ole G.W. Did you have any idea of what was going on inside you?" Gary quietly shook his head no.

"Could you feel anything?" I pried, unrelenting.

"Nothing, " he replied.

"Gary, do you know if the emails were sent? Obviously they triggered the Teranor to raid your home." Gary was not sure, he described how everything seemed to be a fog and he felt like a puppet on a string with no will or independent thought. He said that he knew it felt wrong to come with us to the Void, but he had no idea of why he felt that way. He continued to describe the screaming pain he felt as we drew close to the gathering. He said that his mind went blank as the pain raged, a pain that would have inspired any man to wish his own death if only to end the agony.

Mina broke in to say, "We call this a 'death wish weapon'; they are an insidious creation of mayhem from an innately violent time, now Gary understands the nomenclature."

"Wait a minute," Gary expounded; "I sent emails to a large group of random friends with no scientific affiliation; that was me, I did that independent of any outside affect. In my mind, there is no question that these emails were pulsed out to the recipients unnoticed or traced. There are roughly fifty six hundred people on that list and many of them know me well and are connected in government or the science services; our word did get out there! If just one of those people releases that information, then it will go viral and our quest has made its first quantum leap."

The three of us smiled at each other, delighted at knowing that there might still be a chance that our attempt would not fail. It was time to show Gary around and get some food into him. We settled near a small stream and each ate a nutrition pod while Gary asked Mina a few questions. He knew the answers, but it seemed to help to hear them spoken by another. Jasmina explained to him how fluid memory works within the bloodstream and that the blood of a human body can carry memory in the blood platelets that can be accessed utilizing an octopus installed into the cerebral cortex with fingers attached to the central nervous system. With a nuclear trigger, every atom within the body becomes an integral part of the bomb, Plutonium chargers attached to the iron in the blood operate as the fuse and igniter, the perfect, walking weapon.

Mina explains, "Basically, Gary, you were sleep walking from the day they installed the device. Your actions under this level of influence and control are a testimonial to the admirable strength of the human mind. Even when you were a human robot you still managed to perform independent thoughts and actions sending this separate email pulse, unnoticed and untraced, to a large number of witnesses. Your successful effort is the spark that will ignite a raging fire of change in this world of ours and begin the new era for our peoples. We shall prevail over the Teranor and we shall save our world for the future ages."

Thinking that Gary might wish to see more of New Tera, we walked to the Vug. As we stepped inside, Gary volunteered that he would like to see one of the windows. I had to agree to myself that this was one of the more amazing features of Tera. As we flew through the Void, Gary admitted his mind was in a torrent of turmoil over all of the physics standards that he was taught in school and how many of those standards were being shattered. He still couldn't get his head around the fact that people were flying everywhere at incredible speeds. Soon we arrived at one of the massive windows, and as we slowed and neared the ocean porthole a pod of gray whales cruised across our view into the deep blue brine. Gary's jaw was locked open and his head slumped forward like the true nerd that he is. He was a kid in a candy store and he reminded me of myself just a few short days ago. I could understand everything he was feeling right now. In fact, I could hear his thoughts, which were close to exactly my reaction when I saw all this. The whales were a bonus for all of us. Mina told us that it was rare to see the whales come this close to any of the windows. The Vug took us past the window and off into the Void to view the columns; then we sped into an area filled with lush forest and a scattering of the giant trees. We stopped there to pick some nutrition pods. Mina put several in a bag that hung around her waist. Hmm, were we taking another trip?

Each of us enjoyed a pod as we continued in the Vug through the Void viewing all manner of new creatures. Gary and I were both mesmerized by the view as we traveled for many miles while the terrain changed below and above. The colors and illumination were beyond describing; this was the best way to share the sensation with someone from the surface.

In Gary's typical sharing fashion, he looked over at us and commented, finishing with an inquiry, "I can't wait for the rest of the human race to see this, wow, what a head hack! I don't ever have to leave this, do I?" I laughed with him as we both looked to Mina for an answer. It was a strange mix of emotion as we enjoyed this unbelievable new fantasy world. We needed to remain focused on the serious aspects of staying alive and working diligently to save this amazing world from Teranor devastation. We settled into a deep, detailed discussion about what our next moves should be and where to go next. Gary made the great observation that we needed to set up a protected base of operations where we could make shielded contact with the outside world and where we could produce evidence and proof for the doubting masses we would encounter. We also needed to devise an offensive to throw the Teranor into a defensive mode. We were going to make their lives miserable and do serious damage to their infrastructure wherever possible.

"Mina," I questioned, "Just what kind of infrastructure might the Teranor have here on Earth?" Jasmina told us that the Teranor might be deeply integrated into the human race and we would have to rely on the Elders for a great deal of help in dealing with this matter. She went on to explain that it might take time for her people to adjust to any plan that resorted to a use of violence. Teran abilities were designed for defense and protection and not for aggression. In my mind, I recalled the power we used in Vienna; Gary could see images of our actions. When he saw the Teranor pursuers fly across the hall and slam into the stone wall, falling limp to the floor, he acknowledged that we had a good start. Ghosting and shielding would also be powerful tools and we would need to master those abilities. "But," I said, looking at Mina, "we're going to need a more impressive and powerful weapon to take out the enemy."

Jasmina told us that she could target adversaries with severe memory loss and that she could perform mind control, which the Teranor could not master. "Also," she said, "we can fly and they cannot; we can swim endless distances and they cannot; we can walk the Gray and they cannot. My voice can render them deaf, either temporarily or permanently, and I can turn most anything into a deadly projectile. One last weapon is one of relentless destruction: the particle beam. In our millions of years of learning to master energy, Terans found that we can project our energy in focused, incredibly destructive, plasma energy, particle beams. It is exhausting to utilize but it can stop and destroy virtually anything. Terans refuse to utilize this ability as the taking of even one life may alter the course of the future. A life, human or Teran, is sacrosanct and no matter how evil that individual may be, we believe all creatures have right to the life given."

Gary directed his pointed question at me, "What makes you believe we can win this battle to save Earth?"

"She does," I replied without hesitation, tipping my head in Mina's direction. "She is my guiding star and my path." A murmuration of Mizlets soared above us, changing formation as if painting the sky with their wings, millions of wings beating as one. As they shifted position the colors of their wings changed in a wave that moved opposite the direction of their flight. The flashes of color and movement bounced off the reflective waters below and filled our eyes with the dance of light.

Gary looked at us both and blurted out, "I will do anything to save this Paradise!" We needed a next move. With any luck the information about the brain bone meteorite was out, now working its way into the minds of humans. Soon we would need to back that up with another reveal, and then eventually we would need to meet with world leaders to take this effort to the next level. Each time we went to the surface, we risked contact with the Teranor. It would be fairly ideal if we could perform effective work from here in the Void. Right now we needed to find a way to see if emails got to their destinations. Gary volunteered that he sent a few dummy emails to dormant accounts to which he holds the passwords. If we could get to a monitor, then we would be able to verify receipt.

Jasmina suggested a way we could do this without being approached. "There are closed underground military bases throughout the globe. Many of them have power sources intact and computer systems installed."

Gary said, "That's right, they're all over the planet; I can think of several that might be perfect, deep underground with extremely complex access codes, and some of those are obsolete so that even military officials would have to break in. Let's find one of those and get started on verifying our success." Mina agreed that we can approach a base in the Vug and enter from the bottom so there would be no sign of entry. "Let's do that now," Gary responded with his usual enthusiasm.

We all wanted to know how far we had gotten in our first attempt, and instantly we were under way in the Vug headed for a base deep in the ground below a long closed installation in New Mexico. Gary was certain that the secured bunker entry system was loaded with redundancies and that if we were approached, we would have plenty of early warning. Upon arrival the Vug slowly rose up out of the Gray of solid stone through Corten steel reinforced concrete walls and into the total dark of a room built for just this sort of action. Lights flickered on as we stepped out of the Vug. The room was a command center designed to have everything we currently needed. Gary walked to the wall and flipped open a breaker panel to power up the room. Immediately, he moved to the main monitor to start the computer. He took measures as if he had been here before. As Gary keyed in the startup codes, he announced that this was what he did while working on his Master's and PhD; he did civilian position labor for the military installing computer networks in subterranean military bases all over the U.S. These bases were designed to be powered independently and built deep enough to evade Electromagnetic Pulse weapons.

The link with the outside world was a hard wire separator that could be manually or remotely connected. We needed to get hooked up, confirm our success, and get gone as quickly as possible. Chances were good that very soon military personnel would know that we had compromised this facility and someone would rush to the site. Gary got the computer running and began to log onto the web. He commented with a chuckle that it amazed him that after all these years his backdoor codes were still viable passcodes. Soon we three were staring at the email he sent to himself while he was working as a zombie in his lab at home. A feeling of cheer came over us as we read the first lines of data. I could see Gary's smiling face in the reflection of the computer screen.

Mina slipped her arm under mine and weaved her fingers into my hand. Gary scrubbed our access to leave no evidence behind and shut down the system. We backed out just as we had entered, breaking the outside link and shutting off the power supply. Gary wiped off his fingerprints and we stepped back into our ride, slipping again into the Gray. Our new partner shook his head slowly as we began to travel through the Earth's crust, "I'll never get used to this," he confessed in amazement, "and I will never take this for granted."

I felt the importance of what he was saying. What we were doing right then broke every rule of physics that was pumped into his mind through all the years of higher education. A part of Gary would be excited by the new knowledge and learning, but part of him would be filled with despair over all of the crap he was taught as gospel. In the future it would pain Gary to erase from his mind all of the doctrine he was forced to memorize, even teach as a "farce clone" spewing a tangled web of speculation and theory. The poor guy was in agony as the truth took hold of his mind and spirit.

I leaned over to Gary and whispered to him, "Focus only on our future and let your past be gone. The sooner you let go, the lighter everything will become." I could see the tension release in his shoulders as he let down and began to work this through in his head. Continuing with wisdom from something I had read once, "Free the mind from worry, free the heart from hatred, live simply, give more and expect less."

Jasmina bumped her forehead against mine, and I could feel her smile. She said in a soft, loving voice, "There's my dearest Bryce Monroe." She put her hands on my shoulders and we continued to lean into each other until long after the Vug had popped out of the Gray and soared deep into New Tera. With our heads touching we traveled into a quiet place of pure thought where time stood still. Gary shared his thoughts about an idea that had been stirring about in that brilliant mind of his. His thinking was that soon scientists and government officials would begin to hear of our probe work. He suggested that we make a video of this world below and launch it on the web. His thinking was that we would need to win the help of humanity if we were going to stand against the Teranor for the possession of the Earth.

As we traveled, Mina told us that we must meet with the Elders again to ask their help. She would like the Elders to create a way to survey how many Teranor there were hiding in plain sight on the surface. One of her thoughts was that if we could not travel the ribbon to and from Earth, then maybe their travel was limited as well. That would mean there were a finite number of Teranor present to be dealt with. She went on to say that maybe there was a way to confine all of the Teranor and restrict their movement and communication while we introduce Mankind and Terankind. Our minds and imaginations were limited but with all of the brain power of the Teran population behind us, we might come up with more creative ways to approach this dilemma.

We vugged through EarthUnder making our way to a meeting that Jasmina had called with the Elders. When we arrived, the Elders have already conferred with each other regarding our ideas. They immediately entered into a dialogue with us about what they felt they could do to help. It seemed that they did not wish to generate any form of conflict. The Elders did reveal that they had already seen the numbers of Teranor presently breathing on the surface of the planet. They had also tallied the Teranor population elsewhere in other parts of the cosmos. The Elders explained that they had closed the X-points near Earth and had moved the magnetic portholes close to the sun to seal Earth from approach. Soon the Teranor were going to feel trapped and they would recognize that they too were in danger. They had their chance to be left alone and they chose to be the aggressor, taking lives while destroying planets and civilizations. Apparently the Teran Elders were prepared to draw a line in the sand, and I got the feeling that these people could back it up with more force and conviction than the Teranor were prepared to handle.

As we conferred with the Elders I began to understand where some of Mina's powerful inner strength came from. Having the support of these wise souls is a magnanimous boon to one's spirit, knowing that the strength of all your people can meld into the power of one: that is my Mina's gift to this world. She is the culmination and the epitome of both our races; she is the standing stone. I am in love with a woman who is infinitely more than I can ever be and somehow, magically, she has loved me for many lifetimes. How lucky am I? I love a walking weapon with the power of an entire planetary population at her fingertips.

Jasmina listened to my sarcastic thought. Her response was simply factual and level minded, "The mentors coach us to temper our thinking and to try to see a way out of conflict. If we respond to the Teranor with the same form of violence they practice, then we shall all lose our peace, our lives, and our home planet. If we can inspire the Earthlings to help and persuade the Teranor to depart without doing damage to this world, then everyone gets to live out their lives without memories of war and suffering in their past. In a global conflict there are no winners, even the planet loses."

The Elders implored us to work hard and fast toward a peaceful solution to this dilemma. They knew well the hazards of trying to coexist with these evil doers. As we prepared to depart from the Elders, one of them spoke up to tell Gary that he would have to stay behind. All three of us were stunned and halted by this proclamation. The Elder elaborated, "When we removed the controller from your brain stem, there was severe damage to the cerebrum and the medulla oblongata. The irreversible damage caused during its installation forced us to perform a transplant of your central nervous system. Your knowledge and memories are still your own, but we have given you the brain of one of our most revered Elders; his brain was still youthful and vibrant when his body had run its course. You have within you not only your own life memories, but you also have all of the memories and knowledge of an Elder of our kind. We would like to ask you to remain here with us to help bring our worlds into balance." It seemed the most natural action as Gary moved toward the Elders; when he turned to face us with his broad smile beaming, we knew this was meant to be. There was no need for goodbyes as we would remain in constant contact with one another.

CHAPTER TWELVE

Teranor Captive

Mina and I stayed with the Elders for several surface cycles to receive training in dealing with the Teranor. Brain bone memory of past conflicts and deceptions were brought to mind during our exercises. Tears gushed from our eyes as our emotions welled up from witnessing so much death and loss. The Elders shared with us countless possible scenarios and enlightened us on their numbers, concentrations, activities, strategies, and intentions. It was like getting a mental map of everything that the Teranor thought they were keeping shielded from prying eyes. We appeared to have the upper hand, but deception can disguise a fickle outcome.

Our training finished with wishes for safety and success. I couldn't clear my thoughts of the damage and suffering caused over and over again by the Teranor. My human side could not comprehend how the Terans had endured such tyranny for so many lifetimes. Compassion turned to rage with every image of conflict or aggression now depicted in memories from past generations. It was impossible to know what to do with these feelings. My heart ached with the agony of millions of lost lives and tortured souls. I saw entire planets thrust into a rapidly dying hell when the atmosphere diminished and inhabitants competed for the last remnants of food, water, and breathable air, their pride and productivity long erased from their lives and the last glimmer of hope flickering out like a candle in wind. Memories were filled with dire emotion and despair. Blood flowed, tissue burned and voices cried out in agony as thriving planets were scraped of resources and a dry, dead hull was relinquished. In distant consciousness were the faces of Teranor, proud of their harvest and devastation. They were blind to compassion, deaf to the cries of those they crushed. They were consumers, takers, a greed-obsessed breed of monstrous affliction, trained only on the next bountiful orb. I felt a keenly intense obsession by the Teranor for Earth; they knew we were here. Their seething lust for more had turned to an unrelenting craving for revenge.

Both Mina and I could see what the Teranor would do to the Elders if we failed to protect Earth from their despicable corruption. Wise words of the Elders rang in mind, "The appearance of good from violence is temporary, but the evil of violence will last eternal." My human side kept telling me to fight fire with fire. Mina reminded me that the Terans have survived for many millions of years and that we might have to relocate to evade conflict. My first instinct was to stand and fight, but then, how do we go up against planet killers? The Teranor had developed technology far beyond the scope of my imagination. They had created ways to scour entire planets and squeeze them like a sponge to wring out every last drop of what they find of value to their own continuation. In the mind of a Teranor, mowing down humanoids or other life forms is no more significant than leveling a field of grain or weeds for that matter. And we are to them nothing more than weeds standing in the way of their progress. I could feel Mina searching for an answer to our challenge. For ages Jasmina's people disguised Earth as a dying planet by creating an image from space of desert lands overtaking the lush green while the ice caps melted away, generating floods and storms.

Some 260 million years ago Mars was taken by the Teranor and Earth was left as a less attractive candidate for harvest because even then it appeared as a dying planet. Much of the life on Mars was moved in secret to EarthUnder, where it was shielded from view. Many of those creatures were not able to adapt and expired. Mars, which once held grand oceans of water, lush forests, and grass-covered steppes is the scoured, scorched, rock sphere we see glowing red in the night sky, red with the aura of Teranor devastation.

Now the Teranor have come full circle to return to our solar system prepared to take from this less attractive planet. They find that their passive yet powerful enemy resides within the shell surface of New Tera. The act of revenge is far more important to them than taking this planet for their gain. One can feel the lust they have for retribution for having been abandoned on Tera.

I could not understand how the Elders remained so calm knowing that everything might be lost. "Free the mind of worry, free the heart from hatred" rings in my ears as the words were repeated for me by my lovely companion while she watched my thoughts and shared my concerns. She too appeared to be unusually calm and collected. How could anyone live calmly under conditions of such tremendous threat of imminent harm?

Jasmina saw the same scenes that I could recall from the gift of memory imparted to me. Horror took hold as entire races of humanoids and all manner of creature were made to vanish. I could see individuals explode into vapor and could hear the cries and screams as millions were decimated in a single fell swoop. The Teranor had utilized countless insidious parasites to invade and demolish entire world populations. One creature that I saw in my mind was the Headworm, which infiltrates its host through the ear, nose, or throat and renders the body paralyzed. The host could breathe and communicate, but could not swallow, so without food or water, the host would die in three days, days of anguish and agony.

The Teranor inundated planetary populations with creatures of this type. Once numbers were diminished, the dark ones ignored the remaining few survivors while they ripped the life elements from each planet they destroyed. It appeared that the Teranor were taking these assets and resources to a giant planet that they inhabited in a shielded galaxy. They used gamma radiation burst powered portholes to carry these resources back to their corner of the universe. Utilizing these space portholes, the Teranor could move objects from as small as grains of silica to the size of their massive, ancient, plasma-drive warships. With the power of the Terans pushing these X-points into the sun there would be no arrivals or departures for anyone.

The issue now was how to deal with the invaders who were already here on our planet. Could we isolate them? Could we stop their conspired intentions and could we somehow get them all to go away forever? Maybe we could get inside their brains and eliminate the part that produced aggression?

"That's it," Mina proclaimed, leaping to action! "You've done it, Bryce; we need to present this idea to the Terans. We can enter the minds of every Teranor on Earth and steal away the part in each brain that causes them to aggress. Then we can collect all of that bad energy, thought, and memory and incinerate it. We must meet with our people immediately."

The Elders agreed that there was a way this would work. They revealed a count of roughly three million Teranor on the planet and a large faction of human recruits and disciples. They too would need to be treated for this horrendous behavior with a mental alteration. One of the Elders spoke, "We will need to perform this on an individual Teranor to be certain we can completely remove this part of the memory without risk of retrogradation. Jasmina, do the two of you believe you can capture a Teranor and bring it here for us to test?"

Mina nodded yes, and I backed her up by saying that it was going to be a lot easier than trying to take on the entire invasion force of Teranor. The Terans smiled at my statement. They seemed to be amused by human candor. Mina smiled as well and as we walked back to the Vug, she put an arm under mine and said, "They enjoy one of the traits that I love in you."

We took off in the Vug heading away from the areas I had become familiar with. It felt like we were deep under a continent and far from the edge of any oceans. The pressure in the air here seemed heavier and darker, but there was the same brilliant light and color. People and creatures moved about as elsewhere, but something felt unlike other areas of New Tera. We lowered and slowed, coming to rest in the gaping mouth of a cavern in a wall of rock. We stepped out of the Vug and Mina led me into the pitch black of this stony throat. As eyes adjusted to the darkness, the cave appeared to be a warehouse stacked with crates. Mina explained that we were here to find implements that would help us on the surface to silence and abduct a Teranor for the test. These were tools and artifacts from another time that were not used in New Tera. She opened a crate and handed its contents to me. It appeared to be a halter for a horse. From another crate she pulled shackles and cuffs. Then back to the Vug we went.

Walking out of the darkness and stopping in front of the Vug, Mina took the artifacts out of my hands and bent to place them into the Vug. Just as I stepped to follow Mina into the Vug, something grabbed me from behind. I was abruptly flying back into the cave as Mina screamed, "It's a Taker; ghost, Bryce, ghost now!"

My abilities having grown keener, I ghosted in an instant, the contraption lost its grip on me, and I drifted to a stop. Jasmina sprinted toward me and past, running into the pitch-black dark of the cave. I could hear her voice in my head telling me to follow. If there was a Taker in the cave, then there had to be a Teranor or surface access. She could see the faint red glow of a body fleeing into the depths of the cavern. The Taker was a four-pronged gauntlet on hinges, controlled from a chain that reeled in the Taker and carried the captive to an end. It was yet another evil artifact from a less civilized time. A Teranor was in this cavern and if we could capture it, then we could learn of its origin and use this evil one for our test. If there was one Teranor here, then more would come, which meant that an invasion was certain. We had to catch this monster or rush to the surface to capture another. Either way the Elders had to be warned and the cavern had to be sealed. I caught up with Mina as she took care not to pass by the well-hidden aggressor.

Just then a long spear hurtled out of the dark traveling so fast we could hear the wind sliced by the razor edges of the trident blade. In less than one beat of her heart, Mina repulsed the spear as a gurgling scream emanated from the dark. Mina raised her hand and brought the Teranor out, glowing with the crimson of blood, eyes shining yellow in the dark. Mina commanded it to stand as she checked the narrow end of the cave for a passage, but it was solid stone. She returned to hold the Teranor in place while the Vug brought us the restraints. After wrapping the evil one, we took him back into the open, where he screeched in spite of the halter, his eyes burning from the light of this world. Mina notified the Elders of our discovery and soon we were back with the Elders.

The Vug lowered to the ground as Gary arrived to greet us. "That was fast," Gary quipped. We pulled the Teranor out of the Vug and stood him in front of the Elders. A perpetual flow of Terans formed masses of bodies surrounding our core group around the red, glowing intruder. These Terans had never seen a Teranor. As the crowd pressed closer the Teranor drooled and snarled at the bodies surrounding him. Talleyrand appeared overhead and lowered into the gathering. His silver hair hung over his shoulders like virga rain. Talleyrand's body was sheathed in a mirror-bright metallic skin suit, hands encased in gloves fabricated from woven wire. He strode with deliberation directly to the intruder with no hesitation and slapped his glove-covered hands onto both sides of the Teranor's cranium. There were no sounds and no thoughts from the onlookers as the corrupted captive fell to his knees and screamed out his hatred. He screamed and screeched until sound ceased to vibrate from his vocal chords. His eyes began to bleed as they rolled up into his head and the red aura faded as the Elder took evil from the spirit of this monster. He lurched and writhed as thick, dark crimson sludge oozed from his nose and mouth.

Talleyrand finished his contact as the body of the Teranor slumped to the ground. The Elder turned towards the others and announced that the process was completed. He asked that the Teranor be cleaned and the evil be disposed of. Talleyrand removed the gloves from his hands as I confronted the Elders to speak. The human in me blurted out that if there was one, then there must be more. Talleyrand agreed that while he was removing the evil in the captive's brain, he did see the outline of a master plan to invade New Tera.

Talleyrand spoke, "This was a front runner, there are more, many more to come. We must act now, and swiftly, to counter their plans. I have seen into their minds and I can say what they will do next. There is no time to prepare the humans for what we must now do. The Teranor have prepared Headworms, Ice Flies, and Cordyceps fungi for release into the surface population. We will dispatch the Mizlets to handle this threat. We shall dedicate our population to removing evil from the Teranor, but their leadership has been shielded and we shall require a specialized team to deal with the Teranor imperious elite. Jasmina, you and your Bryce Monroe Sterling will lead a large, swift, trained team to the surface to encounter the Teranor leaders. You will need to make tactile contact with each individual leader to bring this conspiracy to its critical halt. The Elders feel this is our only way to begin saving the planet."

CHAPTER THIRTEEN

Fierce Offensive

Mina and I had begun our work, letting the surface population know that the Terans are here. That effort would have to simmer for a time while the Teran Elders put us to task stopping the Teranor leaders. Gary approached us with a group of Terans, a count of thirty determined looking individuals dressed in metallic, Encounter Skinsuits. Gary handed Encounter Suits to Jasmina and me, and wished us good luck and farewell. As we dressed in our Skinsuits, an ancient, white-haired Elder approached. Her skin was creviced with deep smile lines; she had eyes blue as a clear late evening sky, and as old as she appeared from a distance, her eyes were as young as a child's. Her smile smacked of humor and wisdom, while her broad shoulders hinted at her inner strength. She pressed a hand over each of our heads, pushing us to take a knee. Thoughts and images streamed into our heads: the knowledge and power we would require to perform this task was installed. She lifted her hand and waved it in front of our eyes as if to sign her work completed. She looked up and flew into the Void.

Mina then led me to our recruits, where we then shared our training with them. She told me that it would come as needed and that if I let go and simply acted on instinct, the teaching would control my moves and decisions. My trust in Jasmina made this much easier to accept. As I searched my mind, I could find no apparent changes in thinking or memories. I felt like the lamb being told to play in front of the wolf, that his teeth had no bite. We were venturing into the wolf's den but Jasmina assured, "We are the ones with teeth."

It is always dark on half of the surface. The Mizlets had been dispatched, millions of them sent rushing to the surface to find and obliterate the masses of wicked creatures being unleashed on the sleeping populace of Earth. Like fireflies they flickered their way to the top of the Void and submerged into the Gray. Soon Earth would be engulfed by a silent war, which would follow the sun as it dipped to the horizon.

As the creatures began their night stalk, Mizlets would find and destroy them. Millions of Terans banded together to focus on each of the Teranor on the surface and begin the change. It was our time now; we had to emerge on the surface and begin the quest to find and capture each of the Teranor Imperials. There were seven of the leaders here on the planet, according to the Elder assessment of the Teranor invasion. In addition to Earth, there were Terans working to cognize if other Teran worlds might have invasion hordes present. The Elders shared that some worlds had been lost already. The knowledge of loss added a sense of urgency to our mission. Our team loaded into Vugs and blitzed for the surface.

As we moved through the Gray above the Void, Jasmina and Talleyrand were speaking back and forth while the remainder of our group listened to the conversation.

Talleyrand was telling Mina that the Teranor leaders were not in positions of authority on the surface. They were blended in with the most common of residents, camouflaged as criminals and corrupt executives. Our first target was stationed as a convict in a prison complex. He would be the simplest to approach as we could use the Vug to access his cell through the floors and walls of the concrete structure and ghost the halls in and out. Our mission was to capture and contain, then remove the Teranor Imperial from the surface and deliver him to the Elders for treatment. The Vug put us inside a wall just across from the cell holding this first target.

Half of the team waited outside the cell while the rest of us entered the small concrete cubicle where the Teranor was standing facing us as we entered. We were ghosting, but he appeared to see us just the same. Obviously he was an Elder of the evil ones; his posture displayed that he was ready to resist. Two from the lead group moved in to take him when his chest swelled and they were thrust back through the wall. Four more charged at him and were sliced into four quarters. They lay lifeless on the floor as blood drained from their parts. There were two more from our team in the front row with Mina and me. The Teranor raised his hands to use another weapon from his arsenal when suddenly a fiery shaft of light appeared from behind us and in a flash the beam atomized the Teranor's neck and head, leaving its body standing for a moment, a gaping trough cleft into his torso cauterized and sizzling from the heat of cells disintegrated by light.

Jasmina flipped around in surprise to face a young-looking team member trembling, obviously shaken by his actions. She said nothing, putting a hand to his shoulder to offer thanks and support. The two team members by our sides took the body, which was still standing there as if it didn't believe it was dead yet. Other members recovered the bodies of our fallen companions and we moved back to the Vugs for the journey to the Void. As we traversed the Gray, we all felt the shock of loss. None of us had been prepared for the violence we encountered. Our team was rapidly coming up to speed on how ruthless evil can be when cornered. We were numbed by thoughts of life ending without warning. Much was learned in the blink of an eye. Hearts heavy with dread, the return to New Tera would be a torturous reunion. Deep inside I was relieved it wasn't me that took the shot, but overjoyed that someone did. It was naïve of us to assume that the Teranor would not be prepared to aggressively attack. Our approach would need to be far more careful and more aggressive in future attempts, or our team would not last.

As the Vugs lowered to the gathering I could see and feel the sadness. The illumination of New Tera was dim and the faces of Terans were turned downward, the light of their eyes absent from view. As the bodies of the fallen ones were gently carried away, there were flashes of light and dark waves pulsing through the Void. Jasmina told me that the Mizlets were also losing numbers as they battled to stop the Teranor release of their insidious parasites. Jungles, forests, deserts, and ice caps had become a battlefield. As we prepared to depart again, replacements joined our team. My gut told me that they were meat for the slaughter after what we saw already. The words of George Fitzgerald, a wise old friend, spoke in my mind, "It can always be worse." This time, I questioned his wisdom. He also frequently used to say, "Good always comes from bad." It was hard to see through this pearl of wisdom.

As the Vugs lifted off again, I looked down at these people and pondered why the Elders felt it so important that we not take lives on the surface. They seemed as sad for the loss of the monster as they were for the lost members of our team. The Teran in me was not helping me understand this logic. Trying to figure this out would need to wait while we continued our mission.

Our next target was a noted Wall Street broker. He would be easy to locate but difficult to take. We had to assume that he would take fast action to destroy us and we all felt more prepared to take on this opponent. There were no plans. How do you plan for the unknown? We arrived below street level, early morning, just outside his office tower. We staged the Vugs and entered the building from four sides to hopefully box him in. The Elders conveyed to us that he was already here and waiting in his office. Mina could see him in his office and the floor was littered with his bodyguards. We left our team on the ground floor and Mina and I flew while ghosting to the top floor and the window of his office. Mina reached out with her arms and encapsulated the leader in a tensile energy case, then threw him out through the window. This monster was growling as he struggled within our trap; he threw fireballs in our direction that bounced off the lining of the case and struck back at him. I held my arms out to add power to Mina's creation, and we lowered to the ground where our team waited to join us in the Vugs. It was a loud and violent journey back to the Void to deliver our first captive.

The Terans were there waiting for our arrival. They appeared mournful as we slowed to a stop and produced the first captive. They were gentle as they took him. He struggled to get free as Mina transfered her grip to the group waiting to take hold of this evil monster. I was curious about the pending process, but it was time to leave again on our next attempt at capture. The next target would be tricky since "she" was a mercenary in a war zone in central Africa. We know where to go to get close, but had no clue of how we would make everything fall together. As we rose up to sail away in the Void, the aura of our recent captive was glowing below, illuminating the masses surrounding him. As we soared off Mina saw in my thoughts that I didn't understand the reverence with which the Terans received their new guest. She told me, "He is our brother. We feel compassion for him as he has taken the path of darkness and is lost." She continued, "We hope to save him. Over the millennia Terans have learned ways to save the Teranor from their own destruction and we can bring them back from the dark place they covet."

Now this made some sense, making it a lot easier for me to understand why we were not charging in, guns blazing, to take out our enemy. In the words of another human years ago, "We have met the enemy and he is us." We weren't trying to take out this enemy; we were working to save them. It wasn't the Teranor doing harm to the planets and their inhabitants; it was the evil inside them. The evil had become so integrated into the Teranor that there was no good on the surface. They had become the purest embodiment of evil, their actions unstoppable.

We traveled by Vug through the Atlantic Ocean and

eventually came to rest outside a jungle compound well hidden in a beautiful, lush green, mountainous area. Ghosting, our team began to approach the compound with care. There were Teranor wandering aimlessly outside the walls of the installation. Mina walked to one of them and put her hands on his shoulder. He had already been treated by the Terans as had the others. They seemed confused as they bounced about in the lush forest, heat and humidity making everything sticky wet. We walked, ghosting through the wall around the perimeter of the fortress. As we approached the central building Mina warned us with thought and gesture that our target was inside that structure. A few more careful steps and the one we were after leapt from the roof to land in front of us. Her eyes could not see us, but she knew we were there. When she lunged at Mina, I instinctively stopped her with a stunning blow of force from my outstretched arm. She was quick to recover and sprinted back towards our location when several of our team tackled her and held her down, using their energy to encase her for the ride back to the Elders.

We learned that each Teranor has perfected different abilities, as this one fought back using an energy beam from her hand. The beam sliced out through the hold on her and she began to aim for her captors. She seemed to target me and the two teammates next to me. As the beam came my way, I deflected it into the jungle and dove onto her arm to turn her hand towards her face. When she saw the beam moving her way she ceased emitting. Together with the other members, we carried the struggling leader into a Vug and not long after the encounter, we delivered our new prize to the gathering awaiting our arrival.

While we were there making our delivery, several of the Elders came to inform us that the remaining four Teranor leaders were gathered together in one location. Four of the Elders would be joining us on this final endeavor. Apparently their strength, skill, and wisdom were needed to deal with this many Teranor masters in one fell swoop. The power of this strategy felt good to me. I really wanted this to be over so that we could get to work on the other half of saving the planet: dealing with the enlightenment of Mankind about the pending death of our biosphere.

The final destination is Arcata, California, a fairly remote college town from which the Teranor recruit new Abecedarians during the four-year academic cycle. The Elders told us that in addition to running their operations from there, they have constructed a planet killer. This wicked device would induce a massive earthquake intended to break through the Earth's mantle and inundate New Tera with an uncontrollable flow of sea water, potentially splitting the planet in two. The Teranor objective was to generate irreversible destruction to the surface while distracting Teran attention long enough to begin their invasion of the under-Earth world Terans called home. The Teranor knew that only this would work, and since we controlled Earth's gravity, they had to allow us to live long enough for them to abscond with the resources. Their plan was to keep us too preoccupied to confront them. We had to take the masters now and by any means. These were strong words coming from an Elder. With these powerful members in our midst, the Vugs traveled at hyper speed. We arrived in Arcata almost instantly and emerged from the ground in full view of the town square. The Teranor masters were waiting there for us. It became clear to me that these evil masters must have abilities similar in strength and power to the Teran Elders. The Imperials had recruited an army of human disciples (Abecedarians), but we were ghosting so the humans had no clue of our numbers or location.

Battle began immediately as the evil ones threw everything they had at us. We stood our ground while our Elders deflected the entire onslaught sent our way. The humans scattered in confusion, most running for cover. Fires raged as beams cut through buildings and cars. Everything in the town square became a projectile as the Teranor tried to create enough chaos to cover an escape. A handful of our team jumped into action and tried to capture the leaders, but they were cut down by particle beams generated from one of the leaders. This one was obviously the most powerful and treacherous of the four. If there was a supreme leader, then he was the one. Mina and I joined one of our Elders in concentrating on this one while the remainder of our team assisted the other three Elders with the remaining Teranor leaders.

We closed in on this evil one as he moved swiftly and sent harm our way in many forms. He was able to hit us with a force like being struck by a heavy iron plate. We were dodging bullets and boards, evading fire and car bodies. Our adversary lowered his eyes onto Mina and thrust at her with his arms. I could see a plasma burst begin to emerge from his arms and I reacted instantly to protect my Jasmina. In a flash I cut the master's arms from his shoulders and they fell twitching to the grass. He screamed in anger and frustration at his loss. He began to cry out a tone that built into a roar, beginning to shake the ground beneath our feet. Mina let fly her beautiful voice, forcing the scream back into his throat, where it exploded, rendering his voice silent forever. Still, he struggled to damage our group and destroy our effort. The Elder with us threw his arms around this Teranor leader and called to our Vug to come get them. They left the conflict, heading back to the Void. Mina and I joined the others to finish the battle. Only two remained; one of them died in the fight and the other would live, but he would spend eternity on one leg. This leader was quickly taken away by an Elder with three helpers to keep the Teranor subdued. We had tried to use a more civilized approach, but there was no chance for our plan to work.

Part of our team remained behind to help clear out the town square and to transition the human recruits back into society. Mina said this would be the easy part and that nobody would remember anything when the team left to return to New Tera. We entered our Vug and raced to catch the others before they met with the Teran gathering. At arrival, the Teranor were sitting in front of the Elders. Talleyrand was speaking to those still alive after our confrontation. The strongest of them began to gurgle, coughing blood and smiling as if to laugh. Just then the ground around us shook violently.

"Mina, it's the planet killer," I yelled as I turned to find her looking at me. This archaic Teranor weapon of planetary destruction is a tectonic disruptor. It operates utilizing seismic instigation. Once it was triggered, there was no stopping the planet's reaction. The Terans closed their eyes and silently held back the damage as the harmonic vibration of the earthquake opened a crack in the Earth along the Pacific coast of North America. Water would pour into the Void, but the Terans were there in force and controlled this new window with their minds. They were prepared for this; the Elders had seen it coming. The Teranor had placed a failsafe device in their planet killer and had counted on the distraction to help them get free. There would be many more projects ahead for us to work on.

After the Mizlets finished traveling the globe destroying the infestation of extraterrestrial parasites, we would then need to search the planet for imbedded Teranor and any escaped parasites. We could hear screaming as the Elders began the lengthy process of removing the evil from these Teranor leaders. Once we had distracted their leadership, it was possible for the Terans to remove the sludge from the millions of Teranor, but the process would be much more extensive for the Elders to remove the dark energy and bring out the good in these leaders. For Mina and me, there was another serious project to re-activate: easing Man into understanding he is not alone in the universe. Gary was here and would help us come up with ideas for ways to make this happen. There was hope that his email had already started people questioning the age of the brain bone meteorite.

As I thought of issues yet to resolve on Earth's surface, Mina and I both conceived of our hideaway at the same time. We decided that for a time we would escape reality and go back to our cabin in the mountains north of the Great Lakes to look into the fire pit and watch the sun rise and fall for some cycles, and to spend time thinking with one mind. Thus far, our time communicating has been rushed and frantic under wild conditions, and we both felt the need to do some meditating around the fire and to enjoy watching days come and go. The cabin was calling to us both, and Mina informed Talleyrand that we were heading to the surface for a few days.

Moving to say goodbye to Gary, we heard the agonizing screams of the Teranor leaders being treated to remove the deep-rooted, dark evil they had guarded for many years. As we approached Gary, he greeted us with a goodbye. He already knew we were leaving for a short time. I had forgotten that although it was still Gary, he now had the brain and spine of a beloved Elder from his transplant. Mina touched her elbow to mine; I could feel her suggesting that I turn my head to view Talleyrand coming to speak with me. He seemed more intense and less composed as he approached. There had been much to be dealt with in recent times, but his mind seemed to be focused on future days. His approach was filled with deliberate intent and his eyes were locked in a grip with mine. As he drew near he placed a hand on my shoulder, his gaze sad and his words coming very slowly. His silver hair hung like curtains framing his face, obscuring the light that usually glowed as one peered into the windows to his soul.

His voice, warm with love and sincerity, came to mind with the message, "I will be with you forever and in all ways."

I felt he was the father that my human father could never be. My human father was a great man, but somehow he always seemed more like a stepfather. Talleyrand was a father figure for all Terans, but I felt a special connection with him beyond our brief time together. Thanking him for his mentorship and wisdom, we departed in our Vug for the surface and Mina's home in the desert to visit her village and to see her housekeeper Magna for a time.

CHAPTER FOURTEEN

Love Lost

While we were in Mina's village I can check on people we left in harm's way on the surface. Jasmina and I were both still feeling the cabin pulling us home for time in solitude. But for now we walked the worn sandstone steps to her desert home. It felt strange to be back on the surface in daylight. The desert sun stung my skin with tiny bites of cosmic rays filtered by hundreds of miles of polluted air. Pupils narrowed in reply to the sun's diminished, unrelenting attack. Sand ground beneath our footsteps walking towards the door of the grand house. Moving through the weathered wood door, Mina called out to Magna, who should have been awaiting our arrival out front. Jasmina felt something was not right. We stepped through each room with caution. Returning to the great hall, we split to survey the remainder of rooms.

A shrill scream echoed in the halls as Mina cried; "No, no, no!" Kneeling on the kitchen floor was Jasmina, her arms wrapped around Magna's legs, her tears soaking into the housekeeper's robe. The scene was a sickening nightmare of morbid cruelty; Magna was clinging to the stone wall, her fingers digging into the mortar between stones, eyes rolled up and sunken, life sucked from her body through her skull. A tall, dried, lifeless Cordyceps ascocarp had grown from her skullcap like the stem of a mushroom. Green spores that had leaped or drifted from the knobbed tip were attached to the wall above and beside the top of the stem. The Cordyceps was dead; Mizlets had not gotten there in time to save Magna.

Jasmina would never let go of this memory. The horrid image would haunt her dreams; it would dim the light of her days forever. Jasmina's infinite strength had found its limit. The Cordyceps were released here because they are an equatorial parasite that thrives and flourishes in the heat of deserts and jungles. The Headworms would be found near the forty-fifth parallel, both above and below, and the Ice Flies would inundate the frozen ice caps and any wintery climates of the planet. There was no knowing how much death had occurred before the Mizlets arrived. Our fairy-like friends are fast as light and deadly when needed. They had done what they were tasked to do, but they followed the night sky to work under the cover of dark. It takes the Earth twenty-four hours to turn once on its axis, but night in one area can span twelve hours, during which it was possible that many humans died.

I sat with Mina, her tears puddled at Magna's feet. There was nothing to do or say; all I could do was sit there with her while the pain of her loss tore at heart and soul. Night came and went. The next day was slow to go; the shadows grew long before Mina began to stir. She brought the Vug into the house and we gently laid Magna into the transport where she would be carried to the Void for interment.

Dread and sadness hung heavy in the air like a thick, cold morning fog. Life could not have less value as this loss ruled the day. Memory of this loss would return time after time, and only the distance of time would help heal the wound. We sent the Vug to be received by the Elders, where Magna would be properly cared for in preparation for the next level of her existence.

Jasmina spent days taking long, pensive, contemplative walks through her village, checking with her people to make certain that others were all right. It was hard for her. As strong as I had seen her, she was also equally sensitive and caring, and she was torn apart by the loss of several others in the village. The loss of lives included children, which seemed to bring anger to Mina. I had not seen that emotion in Jasmina, but the meaningless ending of children's lives struck her with powerful emotions of hate and anger. Across the village, families were mourning the loss of loved ones. We had to stay to help her village deal with their pain. It was hard to sleep at night. We worked until exhaustion closed our eyes, but the nightmares woke us both a short time later.

One sleepless night I sat at Mina's desk and logged onto her computer, where I soon learned a surprising discovery. Someone had gotten word out to world leaders from all walks of human life; it was Vanessa: she came through with the reveal. Vanessa had been accosted by the evil ones while we were in London and they had roughed her up and taken the samples we had left. But she had made a thin section of the brain bone. She was mystified by the specimen, and not long after her trouble had settled, she drew together a research team that dedicated their efforts to one task: to learn all they could about the origin of this extraterrestrial specimen. She presented this work to The Royal Society and put her career on the line presenting the findings. Again George's words came to mind, "Good comes from bad." If the evil ones had not been so cruel to Vanessa, she would not have committed to her research with such dogged dedication. The world changed while we were gone. Between the presentation of Vanessa's discovery and the parasite invasion, humans were beginning to awaken.

For a time Jasmina and I remained in her village helping families repair their lives. No days were better than others, as the pain of loss returned over and over in each house. Then a day came that stabbed like a blade through the hearts of us all; it was a busy day filled with visits to homes offering support and assistance. As we walked out into the street, the midday sun burned sweat from our foreheads. We staggered and halted, reaching out to each other as waves of bright energy blew past us, pulsing, one following the last. I could feel that this was tragic, but Mina knew that many lives had just been silenced; multiple body bombs had ignited, taking the lives of many of the Elders and the Terans around them. Gary's voice called out from the Void. The Teranor had hidden a number of agents in areas they had infiltrated within EarthUnder. Somehow they were not prevented from detonation, which leveled and scorched a large area of the Void, ending the lives of many. Gary was at his workstation and was missed by the blast, but Talleyrand's span was ended, along with other Elders and countless other Terans. I felt the tragic loss as spirits streamed through our bodies on their path to the next realm. One could see the light ring of each spirit as it passed, expanding into the Cosmos. The sadness was tactile; it hung in our hearts and in the air like dark matter, dense and unable to bear. Living history and great wisdom were lost, voices silenced forever.

We stayed in Mina's village helping with her people while keeping vigil through Gary. Gary was finding that the work Vanessa had presented was having a huge impact on global awareness of life elsewhere. He observed that people were making assumptions in the right direction and that soon they might be ready for the next level. Days morphed into weeks and months as we did what we could to help rebuild lives here in the desert.

Eventually we took our trip to the cabin in the woods. Insects and animals had also died in the early hours of the invasion, but nature was taking care of the loss and new life was making its way into the world. Mina and I spent seemingly innumerable hours meditating by the fireside. We stood arm in arm at the crest of the waterfall watching the sun rise in the morning mist, while we spent evenings enjoying the last fluttering wing beats of creatures making their way to the night's roost. Hours raced past as we embraced, sharing our memories and hopes. Our lives were changed; the magic of the firelight seemed to flicker on blind eyes. We stared into nothing as fire warmed our faces. We were losing our hold on lifetimes of happiness.

Days passed, and Jasmina agonized over her loss; there was little that could be done for her. Time dragged as life went limp. Weeks into our visit to the cabin, a special evening came. The fire was crackling and smoke drifted with the gentle breeze that caressed the meadow encircling the cabin. Mina moved restlessly in the glow of the flames as if preparing to speak. Words slowly lifted from her reluctant lips and floated to my ears in half step. "She was my mother," Mina slowly confided. "She had chosen to care for me for the duration of her life. This was a decision far outside the boundaries of Teran cultural tradition. Her constant, vigilant presence filled me with strength and confidence like no other Teran has ever known. This loss has left a hole in my soul."

I moved to put my hand on hers, telling her that I could never know how this must feel. Jasmina turned, looking down at the comfort of my hand. She replied, "Oh, but you do." Her gaze moved to mine; as our eyes connected, I felt the rush of sadness and loss cut into my chest as her thought words revealed that my father was Talleyrand. Tears pooled in our eyes, falling with synchronicity as we looked into each other's tear-stained faces.

His last words were etched in my memory, "I am with you always and forever." His memories are mine and a part of his spirit is in me. I can never reach out and touch him, but I feel that he will always be there in my mind. Looking back through the life of an Elder at the thousands of years and experiences, I can feel the magnitude of Mina's loss from the passing of Magna. Jasmina can feel my sadness and compassion. We are drawn closer by the mutual pain of loss and mourning. Where two souls mourn loss in kind, they are one of heart and spirit. There is nothing to do now but for us to share, honoring their time and remembering the love.

Lives begin again many times through the course of a journey through the worlds. An ending like this is still a beginning, but in the lives left behind, it can be the start of inexplicable sadness lived endlessly in the memory of those lost in time like tears in rain.

As the flames provided a place of reflection, we watched the images of memories jump out at us. I listened to Talleyrand speak his wisdom as if he were there. The weight of our loss was an anchor. There was no place to escape our grief. We had brought it with us here to our fortress of solace and yet it grew steadily as does an ancient tree that grows from solid rock. Evil had forever changed the color of our lives.

Mina and I sat quietly beside each other on the ancient hand-carved wood bench at the fire ring. My fingers brailled over our names carved into the back rest as Mina reached out to the pot of tea water hanging above the fire. Talleyrand appeared in the firelight that glowed in the smoke rising from our warming fire. When he spoke the voice came as if from behind a wall and yet he was right there. Jasmina was frozen; I realized we were both seeing him, hearing him speak. He told us that the next life was but a window between worlds. We could speak and see but could not touch. He smiled as he repeated that he would be with us always. As my father's image faded from view, Jasmina's hand filled mine, and we sat quietly in stunned wonder. Night passed nearly unnoticed as the stars yielded their dominion of the sky to the early light of the sun rounding the globe. Time had taken a still stand as we tended the fire through the night and passed our time together deep in thought, our minds folded into one.

Morning brought a brighter day. We both felt lighter as we moved through the day. I noticed the birds singing again. Jasmina hummed a melodic tune as she walked through the meadow barefoot, picking delicate, blue flowers for the vase in the cabin. Parts of us were mending faster now. We both caught glimpses of the other making brief shallow smiles. It was painful to deal with the dread of returning to EarthUnder to witness the damage and loss. With time on the surface, thoughts of past concerns began to creep into the back of my mind. There were rare meteorites to have classified, contacts that may have found trouble along their paths home, and we needed to present the brain bone meteorite research data. Humankind would soon have to begin saving and sharing the planet. And somewhere out there in the world was a dirty dog by the name of Claus Laurent, a fellow owed serious payback for his troublesome ways. I just knew somehow that the worms had not gotten him. He was far too lucky for that. He was put on this Earth to trip me up and get in my way; for him to be gone would be too easy. Even if he was a Teranor recruit, his basic tenor and actions were always wrong and corrupt.

I rested, staring into the light of the fire as Mina headed for the cabin. We had left so many situations unresolved. As I gazed into the glowing logs, my mind was bursting with unrelenting worry about Earth's future. Talleyrand reappeared in the dark beyond the firelight, his face carrying a peaceful, thin-lipped smile. His presence seemed to bring a feeling of peace. He reached out to me from beyond this existence as if to touch. I stood and walked towards his faint, illuminated image. As I drew closer I could hear his voice and feel his energy surrounding my head as if he was cradling my brain. Talleyrand told me that he was going to share his knowledge with me. It would become a tool for me to use when needed.

As the knowledge poured into my memory and he spoke to me, I realized that much of what he was sharing was knowledge he had just acquired from his new state of being. I could see the thoughts of all of the Teran people as well as the thoughts, plans, strategies, and tragic histories of the Teranor and their recruits from other worlds. They had the ability and technology to reduce a planet and all of its living tissue into pure energy, which they could then inject into their own bodies, giving them unlimited power, energy and a huge drug-like high. The Teranor were severely addicted to this intoxicating high and they endlessly craved more. Nothing in their existence had more value or importance than maintaining that level of intoxication, and all life was forfeit to their lust for more life force energy. They were clever in their approach to this system. They had learned that less resistance makes the process transpire much more quickly. The value of Earth as a target was compounded by the life energy reserved in each of the Terans.

I could see through Talleyrand that there were count-less Teranor suspended elsewhere in the galaxy and beyond. These hordes were poised and ready to get their share of the life energy that exists here on our home world. I could also see the other worlds that they were currently sucking the life from, as well as the dead worlds they had left behind. The Teranor had a myriad of abilities in their arsenal for war-like action and evil efforts, but Talleyrand had taught me that they also had weaknesses. The lust for more "high" was one of their greatest weaknesses, and it might just give us an advantage.

As his mind detached from my conscious thought, Tall-eyrand's eyes raised to look beyond me. Jasmina had come from the cabin and was drawing towards us. In the cool, peaceful silence of the night I could hear their thoughts as they shared. So many thoughts streamed between them. It seemed that words spoken were a waste of time when I listened to them share volumes of thought in only moments. Emotions are far more intense when communicating in this manner. One can not only hear what a person is saying, but actually feel the emotion that motivates the words to be released from the mind.

Compassion welled up in my chest; tears filled my eyes as I experienced the conversation between my father and Mina. Soon they were done and Talleyrand's light image began to fade, but Mina's face gleamed as another image began to appear.

"Magna!" Mina called out in joy at the appearance of her lost loved one. It was time for me to walk away so these two could share, alone in solitude. I didn't think I could have handled the deluge of feelings from this encounter. This was all new to me and I felt limits in my human ability to cope. Jasmina and Magna spent hours there, leaning into each other and sharing their thoughts and feelings. In the cabin I was brainstorming where we go from here. Sooner or later, we would have to face the future and deal with what was to come. I could see through Talleyrand's help that the planet was littered with Abecedarians: Teranor wannabes that had sold their souls to the Teranor and were at different levels of recruitment and training. Now leaderless, the Abecedarians had no direction and yet they remained, a treacherous subculture of human recruits craving Teranor affiliation. War was coming, a galactic war, a war of wars to decide who will carry on in the universe.

About the Author

Edwin Thompson has traveled the globe since childhood, in search of rocks from space, fossils, and man-made artifacts. For the past thirty years he has hunted meteorites and lectured on cataclysmic impact, meteorite identification, and meteorite hunting around the world. His efforts in the field have produced countless world-renowned specimens and successful meteorite hunters.

He is a short story author and a science fiction adventure novelist. He has written articles and short stories for *Rock and Gem* magazine and *Gemfaire Quarterly*. When he's not dreaming of ideas for his next novel, he's racing off to find another rock from space. Edwin has a background in Archaeology and Geology, and he is one of planet Earth's leading field experts on meteorites. You can visit him at www.etmeteorites.com.

From the Author

I have taught and mentored a nearly countless number of people over the years how to hunt meteorites. Many of those enthusiastic hunters have gone on to be far more productive and successful hunters than I could ever dream of being. You could say that I taught people to fish. This is a huge network of humans who now support many others within their third world countries. In many cases they now live in better conditions than I do. Mostly, they are desert dwellers who had very little to begin with. Now, many of them live in large homes and have healthy families. This was always part of my plan, to save the children. I went into this part of the world as a child and I saw the hunger and the poverty and hated it. This has all been the result of a decision to help stamp out hunger and poverty. I could never have dreamed of the success it has grown to be.

Acknowledgments

would like to thank my good friend James Tobin for his positive support and encouraging critique.

Book II of The Meteorite Chronicles: Thundering Skies

Connection

The wind breathed oxygen through the trees. Everything from the smallest blade of grass to the tallest tree in the forest waved in a symphony of motion to the beat of the gentle breeze. The air chilled the skin as it carried off the body's heat. I sat warming by the fire, hypnotized by the dance of flames lapping at the logs in the pit. Night air took over the day. Jasmina and I were taking this time to mend from our losses. She was in the cabin getting a few things while I tended the fire. She hummed melodic tones that echoed over the meadow and into the trees. This was the moment of time between day and night when everything goes silent and one can almost hear the turn of the Earth. The final glow of daylight sank into the forest to the west, while the stark white light of the moon hinted at rising in the east. For a time, the stars were so bright one could read by their light.

At any distance, Mina and I share our thoughts and feelings. She silently listens while I pore over endless memories of past events. This new capacity of memory, knowledge, and recall seems to offer no help in dealing with the dread of what's to come. I can see the horrifying technology created by the Teranor for their invasive endeavors. I can feel the heartless greed of their consumption, planet by planet. I can feel Jasmina trying to calm me, but I can also feel that she can understand and relate to my thoughts of extreme concern. It comes to mind that I have some powerful friends here on the surface that might be recruited to help us with what is to come.

As I glared into the flames, the faces of countless friends around the planet appeared while I began to formulate an idea. There might be a way to connect open-minded people from my world with Terans in a way that would allow us to work in tandem. We would empower humans to deal with the Teranor, utilizing the powers and strengths of the Terans of EarthUnder.

I had never forgotten the experience I had years ago when I first traveled to England to spend extended time with my friends Vic and Kathy Roberts. We had met years earlier and ended up traveling together for almost a year, seeing the world and enjoying life in other cultures. When I first met the two of them, they struck me as magical. Kathy appeared to be more than just a human. Her elfin size, her permanent smile, and serene, youthful, sparkling, powder blue eyes and knee-length silver hair struck me as the perfect image of what she later admitted to be true. Kathy shared with me that she was a practicing Celtic Druid from a very long line of the same. Her family line traced back to nearly five thousand years of Druid Shamans. She was teaching crystal healing, herbology, holistic medicine, prayer circles, and all manner of medicine far beyond the western medicine that both she and Vic had practiced for decades as nurses in a London hospital. Vic, a more passive, inert presence, was a tall, silent type of man's man, a gentle spirit always standing by Kath's side as her second set of ears. He was her advisor, her sound wall, her ultimate companion, and her apparent bodyguard. Vic has always been there for Kath in the strongest, yet gentlest, ways. They were the sweetest couple I had ever grown to know. They always had this low-profile comedy routine going on between the two of them; they would banter back and forth.

I felt in my gut that I needed their help. On a long trip around England visiting ancient archaeological sites such as "The Big Man" and touring the ley lines and standing stones across the land, we found ourselves hiking across Dartmoor. I had found an arrowhead on the Moor, which inspired a lengthy discussion about early Stone Age man across the planet. I had puzzled for years over the fact that artifacts found all across the globe, from any period of time, would resemble those of early man from other parts of the planet at the same time period. How could this be? Five, eight, ten, twelve thousand years ago, how did early man communicate these styles, fashions, and techniques to tribes of humans elsewhere? No cell phones, television, computers, airplanes, not even a postal system, nor any kind of global transportation system—and yet I found the same tools from the same time periods on virtually every continent.

While Vic silently listened, as he always did, Kathy opened my eyes to something far beyond my belief system. Kath explained a system which at the time seemed a bit farfetched to my skeptical, scientific mind. But after all I have seen in New Tera and all I have learned from Mina and Talleyrand, what Kathy had shared with me those years ago started to make sense. Kathy explained that since the beginning of the Druids' record of time, they had gone into their fogous or souterrains, as they were known in Ireland and Scotland, built of stone over holes in the ground, and traveled through Mother Earth to communicate with the Shaman of tribes the world over. Kath detailed how she had actually done this with Southwest American Aborigines. She had traveled to their sweat lodges and the Kivas of the Puebloan peoples to participate in prayer circles. Now I had a better explanation to share with Kathy and Vic, or maybe they already knew all about New Tera and had steered me in another direction those years ago.

Vic and Kath had moved from their six-hundred-year-old home in Somerset, England, to a peaceful Welsh countryside farm near the sea, outside a village with a name I cannot pronounce. I had visited them there once and had spent many wonderful days enjoying the lush green Welsh countryside and eating far too many of Kathy's delicious rock cakes and drinking all manner of tea. It was Kathy who had persuaded me to give up coffee for tea those years ago. In her endless efforts to generously share her magical ways with me, she had converted me to the healthful benefits of tea.

Every day with both of them had been a full day of learning a proper lifestyle. Kathy had warned me once to be very careful when calling out to the universe for what one wants. This was one of her lessons that I had taken to heart and had never tried for fear of doing it incorrectly.

Perhaps now it was time for something to be asked. Still, even in light of what was to come, I felt that Mina and I should visit the two of them together to learn all we could from Kathy about what she knew of a relationship between ancient man and the Terans. It may be that there a large number of humans were already in the know about New Tera. Mina and I knew we needed to build a network of resistance here on the surface, but maybe that network was already in place: a network of believers ready to take action in defense of our home. I searched my Teran memories for any limited or extensive contact between humans and Terans, but could find no deliberate, long-term contact. I could see back thousands of years, when the Terans were involved in the construction of pyramids built to cover holes that penetrated into New Tera. Before Man was brought to Earth to populate the surface of the planet, a number of openings into EarthUnder allowed unfettered passage between the underworld of New Tera and the surface. In an effort to allow Mankind to develop their own world community, those openings were sealed. Terans, who were once revered as Creators, Angels, and Gods flying about as if on wings, vanished into the Void. I began making all sorts of connections between Man and Teran in the archaeological record of Man's past. Still, with all of these answers coming to light, there was little evidence of any consistent contact between Earthlings and EarthUnderlings. Could it be that this was yet another shielded aspect of Teran history?

Jasmina's singing still lilted over the meadow as I bent to place another piece of wood into the fire pit. The Moon began to peek over the horizon, its illumination washing out the lesser stars in the sky above. Jasmina's voice came to mind telling me that I must remember to let some things go. Her peaceful nature came through in her words. Being of Earth's surface, I was by nature more aggressive, focused on what was to come. I could see in my mind's eye what might transpire here on my home world and it was terrifying, a huge distraction. In the light of the fire I watched as Teranor plasma ships raided space stations and distant outposts. Planet killers disrupted ecosystems and atmospheres on countless outlying worlds, some with humanoid populations, others populated by alien creatures of lesser or greater levels of evolution. I witnessed the seething deceit and degenerate corruption of the Teranor approach. I could watch as entire world populations were consumed by the evil, seemingly unstoppable, Teranor scum.

Hatred filled my heart and mind as my body tensed from these visions of horror and devastation. I could hear the voices of billions suddenly silenced—from the cries of anguish and torturous pain to the hush of eternity without whisper nor thought. I could feel the Teranor greed pulsing through the cosmos as they traversed the galaxies in their endless hunt for more. They are cold, ruthless, remorseless, soulless, stone-hearted monsters.

I saw that over the years the Teranor have launched asteroids at the Earth, sending them through the magnetic portholes near our sun. These chunks of stone and iron have been sent to test the Teran defenses. For thousands of years the fence has been tested. I could see their battleships drifting out there beyond our galaxy, conserving power as they waited endlessly for their orders to approach. Like great fleets of warships, floating in mothballs, awaiting the next conflict, the Teranor invasion machines have waited in stasis for the climactic, apocalyptic command. Through time, mankind has documented these pieces of asteroid flying through our solar system and glancing the surface of the planet, having been deflected from direct impact by the Terans. Over the millennia these projectiles have grown smaller as the portholes have been downsized by Teran effort to protect the planet. Some of the earlier impacts were devastating to the surface environment. But these were just rocks, chunks of planetary debris hurtled at our globe with vicious intent. What I couldn't get out of my head were the ships. These massive plasma ships carried death; they represented an end to life anywhere they would navigate. My new mental capacity still could not fathom how we could possibly go up against a fleet of these destructors and their planet disruptors. It felt like there was nowhere to turn.

Sitting in stasis, frozen in thought, warming by the fire, I snapped back into the moment as Mina arrived to sit next to me by the fire. One could see the compassion and concern in her face from listening to my thoughts and watching the images that flashed in my mind. Her presence next to me had a calming effect as she began to speak of my thoughts. She reminded me that worry is the mind killer, that fear is the life taker. She placed her powerful hand on mine and told me to continue to maintain my fearless approach to all challenges. Mina detailed how much she had always admired my confidence and composure in the face of adversity. She seemed to know me better than I knew myself. Jasmina saw qualities in me that I just don't recognize as part of who I see in the mirror. Her hand remained comfortably placed on mine, and I felt the energy of her strength flowing from her hand into mine. It was as if she was transferring her power into my body with her contact. There was a sensation of accretion—my body swelling with her power and strength.

Mina explained slowly with minimal detail, "The Teran Elders have shared mental ability and capacity with you. I am sharing some of my physical strength and ability with you, Bryce Monroe. Since you have always leaped into the breach to protect me and you are always there in front of me as a human shield, I feel that you should have some of this gift. This will allow you to move faster, react more quickly, and exercise more force. In like kind you will also be able to think faster." Mina held her hand over mine. I could feel a flow of warmth passing through the back of my hand and surging throughout my entire being. What I was feeling was the tangible input of Jasmina's own lifeforce. In what felt like a mere blink of the eyes, I noticed that the first light of sunrise was beginning to illuminate the leaves of the aspen trees at the edge of the forest. Mina's hand cooled as she gradually ceased sharing with me. My greatest concern was that this action might diminish some of Jasmina's abilities or reflexes.

I could see that Mina was tuned into my thoughts. Without moving her head or line of sight from the flickering light of the fire, she put my mind at ease by telling me that nothing in her had changed. Then she said, "Yes," with a smile in her voice, "we must visit your friends in Wales and then we should pay a visit to my family in Iceland." She went on, "I have cousins in that part of the world. They maintain one of my favorite places to visit, and they are some of my closest friends. It will be a chance to introduce you to Robynow, one of my favorite members of the family. Robynow is even stronger than I am, but in a calm, quiet, cool and collected sort of way. She has many talents uncommon to Terans. She is an artist, she writes and plays music on the piano, she questions everything and yet she has more understanding and resilience than any of us. She is stronger than two of me and she loves everything that lives on this planet. I have watched her communicate and fly with butterflies as if she were one of them. She is one of the rare few who can see into the future and yet she keeps this knowledge to herself. Robynow is different in many ways from most Terans. All of her physical features are darker than any Terans. She has brown hair and eyes, and her skin is an olive color. She has a quiet, thoughtful, gentle, wholesome spirit, along with gifts and abilities that no other living creature possesses. I haven't seen her in a number of years; she and her part of the family line chose to live in a remote part of the planet where they can keep an eye on the rest of the world. I would like very much to reconnect with her. She may be invaluable in the days ahead."

The plan now was to spend a few days more here at Clifftop, our place of solitude, and then we would try to make contact with Ali and then Vic and Kath, followed by a visit to Iceland to spend time with Jasmina's Robynow. Deep inside I could feel that I did not want to leave the fireside and more mentorship from Talleyrand. Life was filled with questions, and he had already proven to be the paramount source of answers. Mina appeared apprehensive about my desire to check on Ali. It felt as though she knew something that I was not aware of. But I needed to find out for myself if this long-trusted dear friend was safe and unharmed.

Daylight was consuming the dark of night to begin another day of warming the Earth and sky as our fire dwindled to a bed of coals. We both looked up at the same instant to see illuminated figures approaching. I glanced at Mina to see the same dread in her eyes that I felt in myself. I felt my chest swell and eyes well up with the flood of tears as we both watched the figure of Kadishya come into focus. Both Mina and I knew instantly what had happened. Talleyrand and Magna stood back while Kadishya drifted towards us. Mina collapsed to the ground in grief, sobbing and crying out to her beloved sister. Kadishya had discovered that one of her children had been Fladed by the Teranor who had tracked us during our journey with the stones. When Kadishya recognized the hazard, she took the Flade from her daughter and escaped to the upper atmosphere, where she was obliterated by the explosion. I had learned from Talleyrand and my orientation that if a Teran is vaporized by a destructive event such as an explosion, or if the head of a Teran victim is removed from the body, there is no chance for the Teran to reincarnate. Part of what gives the Terans their long lives is this ability to reincarnate into one of their own host bodies. This is a ritual process that requires time for the memories and consciousness to transfer. A Teran sacrificing his or her life to save another is the ultimate immolation since it can result in certain finality of that Teran's span of life in this plane of existence.

Mina and I were both stunned by the loss of this closest loved one, a powerful, kind, loving, distinguished friend and family member. It felt as though all of the memories of time with her were coming to the forefront of my mind and then washing out as they appeared. Mina enlightened me that this occurs during the transfer of life memories to the brain bone. She said that over time those memories will return in colorful detail. It is so difficult to fathom the loss of someone who was nearly immortal in many ways.

Kadishya approached with her eyes obviously locked onto mine. She spoke from behind the translucent curtain of shroud between worlds. "Bryce Monroe," she began in her typical warm tone, "as I said in our last encounter, I will be with you always. Do not grieve my passing, I am still with you." She hesitated as if there was much more to say but then turned to Jasmina and began to confide in her. She looked down to Jasmina crumpled on the ground next to me and said, "Mina, the children are with Maryam. They understand what must be done. You must be strong for our family and our people. I was prepared for this, as you well know, and I will be with you." Kadishya drifted back into the morning light and the three figures faded into obscurity.

As the day deepened into its rhythm, we felt each other's sense of loss and sadness. Each of us could feel how the other dealt with this pain and emotion. Neither of us had the emotional tools to handle these feelings. Kahdy was the heart and soul of her people. We all knew that she was destined to be an Elder. Her wisdom and her gentle spirit shined as a beacon of leadership for the future of both our civilizations. We were headed into a new age; it would be an age of two worlds combined. I could see that everyone had felt Kadishya would be the one to lead us into the future of our worlds united in one single, safe home. I felt the sense of loss throughout the entire populace of New Tera. I turned to Jasmina and asked, "Where do we go from here?"

Jasmina turned her tear-covered face to look at my questioning expression. Her face changed from grief to a startled look of confusion. "Bryce, your chest is glowing," she stated as she pulled my shirt open to reveal that I was wearing the medallion coin Kadishya had presented to me on that dark day when I saw her last. The medallion was glowing with a pulsing aura of golden light. Mina knew instantly what this meant. She cried out with exultation in her voice, "This is my sister! She is here with you! Kadishya left her spirit with you; she knew this would come to pass and she entrusted you with her life!"

CPSIA information can be obtained
at www.ICGtesting.com
Printed in the USA
FSOW01n1228150115
4517FS

9 781629 011967